The Lady in the Loch

Elizabeth Ann Scarborough

ACE BOOKS, NEW YORK

THE LADY IN THE LOCH

An Ace Book / published by arrangement with
the author

PRINTING HISTORY
Ace hardcover edition / December 1998
Ace mass-market edition / September 1999

The Penguin Putnam Inc. World Wide Web site address is
http://www.penguinputnam.com

Check out the ACE Science Fiction & Fantasy newsletter
and much more on the internet at Club PPI!

ISBN: 0-441-00666-3

ACE ®
Ace Books are published
by The Berkley Publishing Group,
a division of Penguin Putnam Inc.,
375 Hudson Street, New York, New York 10014.
ACE and the "A" design are trademarks
belonging to Penguin Putnam Inc.

PRINTED IN THE UNITED STATES OF AMERICA

10 9 8 7 6 5 4 3 2 1

Ace Books by Elizabeth Ann Scarborough

THE GODMOTHER
THE GODMOTHER'S WEB
CAROL FOR ANOTHER CHRISTMAS
THE GODMOTHER'S APPRENTICE
THE LADY IN THE LOCH

Books with Anne McCaffrey

THE POWERS THAT BE
POWER LINES
POWER PLAY

Also by the Author

THE HEALER'S WAR
(Winner of the 1989 Nebula Award for Best Novel)

To Lea Day, trusty research assistant and Power Weasel, with gratitude.

Acknowledgments

I'd like to thank Lea Day for mining Powell's bookstore for all she could find that pertained to my topic and sending it to me. Also I would like to thank Jane Yolen for introducing me to Deborah Turner Harris, who I'd also like to thank for introducing me in turn to Elizabeth Ewing, to whom I owe a debt of gratitude for putting me up in Edinburgh while I did my research there. Special thanks to Lady Patricia Maxwell-Scott and her sister Dame Jean for allowing Elizabeth Ewing and me to visit Scott's home, Abbotsford, during the off-season. Finally, my profound thanks are due to copyeditor Carol Lowe who deserves combat pay for editing books with so much Scots dialect.

The Lady in the Loch

Chapter I

THE MOTHER OF the corpse wore solid black as she danced round and round the room to the lamenting *coronach* of the pipes. With her danced the father of the corpse, also in black. The attire of both showed signs of having been recently, hastily dyed for the occasion. Phantoms of the plaid fabric swam beneath the dye of the mother's gown. The mother wept as she danced and the father scowled. The corpse lay in the middle of the room, her claes deid, her funeral garments, concealing the thirty stab wounds in her chest and the dishonor her killer had subjected her body to before she died. All around the coffin, her brothers and sisters-in-law, her sisters and brothers-in-law, her fiancé and her grandmother, all of them weeping, shuffled in their own awkward dancing. The neighbors danced and wept as well. And close by the coffin, the bound and gagged tinkler man was weeping too, less for the murdered lassie than for himself, he who was the accused.

The time was one minute until midnight by the grandfather clock standing in the candle-cast shadows draping the walls, festooning the ceiling and carpeting the floors. The flickering of these same candles lent astonishing expressions to the corpse's face and deepened the dread on the faces of the other celebrants, dancing, singing, eating, drinking, and weeping for the dead lass.

A *danse macabre* if ever there was one, Walter Scott mused from his chair in the center of the room, close to the girl's open coffin. Scott was excused from the dancing both because of his semi-official status in the investigation and because of his lame leg. In a way, it was quite thrilling, this lyke-wake, for it was the first he had attended. Lowlanders and Borderers such as himself, people raised in the strictness of the Kirk, did not practice such rituals, but the girl's family, the MacRitchies, were transplanted Highlanders. So on the one hand, this gave Scott a wonderful opportunity to observe a ritual of which he had previously only read. But on the other hand, there was the girl in the coffin, and though he had never known her, never heard her name, she was touchingly young, younger even than his own eighteen years. She should have been beautiful too, an Ophelia, a Lily Lady of Shalot, but she was actually rather ordinary-looking, robust even in death, the freckles standing out like blemishes on the waxiness of her skin, her eyes, at present, closed with coins, her red hair too festive for her own funeral.

The sheriff-depute of Selkirk, Scott's old friend Adam Plummer, stood beside him, both of them shivering, for the room was chill for more common reasons than the eldritch atmosphere that gripped it. The fireplace was cold, as it must be until the body was removed, and the door was still wide open for the moment.

As the clock gonged the first of its twelve notes for midnight, the dancing wound to a shuffling halt and the piped lament died a wheezing death. Plummer crossed the makeshift dance floor in two long strides and closed the door so that it was barely ajar.

The mourners hushed, except for one man who continued, unheeding, to gnaw on the drumstick of a goose. As Plummer returned to the corpse's side, the clock struck its second gong. The mother, Mrs. MacRitchie, let loose with her eerie keening cry, the *hullulu*, as the Irish so accurately termed the cry, for that was the way it sounded, a long mourning-dove yell.

The MacRitchies' large, pleasant stone farmhouse was wrapped in the boughs of the Ettrick Forest, and both forest and farmhouse kitchen could be entered from the kitchen door. The house was not too far from that of Scott's old friend James Hogg, and his mother. Hogg had been with the search party that discovered the lass's poor body and also with the party that had flushed the tinklers from their camp in the woods and chased the young man through the trees. The murdered girl's fiancé and her brothers had assumed, as had all the neighbors, that the tinkler lad, since he was in the area, was of course the perpetrator of the crime. Had it been left only to them, the young man would by now be hanged. But Hogg, who had some connections with and sympathy for the tinklers, told the accusers that if they proceeded, the current laws of this district would call them murderers as well, that it was best to send for the sheriff-depute and allow him to conduct a proper investigation. Recalcitrant as the younger laddies were, the elder MacRitchies prevailed and allowed Hogg to send a servant with a message to the home of Scott's aunt Janet in Sandy Knowe. Scott was visiting his aunt and uncle for the summer, far away from his studies at the university in Edinburgh. He and Plummer had been whiling away the early afternoon playing chess when the MacRitchies' servant knocked on Aunt Janet's door and told him of the lass's death (never calling her by name. One

never called the deceased by name unless in court or kirk or
on one other occasion, as the sheriff was soon to demonstrate). Plummer evidently was acquainted with the family,
however, and had some idea that the lyke-wake was in
order. He told Scott that this might prove a more interesting
experience than most and urged the younger man to accompany him.

Riding hard, they had reached the farmhouse shortly after
sunset, when the forest shadows gave way to the mist rising
from the creeks and ponds, and that was joined by the smoke
from the kitchen chimney, blowing a solemn ring around the
house.

Plummer questioned Mrs. MacRitchie, who had laid her
daughter out, about the girl's wounds. Scott was relieved his
friend had felt no need to remove the funeral linens to see
the wounds for himself, but he wondered why. Plummer
questioned the tinkler lad as well, but the man refused to say
anything except that he had done nothing wrong, and to
shake his head stubbornly. The brothers and the girl's fiancé, one Robert Douglas, the son of an even more successful farmer than the girl's father, wanted to "bate the truth oot
o' the knacker," and in fact, it looked as if they had already
made progress toward that goal before Plummer and Scott
arrived. Hogg too bore a couple of visible bruises, although
no apparent malice toward those who had inflicted them.

The clock gonged for the fourth time. Plummer began,
"By the power vested in me by the Sheriff of Selkirk and
through him the King, I will noo commence interrogatin' the
victim of this heinous crime."

"What does he mean, interrogate the victim?" Scott
asked Hogg, who had drawn near.

Hogg shrugged. "Used to be done whenever there was
foul play, according to Mither," he whispered back. "Nowa-
days nane but the law know the way."

"Why's that?" Scott asked, but just then, one of the men screamed.

"No! Let her rest in peace! We hae Ma—my bride-to-be's murderer there. We should hang him and be done wi' it!"

"Haud yer tongue, man," Plummer commanded. "Let nane speak but her whose foremost business it is, the last witness to this crime. In the pursuit of this investigation, once more I invoke thy name, Mary MacRitchie," he said, in appropriately sonorous tones. "Rise up, lass, and accuse thy slayer."

Though he had never seen such a thing before, Scott had read of the dead accusing their slayers, but had thought it only superstition. He, with the other occupants of the room, held his breath, waiting, to see what would happen, what, if the victim indeed rose up, she would say.

Even the gnawer of the goose bone had finished all the flesh and, putting away his bone, realized that the room was now completely still except for his ever-more-cautious chewing and the echo of Plummer's invocation, and the heartbeats and expirations of all of those who were *not* now allowed to speak. The first sound other than those was a slight slipping, like jewels against a lady's velvet dress, and then a hollow clink as the coins fell from the girl's eyes and dropped into her coffin as if it were a wishing well.

Even the tinkler was still, as with a sussuration of the deid claes and a long, pain-wracked groan, the body raised itself, hands still bound across its chest, to a sitting position.

With the raising, Scott caught the stench of corruption emanating from her, washed and freshly dressed as she was. On such a warm summer day as this had been, her body had already begun to decay.

Her eyes, which still bore the glaze of unblinking death, slowly examined each person in the room.

"Tell us noo, Mary, was it this tinkler lad who killed ye?"

"Nivver nivver would I lay my love on sich as he," she said, quite haughtily for a corpse, Scott thought. "He'd nae the opportunity tae hae his will o' me."

Good heavens! Just as the ballads implied, the dead *did* speak in rhyme. And Scott had always thought that a literary device.

Sheriff-depute Plummer was not about to be put off by a bit of versification, however. "Weel, Mary, if no' the tinkler, then who? Is the responsible party in this room?"

It seemed to Scott that while the eyes of all were on the animated corpse of the lassie and Plummer, he had heard a small, scurrying sound, but when he tore his glance from the center of the drama to have a quick look around the room, he noticed no irregularities.

"Nay," Mary said without hesitation. "He is no' here."

"Who was it then, Mary?"

The corpse gave a ghastly gasp—or perhaps it was a sigh—perfuming the room close around her with her breath, which was not at its sweetest at the moment. "I thocht ye'd ne'er ask, mon," she said. "Hoo am I tae be avenged wi' sich batin' roond the bush as yers?"

"Don't be impertinent, dochter," the father said from the other side of the coffin. "Answer Sheriff-depute Plummer's question, and nae sass frae ye."

"Aye, weel then," she said, and though her voice had less tone than that of a university poet declaiming his latest masterpiece, she seemed to be enjoying drawing out the suspense, thought Scott. And then he realized that perhaps what she was enjoying drawing out was her last chance to speak to her family and friends before she was once more and forever silent. "'Twas Rabbie, do ye ken? Rab Douglas, he sare entreated me, but I wouldnae lie wi' Rab, and sae he had his will o' me, then drew his dirk and stabbed."

"Douglas! Where's Douglas?" several voices in the crowd demanded. In the commotion, Hogg loosed the bonds of the tinkler lad, now proven innocent in the most profoundly possible way, and the laddie was up and out the door like a shot. Scott seemed to recall Hogg telling him tinklers were extremely superstitious about being in contact with the dead. Though perhaps in light of recent events, "superstitious" was not the correct term.

As for the true murderer, Robert Douglas was nowhere to be seen. The entire wake party trampled each other in running for the doors to effect a capture. Plummer was close behind them. Scott would have run too, but with his lame leg, could not, so only he was there to see that as the door was flung wide, Mary's corpse gave a last wee gasp and subsided into its former inert posture.

When the doorways had cleared and he was quite sure that Mary was not going to rise again to add something she had neglected to say the first time, Scott too started outdoors. But as he reached the window nearest the doorway, he beheld two groups of people. The first were the mourners, who had paused in a clump just outside the front entrance to the house. The second was an angry, concerned group of people in worn and ill-fitting clothing. These were the other tinklers and they carried flaming torches, though probably for no other purpose than to light their way in the darkness as they sought to discover what had become of their kinsman. Some of them were making much over the released prisoner, while others were guarding and containing the hapless Douglas. They could not have known he was a murderer, of course, but they were obviously not in the mood for courtesies to anyone who might have seized their comrade and imprisoned him in this house.

Words were evidently being shouted back and forth, but through the thick walls and sturdy window, Scott could not make them out. Presently, however, Plummer and Mary's father took hold of Douglas, and as they dragged him toward the house, Mary's mother stepped forward and extended an invitation to the tinklers to join them in the wake. The tinklers, folk who seldom needed a second invitation, followed the others back into the house. They backed right out again, however, when they saw the coffin near the food.

"I thought they were hungry," Scott said to Hogg. "Are they squeamish, the tinklers?"

"Nay," Hogg said. "Not as you mean. Death is onclean, you see. The food in this room is contaminated. Perhaps the missus would let them eat back in the kitchen?" He said this loudly enough so Mary's mother could hear.

She looked somewhat offended, but her daughter's murderer had been apprehended by these people and Scott could tell she felt she owed them.

He knew what he owed as well. Much as he wanted to speak with the tinklers, to ask more about their customs and lore, he was a lawyer in training and as such should learn more about this process—besides, Plummer would probably need his help to keep the prisoner in custody as they escorted him to jail.

He was rather surprised, therefore, to find a trial already in progress when he re-entered the drawing room. Mary's coffin formed a sort of judge's bench, across which Plummer presided.

The prisoner, despite the chill of the room, was sweating copiously, making his lank dark hair appear greasy. His chin was square and stubborn, making him, no doubt, appear handsome to the ladies. To Scott, however, he resembled some of the bullies with whom, he, while a child crippled by a form of infantile paralysis, had endured far too much experience. Robert Douglas was a man who would have things his way, whatever the wishes or interests of others. No doubt he had felt that, having declared himself for Mary, he would sample her favors before making the final commitment, and had little respect for her wish to remain pure until the marriage took place. Scott had heard of fellows cut from the same cloth who succeeded at this sort of thing and then, particularly if the girl was of a lower class than they themselves, drop her, and in many cases, ruin her. Mary had been wise, but not wise enough to realize that Douglas denied was a dangerous Douglas indeed. The man's eyes fairly popped with anxiety as one of Mary's brothers placed a noose around his murderous neck.

"The evidence given to us by the victim is uncontestable," Plummer said. "Therefore, it is the decision of this court that the accused, Robert Douglas, should with all dispatch, in the presence of his victim, still above ground, and her family and friends, be taken to the tallest tree on the highest place in this area and hanged by the neck until dead."

Chapter II

SO MUCH FOR learning more legal procedure, Scott thought. He had already witnessed a hanging or two in Edinburgh. It was no novel experience, nor was it one that he fancied. Robert Douglas was a scoundrel, a ruffian, a bully and a murderer and deserved to die, it was true. But Scott did not feel he himself particularly deserved to witness the death. He retired to the kitchen, where the former prisoner was regaling his family and friends with the story of his narrow escape.

All looked up expectantly as Scott entered. Scott said simply, "He's to hang. Immediately."

"Hangin's mak me unaisy jist noo," the former accused said.

"Aye, and wi' reason," another man declared. "Unless there's hawkin' amang the crowd or idle coin tae be freed frae careless pockets, I've nae use for a hangin'."

"I saw me fither hanget," said a pretty dark-haired woman with a shudder. "I've nae wish tae see anither."

All in agreement, they gathered into pockets and aprons what food remained and departed into the forest via the kitchen door. At the last the former accused looked back and said to Hogg, "Mon, ye stood by me tae ca' the King's man when them ithers would hae hangit me. Will ye and yer young friend nae come wi' us?"

"I will," Hogg said, without hesitation. "Wattie?"

"I'll just leave Mr. Plummer a note," Scott said. He scrawled a hasty one on a leaf of the book he carried with him always, and followed Hogg and the tinklers into the woods.

A girl somewhat younger than himself, perhaps fourteen, perhaps sixteen, lagged behind to saunter beside him. She was very small and he was quite tall—a good six feet two inches—and she had to turn her little face up, so it must have hurt her neck to make conversation with him. "Ye're t'lad coom wi' the sheriff's mon, aye?"

"I am," Scott said, smiling at her. Though dirty and with flaxen curls tangled and clothing torn, she was a bonny wee thing. He thought it would take only one of his shovel-sized hands to span her tiny waist. Her wide eyes were the color of the open sky—here, where it was often blue, not in Edinburgh, where it tended to be herring-gray year round. He knew he need not elaborate to her, but Hogg told him that his mother, one of Scott's best informants for his collection of traditional ballads, had obtained many of her songs from tinklers.

"Are ye ane o' them depitties?" she asked. "Is that why ye carry that wee book alang and write things doon? I can read, y'ken, me an Geordie as weel. Oor fither taught us. Are ye makin' note o' a' we do and say?"

"No, gracious, no," Scott said, "but I had hoped per-haps—well, I have heard that some of your people are excellent singers of traditional songs, songs that other people have forgotten."

"*Have* you?" she asked, and he could almost see her ears prick forward like a cat's while those innocent blue eyes coolly appraised every article of clothing he wore.

"Why, yes," he said, and felt foolish at once as he realized that he hoped she might see him as something more interesting than a fool to be bilked of money or goods. "The way it was explained to me, your people are descended from some of the old races—the pre-Celtic and Pictish people who were Scotland's first denizens. Then, when the clans disbanded, the armorers, the metalsmiths, silversmiths, and jewellers among them went on the road to sell their services to the country folk, making pails and plows rather than swords or—er—shining armor." He looked sideways at her, but she had not picked up that the last bit was an embroidery of his own because he liked the sound of it. To the best of his knowledge, the Highlands had never boasted knights in shining armor, but Scott was very fond of the image of knights in shining armor and it was his story and he would put them in if he wished.

"Musta gie 'em an affu chafin', a' that metal worn ow'er their kilts," the formerly accused murderer said.

Scott blushed but the girl said, "Aye, weel, I suppose some of 'em musta known that a suit o' shinin' armor would better stop an arrow than a patch o' tartan." She gave Scott a grin worthy of an elf and he recognized a kindred soul— one who preferred a good story approximating the truth rather than the unvarnished and somewhat grimier truth as it had happened. "Then what did we do?" she asked.

"Why, when the clan chieftains were outlawed by the Sassenach, they went on the road and into hiding with your folk. Also some of the great highwaymen and outlaws."

"Och, aye," she said nodding. "I mesel' am descenet frae

Rab Roy MacGregor on the one hand and Willum Wallace on t'ither."

Though it was possible, Scott thought it unlikely but did admire her taste in ancestors, real or imaginary. "How extraordinary."

"Them auld sangs as ye collectet? I ken them a'," she said with a wisdom that was entirely showing off.

"Remarkable!" Scott said. "But how did such a wee lassie as you learn auld songs sae young?"

"Oor mither, Geordie's an' mine," she said, nodding at the former accused. "She knew aye the best sangs ever was."

"She did that," Geordie called back. "Here we are, then," and with a sweep of his hand that might have invited them to behold a ballroom, he indicated a forest glade, where bow tents made of bent saplings covered with cowhides and sacking stood beside caravans parked near a burbling stream. Lush grass grew plentiful on the banks, and on that grass, Scott was amused and somewhat dismayed to see, the tinkler ponies as well as the horses ridden by himself and Adam Plummer now grazed.

Geordie saw Scott staring at his horse and said, "Wee Alan fetchet it for ye and the good sheriff's man. So's ye'll no' have tae walk back by the hoose—" He shuddered a little when he spoke and Scott saw that Geordie's smile was still rather tremulous and his eyes as skittish as a highly bred horse's. And why not? He had narrowly escaped hanging by hearing his supposed victim accuse her true murderer. Such events didn't happen even to tinklers every day.

Hogg spoke up, saying to Geordie, "Mr. Scott would sair love tae hear some of the sangs ye ken. Me mither has gi'en him some."

"Aye, weel, Mr. Hogg, had ye nae spoken up and made them kinfolk o' yon deid lassie gae fer the King's man and had ye nae stayed by my side to make sure I didnae strangle mesel' accidental-like while waitin' amang the lass's kin, nivver would I hae the chance tae sing anither sang. Aye, I'll teach Mr. Scott a sang or twa he can sing."

Scott laughed. "If you could do that, sir, you would be not only a fine singer but a miracle worker. I fear I'm completely tone deaf. But I would very much appreciate it if you would sing some songs through slowly, so I might write down the words or any variations on words from other versions of the same I have already collected."

Geordie nodded and bowed with practiced obsequiousness before singing several uninteresting versions of ballads Scott had long ago collected all too many times.

"He's heard a' them, Geordie," the blonde lassie said. "'Tis mesel' wha kens the best o' mither's sangs."

"Aye," said a soft voice from beside a fire being kindled in the glade. A spit was erected over it now and women's fingers busily plucked fresh chickens that Scott was certain had not been included in Mrs. MacRitchie's proffered largesse. The doe eyes and lovely face of a dark-haired young woman, heavily pregnant, regarded Geordie with affection and amusement. "Midge Margret learnit a' the unco' ballads o' yer mither's, love."

Geordie seemed a bit reluctant to surrender the central place in his guests' attentions, but perhaps his recent experience as an all too prominent feature of the evening's proposed entertainment somewhat softened his disappointment, for after a moment, he said, "Sing for the gentleman, Midge Margret."

"Wha' shall I sing, Geordie? I'm sae chuffed yer nae hangit I'll sing wha' ye please."

"Weel, then, I'll have 'Young Benjie,' Midge Margret, tae honor the puir murdert *rudli* wha' coom back frae death tae save me neck."

Some of the others frowned, but Geordie stared them down. Scott stumbled over the unfamiliar word but Midge Margret, reading his face, said, "He means the lassie. *Rudli*, we ca' it in oor cant."

Geordie's wife left her tending of the roasting chicken to another woman and came to hold fast to her man's arm. Midge Margret squared her shoulders, threw back her head and began to sing with her whole person the story of a love affair gone wrong, of Marjorie and Benjie who had been true lovers, but whose quarrel unhinged the man so that on their next meeting he determined to take his true love's life. Midge Margret's ringing voice softened as she sang:

> *"Then saft she smiled and said to him,*
> *'O what ill hae I done?'*
> *He took er in his armis twa*
> *And threw her o'er the linn."*

Scott heard a stirring behind him and turned to see Plummer walking softly into the glade, in deference to the song. Plummer's mouth described a line as taut as the hangman's rope and his jaw was hard set. His bushy brows lowered like storm clouds over eyes lost in shadow. Scott returned his attention to Midge Margret.

> *"The stream was strang, the maid was strong,*
> *And laith laith to be dang,*
> *But ere she wan the Lowden banks,*
> *Her fair color was wan."*

Midge Margret was as vivid as the lady in the ballad was wan. Her eyes reflected the firelight, the excitement of the day and of the ballad, causing them to glitter like those of a woodland creature. From beneath her headscarf her tangled pale curls bobbed emphatically over her forehead as she declaimed the words in a sweet, low, dramatic voice, at first standing still and singing with open mouth. Soon however, her hands began to move and she put her whole self into the song, her posture and hands vividly illustrating the events taking place in the ballad. She resembled, to Scott, a somewhat bloodthirsty cherub.

Scott had met some of the tinklers long ago when they came to his grandparents' home in Sandy Knowe and had seen them on the road, but this was his first opportunity to visit one of their camps, though he had heard and read a great deal about them in the course of his ballad studies. Most of the people from whom he gathered his ballads were intellectuals and collectors like himself, who culled the songs from old manuscripts, or else were quite elderly people—it was rare to hear a young person, in good voice, singing the songs of antiquity. He had his pad on his knee, himself seated on a fallen log, and busily copied down the words.

The girl paused for breath and then continued, her voice deep and fierce as she, portraying the murdered girl's brothers, interrogated the maiden's corpse at midnight, as Plummer had done with Mary MacRitchie.

> *"Oh, whae has done the wrang, sister?*
> *Or dared the deadly sin?*
> *Whae was sae stout, and feared nae doubt*
> *As thraw ye o'er the linn?"*

Scott knew that by "stout," the song did not mean the murderer was chubby, but that he was arrogant or haughty.

In sepulchral, wavery tones, the murdered maiden answered:

> *"Young Benjie was the first ae man*
> *I laid my love upon;*
> *He was sae stout and proud-hearted*
> *He threw me o'er the linn."*

Her voice lowered to a growl and she fixed Scott's face with a threatening glare, her fingers curled at her side as if over the hilt of a dagger:

> *"Sall we young Benjie head, sister*
> *Sall we young Benjie hang?*
> *Or sall we pike out his twa grey een,*
> *And punish him ere he gang?"*

Midge Margret crossed her hands over her breast, tried to look drowned, and sang with immense ghastly, ghostly relish:

> *"Ye maunna Benjie head, brothers,*
> *Ye maunna Benjie hang,*
> *But ye maun pike out his twa grey een,*
> *And punish him ere he gang.*
> *Tie a green cravat round his neck,*
> *And lead him out and in,*
> *And the best ae servant about your house*
> *To wait young Benjie on."*

Midge Margret let the last two lines drop, as though she were irritated with Sister Marjorie in the song.

The ballad seemed to have acquired new meaning for Geordie too, who growled, "Noo, saft o' her, weren't that? To let him live but blind him? And hae a servant wait on him?"

Scott continued writing the last few words and looked up

from his notebook, smiling, "Oh no. I hardly think she meant it as kindness. Rather she had the servant there tae be certain he didna trip and end his misery prematurely."

"Hangin' isnae sae chancy," Plummer said wearily, making his presence known.

"Is the murderer dancin' wi' the dawn, then?" Geordie asked.

"Aye. The lass's fither pu'ed the rope and her brothers let him strangle until they grew tired o' his jig and dragged doon his feet until his neck snapit."

Belatedly, Scott noticed Midge Margret still standing as she had when she finished the song. He stuck his pen in his teeth, balanced his notebook on his knee, applauded and shouted "Bravo!" in a garbled fashion, around the pen, which he then removed and returned to his pocket. "That was finely done indeed, lassie, and most appropriate considering the events of the nicht."

Midge Margret grinned and stuck out her hand. Scott fished out a shilling from his watch pocket and ceremoniously laid it in her palm. Her fingers snapped closed over it like a trap on the leg of a wild and flighty beast. The first glimmer of dawn pushed through the trees now. The chicken was roasting with a savory fragrance that tickled Scott's nostrils and he realized suddenly that he had not eaten since noon. He and Adam Plummer had ridden with all haste from Sandy Knowe and even though they were offered refreshments at the MacRitchie home, both were so intent upon the case that neither had supped nor sipped.

The mist rose over the stream, lapping the caravans and tents as the water lapped the banks.

When they had finished eating and were sitting for a moment before remounting to return with Plummer's report, Scott could not resist asking, "Have ye extracted testimony in that fashion often before, Adam?"

"Aince or twice," Plummer said, and gave a great sigh.

Hogg said cautiously, glancing at their hosts to judge their reaction, "'Tis an unco way o' solvin' a homicide."

If Hogg thought these tinklers would be squeamish to speak of the night's events, filled with death and doom as it were, he was wrong. Not only did Geordie make no objection to the discussion, but both he and Midge Margret and everyone else within immediate earshot were listening, while trying to seem not to do so, as intently as if Plummer were about to tell them where a great treasure was buried.

Scott was glad, feeling that they all, and Plummer in particular, had need to talk of what had transpired to put it into perspective and at rest. Plummer had a hard job and in some ways was a hard man, but he had a daughter and a son near to the ages of the murderer and his victim.

"I never have seen the like of your examination o' the witness," Scott said.

Plummer shrugged massively and poked a stick at the fire, then sat back on his heels and began to pick his teeth with a straw.

"The thing is," Scott pursued the subject, "all I saw ye do, Adam, was to close the door until it was a wee bit ajar and ca' the lass by name. If that's a' there was to it, why did ye need tae be ca'd?"

"So that justice would be done," Hogg told him. "It was no' as simple as it looked, Wattie. Aince every mon knew the spell and could ca' forth the deid gi'en the proper conditions, but when the kirk took over, sich things in the hands of ordinary men were deemed heathenish and dangerous and best handled by the law."

"It's nay sae much tha', Jaimie," Plummer told Hogg. "'Tis the misuse the spell may be put tae in the wrang hands . . ."

"What is that?" Scott asked.

"Why, you saw it tonight, Watt. As in the ballad the lassie sang, in auld times 'twas true the family would dae the ritual and pose the question tae the victim at midnight on the day o' death. But, see here, as aft as no', in a murder case, 'tis often a member o' the family has done the deed himself, as it happened in this instance wi' Rab Douglas. Had he ta'en it upon himself tae question the girl, he might hae devised a way tae hide its truth frae the others and accuse some other wretch in her name. For that reason, an official witness is always needed, and in fact, is the sole man can question the victim. That way we always hae the straight o' it frae the horse's mou. And there's anither problem wi' allowin' the family tae question the deceased as weel."

"Is there, noo?" Hogg asked. "I had nivver heard anither."

"Aye," Plummer said, once again briefly worrying his teeth with the end of the straw before explaining. "Jist suppose, say, the victim is the husband of a woman doin' the interrogation. That woman may nivver hae listened tae her man while he was living. Why would she then after he was dead? Like as not she'd pin the murder on whoever she wanted tae be guilty, whatever the poor dead fella taud her."

Scott would have loved to linger longer, and ask Margaret and Geordie more about their songs, but Plummer felt duty-bound to return and make out his report to the sheriff. Hogg, whose horse was also at the tinkler's camp, decided to go with them. The lost opportunity grieved Scott afterwards, and he resolved to return on his own, but when, at long last, he was able to do so, the band had already shifted to another halt.

Chapter III

AS THE CENTURY turned, Edinburgh, the city of Scott's birth, turned as well. From a narrow medieval fortress, pitched steep as a rooftop, crowned at its craggy peak with a great blocky castle, and all surrounded by an ancient wall, the city was spreading its wings to soar into a glorious, enlightened future.

The Nor' Loch, a long, narrow man-made lake, had guarded the northern side of Edinburgh since antiquity. Once swans had glided upon its waters, which were fed by springs beneath the castle rock and dammed at the other end below Halkerson's Wynd. Once only the best houses had retained the water view and access for their boating parties and winter skating. But the Nor' Loch had also, since antiquity, been the receptacle for the raw sewage washed from the city streets. It had become so noisome and polluted that its stink, as well as the pall and smell of chimney smoke, announced to travellers miles away that they were approaching the city. As punishment more severe than it might sound, fornicators and transgressors of other sorts had been dunked in the loch by the righteous religious forefathers of the city. Should the culprits be fortunate enough to escape drowning in the effluvia, disease and infection presented them with other hazards.

For the best part of the last fifty years this great civic cesspool had been in the process of being drained. Disease among the workers, exceptionally rainy summers and hard early freezes, along with other problems, had delayed the emptying of the loch. Eventually, the area once under water would be filled in to create pleasant gardens that would link the old town to the new.

The New Town was laid out on a grid of spacious, tree-lined streets, with fine tall houses linked by long stone façades. The mode was imposing and classical, complete with columns and porticos, grand front entrances with fan-shaped windows above them, each window spoked with moldings and paned with imported glass. These homes would be free from the stench of the Old Town, and while the wealthy new inhabitants would continue to need to employ sedan chairs while visiting in the Old Town, they could now own or hire carriages to drive from their doors to those of their other fortunate neighbors, or into the countryside, or to London if they desired.

The New Town was as long and wide as the old one was, but less densely populated, with little parks and squares and pleasant walks where families could picnic or play games. At present it still looked rather empty and the houses severe and raw, since the trees that had been cut down to build the area had not yet been replaced by the trees that were to landscape it. Still, Scott's own family had purchased a house there, as had most of the wealthier families of the city.

The bridge that now spanned the loch on the site of the old dam joined the Old Town to the new. The bridge's broad

lanes teemed with people carrying supplies from the Old
Town merchants who would provide furnishings and fine
appointments, as well as the usual necessities, for the new
homes. The breadth of the bridge even allowed horse-drawn
carriages to join the sedan chairs and pedestrians on the
High Street, though of course most of the wynds and closes
between the houses were far too narrow to permit access to
such vehicles.

Just beyond the New Town the raw stumps and beds of
new roads marked the beginnings of an even newer town, on
the site of the old Moray Estate.

These streets were not laid in squares, but in crescents
and circuses, and promised to be less monotonous than the
first. The initial crescent of homes and a few stand-alones
had been built but were still largely empty. The foundations
of others were barely mortared when winter came.

At the beginning of winter, the loch was almost a quarter
full, its emptiness being replenished by heavy autumn rains.
The remaining mud and water was so foul and stinking that
the homeowners in the New Town required the workmen to
continue the drainage well into the winter.

Scott observed this progress on his daily walks, where he
thought over either the intricacies of the cases he had heard
and recorded as Clerk of Sessions for the city, or, more
often, the twists of plot and complexities of character of the
denizens of whichever new story or book he happened to be
writing in his head. The first volume of three in his collection of folk songs, the *Minstrelsy of the Scottish Borders,*
had been well received and the second was ready for publication.

On this particular day, he was thinking that he wished to
capture old Edinburgh as he had known it and as he wished
he had known it. His own Old Town was a pokey, busy,
rabbit-warren of a place, as familiar to him as his mother's

voice. However, Old Edinburgh in bygone days had been a rowdy, filthy, stinking, barbaric place in many ways, where a citizen had not only God to fear should he or she put a foot wrong, but the wrath of the mob as well. But honor and glory were there too, and marvelous stories full of mystery, mayhem and magic abounded. Every house and every passage, be it street or close, had its own tale to tell. The structure of the city itself formed the warp and woof of much of Scotland's history. Much of this significance was being stripped from the city with the so-called modernization, and Scott mourned the loss.

He and a few others decried the destruction of one historic monument after another, and now, almost more pitifully, the Old Town's greatest grace, its wee forest of Bellevue, was being denuded of its trees. Now that the work was ceasing for the winter, the endless noise had stopped and only the silence of the raw stumps, and the occasional cry of a bewildered bird unable to locate its former nest, remained. Scott knew, of course, that it was all for progress, that fine new houses would be built here to save the Old Town from being inhabited only by the poor and destitute who were already starting to fill the rapidly emptying buildings. In former times the poor had occupied only the lower floors, close to the slops and garbage that were poured onto the streets every night at ten o'clock to the cry of "Gardyloo!"

Now even the upper stories, once the sole province of the well-to-do, and the back rooms with the long windows facing north and south where they could observe the area surrounding the city, were being overtaken by the lower classes.

Scott himself, though gently born and gaining rapidly in literary fame and somewhat unsolicited influence, was not yet a wealthy man and had appropriated rooms on the fourth

floor of a house on College Wynd. It had a southern exposure and from it he could see the Greyfriar's Kirk, Edinburgh University, where he had attended law school, and
where one of the finest medical colleges in Europe flour-
ished, the Deans Cemetery and a portion of the Grassmarket, where the King's cattle were herded in at night via the
Cowgate. In this little square, since olden times highwaymen were hanged, witches were burnt, and those who had
fallen into such political disfavor as to be dubbed traitor
were drawn, hung, and quartered before their various parts
were distributed across the land. In a way that was pecu-
liarly Scottish, it was also where the condemned would be
given "a last drap"—his or her last drink of liquor from a
tavern that bore the name of the custom. Such an innocent
little plaza otherwise, with shops, pubs and homes facing
onto the square which was, of course, rectangular. It was
marked by a cross at one end, from the time of the Templars,
and a great stone with a hole in it at the other, where the gallows could be inserted for hangings.

Hangings these days were more apt to take place at the
Tollbooth, midway down the main street from the castle.
Scott was glad he was now recording cases, rather than
doing advocate work as he had during his apprenticeship to
his father. While he found many cases dry and hard to concentrate on, he was romantic enough to have fancied himself
in his role as advocate as the knight champion of each client.
Fortunately for his younger self, none of those clients had
been guilty of what were now considered hanging offenses.

As Scott neared the Tollbooth, Angus Armstrong, formerly sergeant of a Highland regiment, presently sergeant in
the Town Guard, and no Highlander but a Borderer like
Scott, emerged from the building. "Mr. Scott, hae ye heard
the news aboot the body?"

"What body would that be, Angus?" he asked with a

smile, leaning for a moment on his cane for support. His lame leg did not trouble him as he walked these days, but he could not stand for long periods without loss of balance.

"The body frae the loch, man. Or bones I should say."

"No, Angus, I've no heard of bones frae the loch. When were they found?"

"Jist a bit ago. The captain is doon havin' a wee look at 'em noo. I was gaein' along meself but when I saw you I thought, Scott would like tae see them bones too."

Scott wasn't sure that he would. He had seen bones before, of course. Had a skull in his study, as a matter of fact. And to approach the banks of the loch in its present condition required a certain facility for holding one's breath. However, it occurred to him that the bones were quite possibly those of one of the Covenanters drowned in the loch for their beliefs. The Covenanters having been holdouts of the old, strict Presbyterianism that didn't hold with the King declaring himself not only King of Scotland but head of the Church of Scotland. The few thousand holdouts who had signed a covenant stating that the king might be king of the country but only God was head of the Church were hunted down, often tortured, and made to recant or killed. Although most of those drowning executions had supposedly been in the sea, with the tides adding an element of agonizing suspense to the death. And there were some people who said that except for a few troublemakers that needed killing anyway, no one was actually executed at all and the whole thing was a gross exaggeration. The other possibility was that the bones might belong to a suspected witch, who had been drowned in the course of interrogation . . . or possibly a fornicator who had failed to hold his or her breath when ducked.

In either case, Angus was correct in assuming that Scott would be intrigued by the uncovering of those bones. Who knew? Perhaps as the level of the loch decreased, the unhallowed bones of even older denizens would emerge, from centuries back when the loch was made and the castle constructed in its original form. ⸻

"That's aye thoughtful of you, Angus," Scott said.

"We'd best backtrack up tae the Nor' Bridge then. Maest o' the bones was found alang the south bank near there, below the gardens."

Back up the long steep street they went, Scott, despite his lameness, managing to keep even with Angus. The sky was gray as ever over Edinburgh, from the smoke, or reek, as it was known in the Scots tongue, pumping out of the hundreds of chimneys perforating the permanent cloud above the city. Its stench and pall stretched twenty miles away at times. But Scott had been feeling, as well as smelling, snow in the air. It was long overdue, the snow, for they had had only a wee sprinkle at Christmas and very little before then, with no hard freezes. The old-timers said that once it started, the winter would be fearsome. Folk coming into the city from other parts of the country spoke of horrible storms in the countryside, and the London coach had been canceled for the last two weeks due to snows farther south. Now the wind heralded the storm's arrival, driving along the High Street its blast of freezing air that licked at the collar and tails of Scott's coat. He had to use one hand to hold his hat on and the cobbles beneath his boots were slippery, beginning to ice over even as they walked.

Approaching the bridge, Scott saw James Hogg approaching from the other direction. Hogg had become quite well known as a poet, admired for his rustic wit and behavior by some, disparaged for it by others. Scott did not care. His old friend kept the home of his heart close by here in the city. Like Scott himself, Hogg was a tall man, but whereas Scott's face was full, Hogg's was lean, and his frame lanky as compared to Scott's more raw-boned build. Hogg's hair was already a bit less plentiful than it had been when they roamed the Borders together, though perhaps it was literary fame that was causing his forehead to seem higher these days. His eyes betrayed not only intelligence, but humor and shrewdness. He hailed Scott with a wave. "Watt! Come to see the bones, have ye? I was just comin' tae fetch ye. Taud him aboot it, did ye, Angus?"

"Aye, Jaime, I did." Hogg joined them as the men swung down the new broad street that became the North Bridge.

Just before the bridge left the land to cross the loch, however, Angus scrambled down over the side and through the mud of the portion of the former gardens that had been ruined in building the bridge. Unmindful of their clothing, Scott and Hogg followed quickly behind, and slipped through the freezing mud to the foot of the gardens where the loch now showed ten feet of bank above the level of its stagnant, stinking water. Scott had never allowed his lameness to interfere with scrabbling up and down hills and across difficult terrain.

A small group of men were huddled at one point, including the Captain of the Town Guard.

Two of the men in particular, Scott saw as he drew nearer, were squatting in the mud, discussing the bones with gestures that pointed out this or that feature on a skull and what he, for the little he knew about it, took to be a femur, or thigh bone.

One of the fellows was young, a medical student Scott recognized from literature classes he taught part time at the university to make his meager salary stretch a bit further. This was William Murray, a lad whom Scott knew well as one who did not believe literature classes were a waste of time for men who wished to become doctors.

" 'Tis a woman's skull," he was telling his companion, who nodded his head of curling red hair, cut to collar length.

"An accused witch perhaps?" Scott asked.

"No' that," said the redhead. "The last witch was burnt mair than fifty years ago and nane drooned since then. This lass hasnae been in the loch sae lang as a that."

"Mr. Scott!" Murray said, and rose quickly to his feet, slipping in the mud and nearly tumbling, skull and all, into the loch, except that James and another man gave him a hand. The second man looked familiar to Scott but he could not recall why. "Dr. MacRae here was just explaining to me how one can tell the comparative age of bones. Mr. Walter Scott, may I introduce Dr. Douglas MacRae?"

Scott nodded. "Dr. MacRae. This is fascinating. How did you come by this information?"

" 'Tis a study I've engaged in for years," MacRae told him. "When I was at university, I became interested in the differences in the bones of pairsons of one sex frae the other, one race frae the other, and of certain ages. Later, when I served as an Army physician, I spent time wi' specialists in Egypt who study what they call archaeology and anthropology—they have ways of dating fragments of the past, bones, auld pottery, writings and such, sae they can tell when a pairson lived or a thing was made. Wi'oot tests, of course, I couldnae say exactly when oor lassie here went intae the loch, but it wisnae sae lang ago as fifty years."

"Whereas these bones, y'see here, Mr. Scott?" Murray said, holding up one that was quite a bit more decrepit. "These are sure muckle auld. Auld enough tae be frae yer witches or heretics."

"Hmm, you'd think they might be found at different levels in the mud," Scott mused.

"Weel, oor lassie here had on some heavy jewels," MacRae said, picking up another long bone. "See ye these marks near the end o' her fibula? Until the bones separated and it fell aff, she was wearin' these." Now he pulled up from beside him a mucky, stinking, weedy mass that was nevertheless identifiable as a rusted leg iron, with a ball and chain attached. "Wouldhae sank tae the bottom."

"One odd thing, however," Murray said. "We cannae find her arum bones. Her radius and her ulna are missing, and nae sign of hand or finger bones neither, though it's possible such wee things hae floated awa' or are buried deeper in the mud."

"A murder, then?" Scott asked. "You're quite sure these bones are too recent to have been one of the Covenanters?"

MacRae shook his head. "This lassie has been dead maybe five years at the langest."

"'Twould have tae be murder then, as you say," Scott agreed. "The Crown hasnae been sae unsanitary as tae droon any puir victim here for half a century. And likely she'd have been someone important enough to have been missed, and recognized," he said with a significant glance at Murray, who nodded and returned a grim smile.

"Aye, had she been some penniless drab, she'd hae ended up on the dissection table in the lab, and the murderer wouldhae been seven poonds fifty richer for her cadaver."

Everyone nodded. It was well known that the medical school, while bound to report bodies coming their way that had obviously met a violent end, were otherwise none too choosy about where their teaching specimens came from. The school was allotted one body a year from among the condemned, and occasionally the police might donate the corpse of a derelict who died in the streets, but generally, human remains were difficult to come by in the ordinary way of things and the students could hardly learn their anatomy without fresh specimens to study. Families, even in these scientific and enlightened times, were more likely to

wish their dead underground than exposed to the bright
lights and scalpels—and the practical jokes and japes—of
the medical school. The idea that they might be contributing
to the future health of mankind made very little impact on
such attitudes and Scott, a good kirk-going man from the
time he was a boy, could easily understand why. His brain
might be enlightened but his soul cringed at the idea of such
intimate scrutiny after he was helpless to defend his earthly
vessel.

One of the men looking on, the fellow who seemed familiar to Scott, spoke up now, his voice grave with concern,
but gentle in respect to the remains of the woman who could
no longer hear him. "Puir lassie, whoever she was. I trust
you'll be turning these bones over to the kirk for a decent
burial, gentlemen?"

The Captain of the Guard, a drinking companion of
Scott's named James Laing, hurried to reassure the man.
"Have nae fear, Deacon Primrose. As soon as she's no
langer evidence, we'll see her bones are gi'en tae the
Kirk. It'll be up tae them tae decide was she a Christian
or no."

The man smiled slightly at Laing, his eyes overcast with
sorrow in the same shades of pewter as the sky. Hearing the
fellow's name, Scott recognized him now. They had been
school fellows prior to law school and university, but Cornelius Primrose had grown and changed remarkably from
the moody, sometimes electrically charming and sometimes brooding schoolboy who had seemed to Scott always
to be nursing some secret wound. The boys had not been
close friends, but Scott had felt they shared some understanding known only to brooders and dreamers. Primrose's
family had attended a different church, and had been quite
active in it, and were far wealthier than Scott's family as
well. He thought he remembered that Corey, as the boy had

been called, though more inclined toward poetry and theology, had first gone to medical school, but though Edinburgh boasted the finest schools of that kind, his parents had preferred, after the first term, to send him abroad to continue his studies, considering him too advanced for the local college.

Now, seeing Primrose as an adult, Scott realized that his former schoolmate had been the prototypical romantic hero in the making. The gangly boy had grown into a tall man with a fine, sensitive face, the storm-cloud eyes long and thickly lashed, the brow noble as any martyr's. In repose the man, even in workclothes, was elegant and in his slightest movement graceful. Scott thought that the knight in the book he was thinking of writing might well resemble this man.

"It's good of you to concern yourself ower the bones, Deacon Primrose," Scott said by way of reintroducing himself. Scott was by now a well-known figure in Edinburgh, practically a "kenspeckle" according to some wags. But if Primrose had only lately returned, or moved in circles that eschewed popular literature, he could be unaware that Scott was his former schoolmate, particularly since theirs had not been a close association. Scott was rather relieved, in fact, to find that there was at least one person in the country who did not consider him famous and no doubt, wealthy, which was not the case.

"No Christian man should do less, Scott," Primrose replied with a diffident shrug. "I'm sure you would have suggested it yourself, had I not. I will, naturally, pay for the burial from my own purse. How unfortunate that we have no name to put on the poor lady's stone."

"Even more unfortunate," Hogg said, "that she hae lost her name and coom tae require a stone through such circumstances."

"Of course," Primrose said with a trace of annoyance.

"Deacon Cornelius Primrose, have you as yet had the pleasure of meeting my dear friend Mr. James Hogg?"

"It seems I just did," Primrose responded, with only a hint of a sardonic smile and a nod, not a proffered hand, in Hogg's direction. Corey still seemed prone to brood a bit, Scott decided, unsurprised, for although one's accomplishments may increase and abilities and talents develop, one's temperament did not seem to significantly alter from childhood on, from what he could observe.

Hogg nodded as well and when his hand was ignored, used it to gesture. "So, Deacon. I understand you've a building contract for all of this new town of ours."

"Aye," Primrose said, relaxing into amiability. "It's the family business, you see. I'm the head of it, now that Fither has passed on."

Scott said, "But what of your studies?"

Primrose shrugged. "They were none of them of a practical nature. The medicine was, of course, but my interest was too theoretical for what the colleges could teach me. Theology was more to my taste but I found that I wished to serve the Kirk without taking the lead. And this is a very good business. My locks and latches are quite handsome and in keeping with the architecture. I have in my employ two of the finest metalworkers in all of Britain, men who have built fine swords and firearms and jewelry for the adornment of royalty, and others working day and night to duplicate and install their designs. I find the creation of a new city a most rewarding endeavor to be a part of."

"Oh, as you should, as you should," Scott said quickly, as he heard a note of defensiveness in the other man's tone. "I am very sorry to hear of the passing of your fither, however. What of the rest of your family? Your mither? Mine is still living, I'm happy to say, although my fither recently passed on. Have you married?"

For a time the deacon stared across the loch, watching as snowflakes began to sift down upon the foul black water and the foul black mud. "My mither has also passed away. As has my beloved wife, I deeply regret to say."

Scott did notice then that Primrose's suit was black, but many men's suits were. "My deepest condolences, my dear fellow," he said. "It must be lonely for you. I do hope that when you've finished work today you might join us at the St. James Oyster Bar. Several of us meet there almost daily, including the Reverend Erskine and Captain Laing here. You'd be a welcome addition to the company."

"Yes, do come," Hogg said impulsively, and clapped the elegant man on the back. "You too, mates," he added to Dr. MacRae and William Murray. Captain Laing added his invitation as well.

"That's very kind of you," Primrose said with a warmth that made Scott recall why he had felt a sympathy for the man as a boy. "I usually spend my first available hour after work in prayer, but I should be free enough to come along afterward."

They returned to the matter of the bones, which were gathered up, old and new, along with the leg iron. Dr. MacRae, Murray, Captain Laing and Angus took charge of the newer skeleton. Scott and Hogg continued down the bank until they came to the unruined portion of the terraced gardens lining the cliffside from the High Street down to the loch. Using the paths constructed for viewing the gardens, they made the ascent back to the wall and the gate through it leading into the nearest wynd that would take them back to the High Street.

At the top of the steep ascent, both men stopped by the wall to catch their breath, panting and staring out across the landscape, which had paled with snow while they were conducting their gruesome errand.

"Look ower there, Watt," Hogg said suddenly, pointing to the northwest, along the outskirts of the Moray Estate where the newer New Town was being constructed. "Ower by Moray Wood. See the folk trampin' alang the lane there?"

"Aye," Scott said, making out the small figures walking beside their wagons, heading toward the remnants of the once extensive forest that had been part of the estate and now formed much of the timber for the beams of the new homes being built.

"The winter is turnin' hard indeed. The Traivellin' People are coomin' in for shelter."

PHYSICIAN'S NOTES:

Another season commences and this time I feel I am very close to the answer. She is always with me, urging me to carry on, telling me how she longs to live once more, and that she trusts through my skill I may bring her back.

The central problem remains that I must rely on wholly inadequate sources for such materials as are required. Early on, experiments determined that the bits harvested from persons dead long enough to have been buried and resurrected were not suitable for transplant. Derelicts, sluts and slags, for the most part, are the only alternatives and though the procurers of such reluctant donors are hardly difficult to find, again, the necessary materials are of an inferior quality—disease-ridden, malnourished, underdeveloped or of so rough and wretched a nature that they are totally unusable. Such creatures as are available to provide these were born and have lived far outside of God's grace that they have permitted themselves to fall into such disrepair. If only they had the wit to appreciate that their parts will someday contribute to making a far more wonderful whole than any of them had ever thought possible.

    Imagine then how hope sprang in my breast when my most recent and faithful procurer, a gypsy of Irish extraction, a rather scarred countenance, and a manner that is not without charm when he is sober but quite clinically ruthless when in his cups, gave me a bit of intriguing information. According to this man, the gyppos must in hard winters take refuge in the lands closest the cities, or within the towns themselves. The families are large, with young women outnumbering the men. These people, he claims, have complained of being ready resources for the anatomical studies of my colleagues over the years, particularly in the Aberdeen area. A large number of such people recently have settled in what is left of Moray Wood. This gypsy makes the undoubtedly spurious claim that the young women of his people stay pure until marriage. If so, this would be a most useful quality. If not, well, while one can make do for a time with baser creatures, it has always been evident that at some juncture, for the final assembly, a lady of gentle birth and breeding would be necessary to supply the elements not otherwise attainable.

Chapter IV

THAT NIGHT SCOTT'S dreams were less than peaceful. As he had several times before, he heard the slipping of the deid claes and the sigh as the body sat up. When he turned to look at the face, he saw nothing but the moving mouth with its foul breath and the corona of bobbing blonde curls.

He was wearing a noose around his own neck and screaming silently at the risen corpse, "Who was it? Who did this?"

The mouth moved again but he could not hear the words. Then the arm disengaged itself from the shroud and slowly raised a long black sleeve to point—but the sleeve was empty and he could not see where it pointed.

He awoke shivering in the middle of the night. Outside the long windows of his bedchamber, the snow flung itself at the building in great waves and its whiteness turned the night bright ivory. And cold. Cold as the grave, Scott thought, and immediately dismissed the metaphor as trite and unworthy. Nevertheless, it was very cold, the dream refused to leave

him, and before slumber would return, he was compelled to
rise to attend to physical necessity and also to hunt for his
nightcap and a spare blanket. He found the nightcap but had
to settle for laying his coat on top of his other bedclothes to
add warmth for the rest of the night.

This time he slept very well except that he thought that
he could hear the howling of dogs, far off, and a short, shrill
scream, choked to silence before it reached its crescendo.

THAT SAME NIGHT the four families of tinklers Walter
Scott had observed walking into the forest were trying to
make themselves comfortable there. As some unpacked and
tended horses, others went in search of fuel while still others began to hunt for game for the cookfires.

All the while the snow piled and blew into drifts as deep
as the wagon wheels.

Bella Bailey had made herself a stout basket with a long
pull on it for hauling wood, way back when it first started to
snow, down by Dumfries. She could load her basket up and
drag it across the snow without having to hoist the wood up
in her oxters, as the tinklers called their arms, and haul it
back to camp, getting splinters in all her tender bits.

There were boys as would be disappointed if that happened, and among them were two that were here in this
camp now, Murdo the Mugger, so called because his mugs,
his pots, were the finest made by any of the Travellers. He
was a grand catch indeed, was Murdo. His first wife had
died and it was said he was in the market for another. Bella
knew she had caught his eye. With her foxy hair and voluptuous body, she caught the eye of all the lads, and since she
had become a woman well before her official time at the age
of twelve, it had been a full-time job just to stay a virgin
until marriage. But it was as much as her life was worth to

do so, so she did, by being faster and more clever than her suitors and playing them off one against the other. Murdo could barely stand to look at the other admirer she was considering, though her parents leaned toward Murdo. But Tam the Catcher was better looking than Murdo, and had no bairnies already born for her to care for. He could play the fiddle as well as doing the jugglin' which gave him his name, and his voice was sweet as honey. He could kiss without drooling all down the front of her as well.

She thought she would find camp ae excitin' this winter, and that things would heat up even if they had to stay camped in the snow.

She was so full of these thoughts that she scarcely took notice when she came out of the forest and into a clearing filled with snow-covered stacks of building materials. But among the materials were the logs that had once been the rest of Moray Wood, and stacks of coal for the workers to burn fires for themselves. She gathered into her basket the smaller bits of wood, two of the logs that would have to be split, and for which she had no axe, and a pile of coal, going from heap to heap, farther into the open as she went.

It was growing darker all the time but she wasn't worried, because camp was very near, and besides, no one would be about now except her own people. It was other people were afraid of meeting them, not they that should fear others.

Besides, the snow was falling heavily enough that very little, including herself, could be seen.

In fact, she failed to see, or to hear, the snow-muffled hoofbeats, the creak of the harness or the shushing of the sleigh blades, until she rose up to find a black-covered sledge-coach between herself and the forest. She panicked for a moment, then regained her composure and said in her beggar's whine, "Please, sir, I didn' mean nothin'. I'm not a thief, I'm not, I'm a good girl. But there's a' the wee bairnies back tae the camp and they're freezin' somethin' horrible. I didnae think ye'd miss just a wee bit o' this auld wood with nae one aboot tae use it."

The voice from atop the coach said, "Of course not, puir lassie. In fact, load it inside and I'll gie ye a lift tae yer camp. Maybe can tak' a load on me sledge tae help them. There's a lass. Hop in noo."

She smiled her most fetching smile, and dropped her beggar's stance to charm him further. She had help with her basket and assistance into the sledge's coach so she could return to camp like a fine lady. Maybe Murdo and Tam were not the best she could do after all.

Her new role as a lady who rode in closed sledge-coaches in warmth and comfort and brought bounty to her people by means of her charm and power over the men chuffed her so that she did not notice, until too late, that the horses had swung around, the sleigh was going the wrong direction, and the air inside the carriage had a peculiar odor. It was sweet and sickly at the same time, like the inside of the surgery in Selkirk the time she had peeked in while waiting for the doctor's wife to bring her a fresh-made cake. It smelled like that, and worse, and the smell was overpowering. She reached for the door to unlatch it, but it was latched from the outside. Her hand fell away and she sagged in the seat, sleeping for the last peaceful moments of her life.

PHYSICIAN'S NOTES:

An excellent subject was acquired this morning. A gypsy lass, healthy, and despite a lusty gleam to her eye and a buxom figure, pure, as the man said she would probably be. Much of her is useful so that there will not be enough to send along to my colleagues for disposal without arousing questions about the causes of her demise.

But winter brings a boon other than fresh supplies and that is the cold itself, which keeps the flesh from putrefying and the cells from decaying. This new subject's clothing was disposed of so that her family will give her up for dead, but since she will prove to be so entirely useful, she, like my beloved, is within a preserving circle, until such time as all of the necessary ingredients have been gathered and the moon and stars are aligned correctly according to directions.

Chapter V

THE SNOW CONTINUED to fall over Edinburgh and the small townships lying on its outskirts. To Midge Margret Caird's nearly snow-blind eyes, her family's caravan tracks were filled in as quickly as they were made, so that the wagon seemed, every time she glanced back at it, to have popped up from the middle of the road. The horses were all done in from lifting their hooves out of drifts and shoving them back down through the midforeleg-deep snow. Their owners were not in much better shape.

Midge Margret heaved a sigh of relief when at last she saw the castle rock with the stone-and-iron barracks buildings that formed the bulk of Edinburgh Castle, squatting like a gargoyle atop the rock. Two days ago her family had walked into the nasty pall of smoke darkness of the city, blacker even than the grim and threatening sky behind them, and smoky as the upper reaches of hell. Now, with the castle in sight, the forest they sought would be near. Other Travellers would be there, as she knew from the road signs, a rag tied in just this way, a weed tied at another angle to a tree.

Geordie's little ones were knackered from the trip, happy as they'd been to have snowball fights earlier. And Jeannie was so near her time now, and so big, it was terrible hard for her to move. She it was who sat in the wagon to drive the horses, Star and Button, while Geordie and Midge Margret walked along beside. Midge Margret wore Geordie's old trews under her skirts, and the skirts she had kilted high above her knees. Even so, the ice crusted at the hem like diamond ribbon on a fine lady's evening dress, and weighed her down something awful.

She would be glad to be among other women more experienced at bringing forth babies than she was. Not that it wasn't always grand gathering with the other friendly families, catching up with old mates and meeting new ones. Perhaps later they might find a barn to sleep in, but for the time being they would all camp together and build fires and, with the snows so deep and themselves hidden in the woods so far from the city, maybe the constables would not trouble them for a time. They could use deadfall from the forest for fuel and would have no need to beg coal or peat; the trees would give them some protection from the snows. The woods still teemed with game, though it was not so plentiful as farther from the city. In the evenings, when she and hers returned from the hawking and the begging, there'd be the fire, food, friends, songs and stories.

The countryside near the forest still had farmsteads and small villages scattered about, so there was no need to trudge into the city. She shuddered with more than the cold thinking of that crowded, dirty, stinking place. Villagers called *her* people dirty and stinking—obviously they had never been to Edinburgh, where the slops were emptied into the streets every evening at ten o'clock. In truth, she had been there only twice, once as a bairn of five or so, holding on to her mother's hand, and again when she was sixteen and just newly married.

That was a time she didn't like to think about. True, it was strange for a woman as old as she to travel with her brother and his children instead of her own brood, but she had no brood and did not think she would ever have another man. She had left Geordie and Jeannie and the bairns with hugs and kisses and presents, to marry a man whose people were newly come over from Ireland. It was a family long allied to their own, and she had seen the man and he was good to look at, quick with a song or a story, and seemed happy with the looks of her as well. The long, challenging looks from his black eyes and the curl of his lips back then had seemed to her promise of something exciting. It had been exciting enough. He liked the cities, as it turned out, and brought her into Edinburgh. He didn't have to tell her what her job was; she knew well enough how to beg and was good at it. He found them a nasty place on the lowest floor of one of the rundown houses in a filthy close behind a butcher's shop, and the first night they were there he took himself off to a pub and returned in the middle of the night to tear at her clothes and beat her senseless. Fortunately, he didn't break any bones, and she waited until he returned to the pub, packed her bundle together, and took off down the road alone. Had he wanted to follow her, he could have done so easily from the trail of blood she left behind her. A farmwife she had begged from recognized her, and much to Midge Margret's surprise, cared for her, but she knew that though her bones were whole, something inside had been broken. Later, when she was back with Geordie and Jeannie, they met with an herbwife who told her she would never bear children.

Under the laws governing their people, a man could beat

his wife, even kill her if he wanted to. By law, Midge Margret's own people should return her to her husband. But no one had ever known her father to raise his hand to her mother, nor Geordie to raise his to Jeannie nor any of the other men of their line to beat their wives. Her father had said that if a man could not get his woman to do as he wished through charm or by winning her respect, he might be best off following her lead until he could.

Geordie had left them for a time then, and when he came back said nothing. But from the fierce nod he gave her and the way he had to protect his hands, which could not play the guitar for a year after, Midge Margret did not think she would ever see her husband again. From that day until this one she remained with her brother's family. Jeannie was sweet and meek by nature and Midge Margret's stronger and more practical hand at the women's tasks was a boon to the family. For a few years, other men had looked at her as if maybe they thought to ask for her, but talk from Geordie or from others warned them off, and now that she had reached her current great age of twenty-four, no one ever asked, and she was glad of it.

Nor, until now, had she ever had to see the smoke around Edinburgh again. Since she walked down the castle hill and out the town that one day, the winters had been mild enough there'd been no need to come so close to town. But this winter was hard and brutal cold, with no feed for horse nor fuel for fire to be found. In some parts of the country, no farmhouse door would open, even were the owner so inclined, for the snow piled up against the house. The nearest city, this city, was the only choice.

The trudge to the forest was a long and exhausting one, but at last the river of snow flowed between two banks of trees, both of the tall skeletal sort and of the evergreen kind.

"There's something wrang wi' it," Geordie said.

"What could be wrang wi' a woods?" Jeannie asked, barely looking up. She was preoccupied with rocking and shushing her youngest, wee Martin, who was as tired as the rest of them though the bairn had at least been spared most of the walking. Jeannie was good as gold and knew a great deal about matters that Midge Margret didn't remember, was very bad at, and mostly didn't care about. Midge Margret seemed to be the stronger and the smarter and the better at things, but there were a few things that she was downright stupid about. And there were times she was not so proper as Jeannie, who was quite the madame for a tinkler lass sometimes, and would not have coarse talk or behavior at their camp. Her airs made some folk laugh at her, but Midge Margret respected Jeannie for her ladylike ways and Geordie was clearly proud of his refined wife.

He was shrugging now in answer to Jeannie's remark. "I dinnae ken. Something. 'Tis nae so dense as last time."

"The trees are bare," Jeannie said.

"And weren't they last time as weel? We nivver coom by here other than in winter."

His steps slowed a little as he puzzled, but then they saw it—a thin, pale column of smoke rising from the trees for a short space before its faint reek blended with the greater smoke of Auld Reekie.

Then they began to move faster, for inside the woods the trees had sheltered the road and the snow was no' so deep.

Nor did they have far to go before they came upon a very large clearing—so large that the bare land was visible through the trees on each side. Within the clearing were several other caravans, each with its family and each with its fire. The camp was strangely quiet, not an instrument playing, no one dancing, no one singing, no one quarrelling or speaking either, for all Midge Margret could tell at that distance.

She thought perhaps the noise was snow-muffled.

Closer up she heard the voices in their murmurs and whispers so low she could hear the crackle of the campfires as well, and the creaking of the snow-covered branches shifting in the sharp little wind that had suddenly come up. It blew like knives through her clothes and all.

They parked their caravan beside the others, and though two of the men from other families came to help with the horses, they barely spoke. The horses were led to where the trees grew thickest and the snow had not penetrated. The children had cleared away what snow there was to give the beasts access to the grass beneath. The men took axes to the narrow ribbon of ice twisting through the trees. Under the ice was water cold and clear, and from this both beasts and people drank. All these tasks were done with nods and looks and gestures, with none of the horseplay and fun that usually attended arrivals at tinkler encampments. The men who helped Geordie looked back at the wagons often, and their eyes scanned the woods. Only the dogs fought and snarled, barked, and played in the normal way.

Midge Margret realized suddenly what made everyone so still. They were frightened, was what.

Wasn't it just the way, when here she thought she and hers had made this long weary jaunt in order to winter all snug with plenty of their own about them, that something would have gone so wrong that it scared the talk right out of the whole camp? What could do such a thing? Not just the poliss, or the city guard. They just angered people. Ah well, first things first. She'd do what was needed and then she'd get to the bottom of this.

There was fuel that needed gathering. Firewood to be picked up, since it was ower late to go begging for a bit of coal at any nearby houses. Midge Margret walked slowly through the woods, checking every tree to find deadfall for the fire. The woods were well picked over by now. She went farther in and found a few bits and pieces on the ground. She also looked higher up on the tree, where the snow was heavy enough on the dead lower branches to break one off.

In this way she circled round to the front of the camp. And beyond, through the trees, just as the last of the day died, she saw why the forest was smaller than Geordie remembered it. Many trees had been cleared, as she could tell by the stumps remaining from some of them. Raw new houses of raw cut stone, raw new roads cut in circles and semicircles, piles of building materials, and stacks of the felled trees, lay half covered by snow. That solved the firewood problem. They could come out here by night, cut up one of those trees and haul the wood back to the camp. Traffic didn't seem to be heavy out here yet. One set of sledge tracks alone she saw, and those mostly filled in by the new snow.

She took what she had, walked back into the woods and into the camp, where she laid the firewood at Jeannie's feet. But before they could start a cookfire, the woman from the next caravan approached them and said, "There now, puir pets, you'll be knackered. Coom by us, we've plenty."

Gratefully, they shared the rabbit stew still simmering in the pot tended by the woman, Mrs. Chrissie Stewart, and her oldest girl, Leezie. Mrs. Stewart said something to Mr. Stewart, who gave Geordie a hard look across the fire. "You maunnae let yer women folk wander far frae your sight at night, laddie," he said.

Geordie bristled because it was expected of him, not because he had the energy. Mr. Stewart made a calming motion with his hand and added, "I'm no' tellin' you how to run yer family, mon. It's just that Bailey's girl Bella ne'er came back frae her gaitherin' last night. We found her tracks, and sledge tracks, but nae sign of her. We reckon the noddies got her."

"I saw sledge tracks," Midge Margret said, talking to Mrs. Stewart only. Tinkler women, though it was perfectly all right for them to talk to *gorgio* men, settled men, and even flirt a bit if it helped in a transaction, did not usually speak to the men of other families. Of course in this case, with her own family around and Mrs. Stewart right there, Midge Margret wouldn't be thought loose or her intentions misinterpreted in any way, but it was usually easier to talk to the other women.

"Aye, tha's how they travel, them noddies, in the winter. I used to know a fella lost his granny to 'em up by Aberdeen. Sledges in the winter's what he said too, though 'tis yer wheeled carriages in the summer, o' course. And never sae much as a whimper frae the lassie wha' got snatchit, for we was all here and as ye can see wi' yer ain een, 'tis nae far tae the clearin'. Her family left this mornin', took off like demons was after them. Noo, ye mind it coulda been the noddies, but she was a vain little piece and she might hae run off wi' some lad or the ither . . ."

A scowling dark-haired man a little younger than herself, Midge Margret guessed, spoke up. "That didnae happen sae pu' it frae yer head, Chrissie Stewart. If Bella Bailey'd run off wi' a man, it would hae been mesel'."

"Or me, mair likely," said a redheaded lad of about the same age.

"Is that true, then, Tam?" sputtered Leezie Stewart. "If it is, and she'd a rin off wi' ye, why are ye no' oot lookin' for her?"

Tam shrugged and looked at Murdo, whose Adam's apple ran up and down his throat a couple of times before he said, gently enough, "It's no' that we're no' brave men, lassie. But if the noddies hae ta'en Bella, she'll be deid a'ready . . ."

"Aye," Tam said with a certain amount of ghoulish relish. "Deid and hauled ower tae the college, where the dochtors will pay for her body, so they can cut—"

Leezie let out a little yelp and hid her face in her apron. Jeannie said "shush" and her mouth set in a hard line as she glared at the men. The younger children huddled closer to the fire, as if they were being told a good story.

But Mrs. Stewart barked, "Enough! It's clear enough what fine protectors you two louts were for the puir lass. Nae need tae gloat ower her death too, snooty little slag that she were."

Midge Margret shook her head sadly and hoped poor Bella had found someone finer than those two to run away with.

That night the snow stopped falling but the stars and moon stayed hidden behind the shifting draperies of cloud and smoke. The children dug the snow away from beneath the wagons, laying bare the hard ground. In the snow banked against the wagon's bed, they made entrances. Spreading hides on the prepared ground, the families wrapped themselves in their warmest clothes and blankets and huddled together in sleep, the snow making a windbreak for them. At the last minute Geordie's wee dog scuttled in after them and its sharp claws bit into Midge Margret's legs and called forth yelps from Jeannie and Geordie's two children as it walked across them to lie at the feet of its master and mistress. Midge Margret shivered herself asleep with the reek of the city in her nostrils.

She did not sleep sound, and her dreams were wild and fitful and full of ugly images she could not recall when she awoke to the neighing of horses, the barking of dogs. She

knew at once it was not morning because the whole family
lay sleeping beside her.

Any feeling she might have had that the animal noises
were in her dreams disappeared when the dog at Geordie's
feet stirred and scrabbled and barked sharply.

She lay closest to the entrance and had just poked her
head out as a bark was cut off in mid-yelp, to be followed by
piteous whimpers. She saw a dark bundle lying in the snow
in front of the wagon next to theirs. A satiny puddle glis-
tened in the snow around the bundle. All of this her eye saw
in a heartbeat, and only then, within the shadows among the
trees, did she spot a large moving darkness, dragging behind
it something large and limp.

She was about to yell when from the next wagon someone began to scream.

PHYSICIAN'S NOTES:

*What exquisite irony that work such as mine, which re-
quires the most precise skill and such an enormous amount
of education and even, in order to regain the woman for
whom I felt the greatest passion of my life, a dispassionate
view of all else, requires as well that I work with servants of
primitively ferocious instincts.*

*Although we had only just acquired a most suitable sub-
ject, one from whom it will take some time to glean all of the
usable ingredients she has to offer, my procurer, in order to
satisfy some personal vendetta, returned to the gipsy camp
and acquired another subject tonight. When I berated him
he responded that he was most upset, since this lass, barely
more than a child, was not his intended prey, that he had
confused the wagons and had meant to take from the camp
a woman known well to him, who he thought would be admirably suited to our work.*

*The young one was in good health, however, and though
externally she was not well grown enough to suffice, some of
her internal elements were most useful and their absence
will perhaps not be noticed immediately by my colleagues,
who may then assume that others of their profession have
made use of the cadaver before themselves, which is, of
course, true. Next time, as I told the fellow, I shall personally choose the subject, as requirements become more
specific and specialized.*

*The remains of one of our earlier subjects has been un-
covered as Nor' Loch is drained. It seems sometimes that
the apparitions of these specimens join that of my beloved in
a quiet circle, all urging me not to have allowed them to be
sacrificed in vain. By this I know that they, at least, are illu-
sions created by overwork, as my dear one would never sur-
round herself with such creatures, except, perhaps, to
bestow charity.*

Chapter VI

BY THE TIME Midge Margret scrambled out from beneath the wagon, so had the others. Chrissie Stewart was the one screaming, for her daughter Leezie had been taken from her own mother's side. Torches were lit, the area examined for signs and tracks. Where Leezie's head had been was a sprinkle of blood. The Stewart dog it was who lay with his head crushed in his own gore, having valiantly tried to defend his family.

"I saw somethin' gae intae the trees there," Midge Margret said. Geordie and the others ran in the direction she pointed and did not return for a long time.

Meanwhile, no one could sleep and the women made a single big fire and all huddled around it, the children to the inside, the women's shawled backs to the cold and darkness.

Jeannie asked, "Who are these noddies and why should the college dochtors want us dead?"

"Ye mean any mair than everyone else?" Midge Margret asked. She felt restless and sour. Had she been able to get

out from under the wagon fast enough, she might have saved
Leezie. Or got killed in her place, her more sensible voice
said. But then, here she was, an old spinster woman with no
husband or children and there had been Leezie, young and
fair with her life ahead of her. Maybe it would have been
better. But more likely she'd have had the lassie free and the
beastly man's heart cut out. She had learned to fight since
her "separation" from her husband.

"'Tisnae jist us, lass. The dochtors them noddies work
for jist wants deid folk. They're nae partikilar who," said
Johnny Faw, the oldest man in camp, and by virtue of his
age, their leader. He was, in fact, too old to search with the
other men. His grandsons had gone, though.

"Aye," said his wife, a skinny body with no teeth at all
left in her head and a good quantity of gold jewelry worn
under her hat and on top of her overcoat and gloves.
"They're aye needin' bodies tae cut up."

"And they've nae care where the bodies come frae," another said.

Chrissie Stewart, squatting by the fire and rocking on her
heels, clutched the blanket Leezie had been wrapped in. A
low whine was coming from her throat but everyone was
talking so loudly, no one seemed to notice except her other
children, who crowded around her.

To make matters worse, it began snowing again and the
men returned without being able to follow the tracks past the
construction site beyond the woods. Mr. Stewart and his
oldest son stayed out alone, calling and searching, but even
they had to return before dawn.

"Hawkin's tae be done ainly in pairs," Johnny Faw said.
"Lassies tae the door as always, but a strappin' lad will gae
wi' each lass, and stay oot of sight and keep his een peeled."

Faw and the older men remained in camp to mind Jeannie and the others who stayed to tend the fires and fix the

food and care for the children. Normally the children went along, as they were the best hawkers and beggers of all, but on that day the babes and the younger bairns stayed at the fire, tending to the horses and dogs. Midge Margret with Geordie and Mrs. Stewart with her second son, and other similar teams slogged through the snow, across the barren mutilated plain that had once been forest, toward the outlying farmhouses and the village to sell laces, broom besoms with which to scrub the dishes, tinwork, scraps and baskets, and to beg bread.

All the while they watched and listened.

THE MORNING WAS cold and clear. Murdo and his brothers would search the construction site, while gathering fuel and anything else that might be useful. The Stewart family would knock up every door in that fine new lot of houses below the Old Town. Others would take on the estate and the servants there, keeping an eye and ear open for traces of Leezie and Bella while begging and hawking.

Midge Margret and Geordie, both young and strong, were to walk to the edge of town and suss out whatever they could about the climate there now, particularly as to folk such as themselves. What with the snow and the kidnappings, they might have to take shelter in the town, Johnny Faw had said. It was an idea they all hated.

Midge Margret tried to tell herself that as long as Seamus would not be there, she would not fear anything in the city. With her dirk in the fold of her shawl and her as quick on her feet as any hare, and as full of fight as a ferret, she could hold her own. It was a terrible thing about the lassies, and it made her angry. She itched to find them, to punish whoever had taken them, to set the minds of their families at rest, but she knew that it was unlikely that the poor little cows were still alive to save.

"You don't have tae coom this day," Geordie told her. "It will be dangerous."

"I don't care," she told him. "Just let the bugger try anythin' on me. I'll hae his een for earbobs and himself deid as Stewarts' poor dog before he knows I'm ontae him."

They tramped around the marsh at the end of the loch. For a long time, they studied the draining process and all the men clustered around the banks, or squatting and looking into the smelly, filthy thing for what—buried treasure? Nothing but money would move these settled people to be very interested in anything.

Along the way, they stopped at some of the scattered houses, and Geordie held back while Midge Margret went to the door to hawk the laces and ribbons she had brought this day, as the wares were light and cheap and easy to hide somewhere and abandon, if the need arose. No one bought such fripperies in hard weather such as this, as a rule, but if they refused, she would then beg.

To the tinklers, there was no shame at all in begging. In fact, even the ones who were settled in towns and only travelled some of the summer would beg, though they had everything in the world a *gorgio* would have. They didn't want to forget how to do the begging. It was something to fall back on, if nothing else. Ordinarily, Midge Margret enjoyed the game of it, the householder saying oh, no, they couldn't spare a thing and her questioning and wheedling until finally in shame they parted with a cake or an egg or even a chicken. Or they would buy what it was she was selling, after swearing that they needed none. She was very good at selling because she did not do the whine many of the women employed. Instead she just looked sad and could make her stomach grumble at will. Usually, this was not hard to do, as she and hers often went hungry. If that didn't work, she would just sigh and say how she hated to disappoint the little ones again, now that their father had gone to heaven to be with sweet Jesus. They'd often overpay her, as a matter of fact.

But it was a rare chance to go out with Geordie alone, to speak with him private, without the family, as they did when they were kids. He always had been her favorite brother, five years older than she, big and strong and handsome, kind to the old or feeble and quick at the skills to make a living.

He was a good smith, and his fiddle was renowned even among the settled people. Their mother had taught him most of the songs, and he knew the stories from their father, who died while Midge Margret was still a bairn.

Since the time he was nearly hanged, Geordie had a story of his own about the sheriff's man and his friends who came to raise the deid in order to save Geordie's own neck, and about how the younger of the two men was a fine gentleman who had left his fancy home to come and visit for the sake of the old songs. In the story, Geordie repeated what the young gentleman had told to them, how they were the bearers of the culture of their land, which was true enough.

Did not the blood of the Highland lairds run in their veins from the time when the lairds and all their kin had been hunted like wolves by the foreign armies? Even their fine settled friends would betray them for the sake of old rivalries and wrongs, and the only ones who escaped were those smart enough to put rags on over their plaids and take to the roads with the tinklers. Even then, it was only for a time, but that time was long enough to pass on the tales and get children on the likeliest of the lasses, which was how Midge Margret and Geordie came to be descendants of Rob Roy on their mother's side and William Wallace on their father's.

Their father, James Caird (whose christened name was

Thomas, just as Geordie's was Angus and Midge Margret's
was Mary Margaret—tinklers were never called by their
true christened name; knowing someone's true name gave
you power over them), had been descended from the same
branch of the MacDonalds as Flora herself and bragged that
he also had the blood of the Scottish royal family in his
veins. Geordie himself was a fine example of what such brilliant lines could come to, properly mixed. He was the best
of both their parents. Midge Margret was glad he had found
someone so fine as Jeannie Robertson to marry. Now with
both parents gone and all of the other brothers and sisters
married away to other families, he was the head of the family that was himself, Jeannie, their three bairns and Midge
Margret.

They had walked a very long way indeed, around the
marsh and down the road and past the castle on the hill.
They crunched over the snow, wondering at the landscape.
Although the snow had stopped, the day was still bitter cold
and the wind whipped their clothing and hair around them
and knifed through Midge Margret's shawl as if she were
naked.

"Geordie?" she asked.

"Aye?"

"About them noddies and dochtors? If they gae aroond
killin' folk, are there nae sheriffs tae mak' them stop?"

"They dinnae bother settled people much, the noddies.
Nane that the law think are worth their time." His voice held
a bitterness Midge Margret well understood. The only thing
tinklers were worth to the law was to blame for every crime
committed where they were, to be beaten or pilloried or
hanged.

"Not even murders of young anes like Bella and Leezie?"

"No, and we'd best no' mention them by name again, or
risk summonin' their shades."

"Puir creatures," Midge Margret said. "But ye ken, Geordie, what's said aboot shades mak's nae sense tae me when I think on the shade o' that lassie at Ettrick as saved your neck, when Sheriff Plummer ca'd her."

"It's a complex matter," Geordie told her. She knew it was and honestly didn't believe Geordie knew much more about it than she, but he was the eldest, and the man, and besides, she liked the sound of his voice. If he cared to accept all that was said about shades and spirits, despite proof to the contrary, rather than considering for himself what he had learned firsthand, then she would not argue with him. "Thon lassie of Ettrick wisnae yet quite passed over, ye ken? Not until past midnight on the dee o' her death. But a true shade is tae be feared."

She ignored the lie he was telling himself. The girl had more holes in her than a cheese after what her man had done to her. She had been plenty dead all right. But Geordie believed what he'd been told about ghosts and was still uneasy to have had his life saved by one. So she asked instead, "Why would the dead want to bother us?" The worst face she saw in her dreams was her husband's, and he'd been alive when he hurt her, not a ghost. Or at least she didn't think so. She had asked Geordie outright if he'd killed Seamus, but all her brother would say was that the man would not bother her again.

Geordie very quickly told her the same as the stories always said, without thinking on her question and giving her his own answer. "Why, they're lost, ye ken, and they're lookin' for something."

"Like what?"

"Maybe their goods. Maybe their dogs or horses if they've nae been burnt wi' 'em, or sometimes, when the body's no' been found, they're calling oot for a decent burial and willnae rest until they're found. Sometimes, even if

their body is missin' something, say, if they've been be-
headed or had a limb hacked off, even their hair cut away,
they'll need it tae rest aisy."

"Don't the noddies ken this? Ye'd think they'd be
haunted oot o' their minds."

"I don't think most noddies hae minds at a'. They're
verra clever, and they're mostly thieves and such onyway.
They're no much fer belavin' in what they cannae drink nor
spend."

"How about the dochtors, then?"

"Ah weel, they're college men, the dochtors. College has
taught a' the fear of God oot o' them."

She shook her head. She did not understand how that
could be and said so but Geordie only answered, "Come, I'll
show ye somethin', as it's afternoon noo."

The snow had blown clear here in the open, and was not
so deep in the middle of the road, having drifted to one side
or the other, or making a sparkling hump, like a great crystal fairy knowe, in the middle. Then it could be walked
around. As Midge Margret and Geordie drew nearer the castle rock, there were folk abroad on the roads, on foot, snow-
shoe, horseback and a few hearty carriages that tracked the
snow and made for better footing.

They approached the castle rock along a good road
Geordie told her was called the Lothian Road. As they drew
nearer the town, they passed a high wall with a metal fence
atop it, and little towers. "Y'see yon wall?" Geordie said,
pointing to it. "D'ye ken wha's behind it, Midge Margret?"

"Can't say as I do," she admitted.

"'Tis the West Kirk buryin' groond, that is. And why do
ye suppose they've the wall and the fence and the wee
toower hooses upon the wall? I'll tell ye why. 'Tis tae keep
them dochtors frae diggin' up the bodies frae oot the new
graves, is what. Ca' them young dochtors 'resurrectionists,'

folk do, 'cause nae sooner dae they pu' a pairson i' the groond than alang coom them fellas tae dig him up again. They hire guards tae keep watch frae the wee toowers an' pay 'em wi' whisky, but wha's bought wi' whisky can be unbought as weel wi' whisky."

"Ony fool would see that," she said scornfully. But she thought it strange nonetheless that such care had to be taken to save the dead, as if they were in their own wee walled city. She couldn't help thinking that if Seamus had killed her, he might have sold her to the noddies—and she shuddered and realized that she did believe in ghosts, because if he had done such a thing, she'd have haunted the hell out of him, she would have.

Beyond that wall rose the higher wall of the castle rock and atop that, a wall within which was another wall of the backs of buildings, this being the old walled city of Edinburgh. She could smell its stench, she thought, even from here.

"Why do the people allow them noddies and resurr—the dochtors tae get awa' wi' it?" she asked.

"Why, the folk whose word would matter are nivver the ones murdered. And I think they must be used tae it. Body snatchin' has aye been an institution here in Edinburgh since right after t'univairsity was built. The snatchers mostly take them as the rest o' the town dinnae mind losing—ither thieves and murderers and hoors and o' course, us tinklers. You mind the story I tell o' Mither's granny that was ta'en while she and her man were sleepin' in a barn and the farmer's son sold her to some men?"

"Aye. I thocht they wis buyin' her for a servant."

"Aye, an' I nivver told ye different. But thon story is aboot body snatchers. They'd hae murderet oor granny and ta'en her tae the dochtors to be cut up just to see how her parts worket."

Midge Margret shivered even harder. The face of Leezie Stewart loomed in her memory—a bonnie lass, from what Midge Margret had been able to see in the dark. Her hair was light and thick and her face a pale oval, with big dark eyes. She was only about fourteen, the age Midge Margret had been when the murdered farm corpsie lass's folk in Ettrick came for Geordie. It was old enough, just, to be married, and Leezie's body was still slim and yet womanly seeming. The thought of those dochtors looking down at her when she could no' cover herself, picking her apart . . . this was an evil place. She tugged at Geordie's hand to pull him away.

In a step or two she asked, "Is it ainly the lassies they snatch?"

"Nay," Geordie said. "Must hae been the aisiest, I s'pose. The Bailey lass were awa' frae the camp when she were grabbit. And puir Leezie prob'ly had the awfu' luck tae be lyin' closest to the entry when he pu'ed oot a body. The snatchers are nae sae particular as a rule."

The sun had come out as they walked and now the snow was melting to sooty, muddy slush beneath the weight of the traffic on the road. Wagons and coaches became stuck and were pushed out by mud-covered farmers, merchants, coachmen and good-hearted passersby.

They walked down the Queensferry Road and into the Grassmarket Square, a wide bit of road with houses and shops in a rectangle around it, the shops on the lower floors, making the market, the dwelling places above. High above it all loomed the outer walls of the castle. Midge Margret eyed the buildings on the square and would have done a bit of begging but Geordie was preoccupied and seemed to want to continue without stopping. She saw a thing she'd not had time to notice here during her brief time in the city.

At the top of the street was a wee fenced-in area, with a

great sandstone boulder that had a hole in it. "Wha's thon stane got a great hole in the middle?" she asked him, pointing.

He pulled her back and crossed himself. "Tha's the hangman's stane. When a gallows is needed, they pu' it in the hole. Made the stake for burnin' witches here as weel. Och, mony's a bluidy dark deed done here."

They continued up on a street that narrowed and twisted its way between the houses of the area Geordie called the West Bow.

"Were they drunk when they laid oot the city?" she asked. "Could they no mak' their streets straighter than this?"

Geordie gave her a pitying look. "It's clear ye've ne'er been in battle, lass. If a toon is under attack, ye'd nae want the streets broad and straight and aisy, would ye noo? Yer Sassenachs could just hie their cannon up thon street, were it straight, and blaw awa' the castle before it could be defendet."

"Oh," she said, "and here I thought it was because the place is so crowded and crawlin' wi' folk, like, that there was no room for the streets because o' the hooses."

"That too," he admitted.

At the top of the street they came into the Lawnmarket, another, slightly broader bit of the main street running from castle to palace. Here folk bustled about their business and hawked their wares in the shadow of the castle.

A fellow almost more shabby than they held aloft in one rag-wrapped hand a freshly printed sheet, "Read all aboot it! Woman's body found in loch!"

Chapter VII

THE DAY AFTER the skeleton was found, Scott's appointment as Sheriff of Edinburgh was announced. Scott wondered if Angus had known about it when he invited him down to look at the grisly discovery in the loch. Appointments came from on high, of course, but in Edinburgh, where the high and the low rubbed elbows regularly, it was not unthinkable that the constable might have overheard something.

In many ways, a sheriffdom meant much less here than it did in Selkirk or Roxburghshire. Out in the provinces, the sheriff and his men were the sole representatives of the law and jurisprudence. The sheriff maintained a court and a castle on behalf of the King. Here in Edinburgh, every other man of means was a lawyer and every other son of the same was also a lawyer or studying to be a lawyer. Of judges and courts and kirks and legal opinions they had many. Also representatives of the English King now had headquarters in the castle. The Town Guard, that pack of retired soldiers who needed a soft job with a good pension, were there for whatever they were worth to police the town.

The sheriffdom was at any rate awarded to Scott not for any outstanding merit at the law, which he knew very well he did not possess, but probably because he offended fewer of those in power than did other candidates. His ideas tended to be a bit to the side of everyone else's—he was more concerned with why the castle looked like an ugly barracks instead of what he thought a castle should look like than with what actually went on inside of it.

No, the position had been awarded largely as a favor from grateful friends in high places to his late father, Scott suspected. Father had died a few months earlier, leaving his business and property interests to Scott's older brother. Scott knew his father had confided his worries about his younger son, with his head full of dreams and stories, to friends such as the Dundas family, and Lord Dalkeith and Lord Montague, sons of the Duke of Buccleuch.

This did not offend Scott in the least. In fact, it pleased him very much. The sheriffdom paid a small, steady income that would not unduly take his attention away from his writing. He had just published the first volume of his *Minstrelsy of the Scottish Borders,* and privately, it was this publication, of so little importance to most of those gathered, that he personally celebrated.

The scene of the party was a *laigh* or oyster house, where oysters and good claret were enjoyed in the shabbiest possible setting by men and women in all walks of life. Chiefly, which was rather surprising, the places were frequented by the upper classes—everyone from university students and poets to judges and businessmen, even some of the nobility. To Scott's mind, these places and the taverns were the most cordial of meeting places to be found in Edinburgh. Unlike the parlors of the gentry, no studied manners prevented one from observing mankind in all its infinite variation of mood, temperament, foible and even at times (though far less often) splendor.

This freedom of expression (and observation) was amplified not only by the presence of much strong drink, which relaxed the stiff social structure to a degree, but also because anonymity was, if not actually maintained, at least respected. The men cliqued together in clubs, whimsically called by nonsense names, as were the men themselves, who invented sobriquets to conceal their identities and protect their professional lives and private secrets from any follies they committed while under the influence of liquor and convivial company. Some of the ladies went further to maintain their respectability—they wore masks, so that matron or maid might partake of refreshment and mix among the men with freedom from censure and please herself without loss of reputation. Women who did not wear a mask might cowl their heads and faces with a tartan shawl, as the servant class did.

It was not that these disguises actually fooled their intimates, for the society of Edinburgh was relatively close, but the feeling of privacy it provided within the close confines of the city did much to aid the relaxation afforded by the drinking establishments.

Scott was not very fond of liquor, truth to tell, but he was fond of the company of others, when he did not urgently require solitude. Having just completed the second volume of his balladry collection at the time his first was published, he had had overmuch of his own company and was eager to go among his friends and learn what joy and trouble now concerned them and what events of their lives and the life of the city and country he might have missed while preoccupied with his own work.

The *laigh* was cavelike in its darkness, save for the glow

of the fireplace and that emanating from a pair of candles on the table where Scott and his friends shared oysters and claret in their third toast of the evening. Outside it was dark too, and had been since early afternoon. Midwinters in Edinburgh were gloomy indeed and it had been snowing heavily when Scott left his office. Not only did the night stay like an unwanted guest late into the morning, but it arrived all too soon in the afternoon. Coupled with that, the smoke of the many tall chimneys, the lums from which the smoke fouled the air for twenty miles or so from the city and lay upon it like a smelly blanket.

The darkness inside was preferable to the darkness outside, especially when there was claret and good whisky to be had inside, and company such as that in which Scott now found himself.

His companions were a mixed bag, some more suited to the drawing room, others to the barnyard. Scott had dubbed himself "Ivanhoe" after a knight he was in the process of creating as the hero of an upcoming book. James Hogg and the Reverend Erskine came, bringing with them Dr. MacRae, young Murray, and Corey Primrose, who had joined their company in the tavern on the previous evening. Lord Dalkeith was present, and already well into his cups, and Robert and Willie Dundas, sons and nephew of Henry, Lord Melville, who had been so influential in bringing about Scott's good fortune. A few of Scott's literary acquaintances attended, including Miss Gordon, Miss Ross, and, closest to his heart, the beautiful, the sweet, the charming Miss Williamina Stuart.

Inside the taverns, Hogg styled himself the Ettrick Shepherd and Dr. MacRae insisted on being known as Lang Davie, which he said he enjoyed because his physical stature in no way matched the magnitude of his mind, heart, talents, personality and appetites. The Reverend Erskine was laugh-

ingly called Father, since that good man had a hatred of all
that was Popish. Miss Gordon was called Dulcie, Miss Ross
styled herself Green Mantle, and Miss Stuart called herself
Columbine. Captain of the Town Guard James Laing called
himself St. Peter, since in his present position enforcing the
laws of the city he too, he said, was a fisher of men. With a
rather regrettable lack of imagination, Corey Primrose asked
to be referred to as the Deacon.

A few of Scott's intimates were missing but the little
room was crowded, nonetheless. And lively.

MacRae—Lang Davie—was regaling those who had not
been there with the uncovering of the skeleton, while
Laing—St. Peter—and the Ettrick Shepherd added their
own observations. Miss—Columbine—Stuart had been listening raptly, and smiled at Scott when Laing told of his arrival on the scene. But then the oysters were served and the
Deacon, sitting next to Columbine, playfully insisted that
she open her mouth like a baby bird while he poured one
down her throat. That led to a great deal of hilarity all
around, followed by Miss Stuart offering the Deacon an oyster in the same way.

There were toasts and speeches, but Scott could not help
noticing that Miss Stuart had stopped favoring him with the
odd glance or smile but instead leaned back from the table,
as did the Deacon, and exchanged with him half-whispered
remarks at which he sometimes grinned and she sometimes
giggled. Scott reminded himself that his career had been assured for him this evening, and fixed his attention more
firmly on what Lord Dalkeith was trying to say. It took some
doing, as Lord Dalkeith's words by now were so slurred that
they were as unintelligible as a Glaswegian's.

Miss—Green Mantle—Ross listened intently to Lang
Davie expounding on how to determine the age of bones and
beamed at him as if he were the cleverest person she had

ever met. Lang Davie reciprocated with hooded eyes and a bleary smile and lifted his glass to say, "To oor ain Green Mantle, the most charming and intelligent lady in all the world!"

Oh dear! He was "saving" her. His public comment was a signal to all the other men in the room to "save the ladies," by making similar extravagant public remarks to all the other ladies and forget no one, lest she be slighted and shamed by the omission. Scott personally disliked the custom. It invariably caused friction and stopped whatever intelligent conversation might be occurring. However, he was a gentleman and one with a vested interest in a lady he wished to compliment.

But this was Miss Stuart's first appearance at the *laigh* house and with his head full of fumes and confusion, he could not at the moment seem to recall what Miss Stuart was calling herself.

"Sweet Columbine," declared the Deacon, with no such lapse of memory and with raised glass and a long look at Miss Stuart through eyes that seemed to see only her. "Surely the most beautiful lady under heaven."

"And our Dulcie, the soul of compassion, wisdom, and all gentle and womanly virtues," Scott said quickly, toasting Miss Gordon, who was an old and dear friend and who gave him a glance that said she understood perfectly that he had not been able to make the toast he wished, but appreciated the gesture.

Others toasted their wives, the barmaid, the woman who ran the oyster house, but at length Miss Gordon said to the other ladies, "We'd best be off if we wish to be hame before the 'gardyloo,' lassies."

"Aye," MacRae said, "'twould nae suit such fair floowers of womankind tae be scented wi' wha's poured oot the windas when the man gies the signal. And it's close on ten o'clock noo." Ten o'clock being the hour when the cry was given and all throughout the streets of Edinburgh, windows were opened and slops poured out onto the pavement and—if they were not careful to have an escort to precede them and cry "Haud yer hand!"—onto the heads of the unwary passersby.

"Aye," said Miss Ross. "It's weel tae find a chair before the chairmen are too drunk tae see the street beneath their feet." Transport at night, in particular within the confines of the city walls and Canongate's narrow wynds and closes, was by means of sedan chairs, carried by the chairmen of the city. The chairmen, like most business people, drank in the evenings, some of them so heavily as to make a ride in their chair an adventure rivalling that of being in a carriage conveyed by runaway horses.

"I'll call chairs for ye, ladies," Laing said, plucking up his hat and coat while others helped the ladies on with their wraps, "and provide a pairsonal police escort."

Scott looked after Williamina longingly as she took her leave. When he turned his eyes back to the table, he was relieved to see that the Deacon was not likewise looking after the lady, but staring instead into his oyster shells.

PHYSICIAN'S NOTES:

A revelation has come to me on the heels of despair, for what I at first took for a rebuke now seems but His gentle example, a reminder to me of the perfection of his creation, the perfection I must strive to emulate with these poor parts to do justice to the fair face I shall attach to them.

He commanded my attention by putting in my way a creature so similar to my love in countenance that, had she my love's voice, my love's accent, my love's expression and laughter, she might be taken for her. Her grace and air of breeding reminded me once more of the sorry origins of my materials. Even as I was lifted up by her loveliness, I was cast down by the seeming impossibility of regaining such a harmonious wholeness for my love from so many diverse parts.

I see now that my doubt, my despair, was actually helpful in prompting me to formulate the questions that needed identifying before I could implement answers.

My angel and I were sitting quietly before the fire, as is our custom when I am safely within the walls of the home I made for my love and for her alone. A single candle flickered between us while the snow fell gently beyond the drawn velvet draperies she had found in Paris for this room "in a burgundy color, my love, which complements that in Mama's Persia carpet to perfection." What pleasure she took then in planning these small details of our future home!

But on this night we sat conversing. The housekeeper was attending to one of her church committees and so we were quite alone. The housekeeper does not see my beloved, of course, nor does anyone else, but they shall—they shall. Meanwhile, the spirit of my dearest remains always near to bear me company until I can construct for her from my science and art a new body worthy of containing that divine spark. I did not speak to her of the other lady, for fear she would mistake my interest for disloyalty. I spoke to her only indirectly of the doubts to which my encounter with the lady had given form.

"Are you cold?" I asked my beloved, who I felt to be even paler and more distant than usual, perhaps in contrast to the vibrant and living creature who so resembled her.

It seemed to me my dear one sighed and the candle flame dwindled for a moment.

"Of course you are cold, consigned to wait in limbo," I answered my own foolish question, and felt that I was in-

deed disloyal to make such comparisons between a living woman and she whose life had been so cruelly taken from her. "I wish you could speak to me, tell me what it's like there," I said aloud. "Does our Lord watch over you? Or must He wait for His best angel until I can bear to release her?"

A gentle smile seemed to play on the shadow that formed her full soft lips as the fire crackled.

"Ah, beloved," I said, leaning forward, longing to take her hand in my own. "You could not be more alive to me if it was the day before your death. I do wonder, though, you know, if this is a black art I perform, to seek to bring you wholly into our world again." And as I said it, the other lady's memory faded as if it were she who was the ghost, for my words were true. What I could not see of my love before my eyes is indelibly imprinted upon my heart and the other lady is but an echo of Her.

One white shoulder made of frost and velvet swivelled slightly toward the gloom and returned, a pretty half-shrug. My love found my doubts trifling, and I was encouraged by her confidence, and continued my discourse.

"To seek to create life, to preempt the Lord's own dominion, that would be a great sin indeed. But—and this is a very great difference, to my mind, to seek only to house such a bright spirit as your own left bereft of its shell because its body has been sorely ruined, surely that is a task not beyond a physician such as myself, or rather, a metaphysician? Why would the Lord give me such skill and knowledge if not to use it? Why would He give me such travail if not to motivate me to learn what I need to know, though I must do it in spite of my colleagues, in spite of the law, in spite of so-called natural law? Your shell I shall assemble from these rude bits I have gathered. It is only a matter of time, my dear."

She, who would never contradict me, seemed to raise one elegantly curved brow, not so much to question me as to prod me onward, to explore my thoughts further.

And at once I saw what she must have known was a flaw in my plan. "Aha! But what of that moment before you join, when this home I will build for you from the best flesh of others is still dead for want of the souls that once moved it, and you, who have been without a body are not yet wholly alive, how to join the two with the spark of life? What is required for that?"

She seemed so sad that I left off my own meditations and said, "Never mind, dearest, I shall think on it, experiment if need be, but I'm sure the answer is near at hand. Perhaps in one of my books, perhaps elsewhere, I will find some clue, for surely this same question has occurred to other, earlier scholars."

She gave me only the sweet melancholy smile I have seen so often and it sent me to my books at once. And there I found an allusion to a work by an alchemist who was a friend to the Virgin Queen's famous Dee. I believe I know where I might learn more of this, but in the meantime, I have a few little ideas of my own. I cannot be wrong, actually. Where else to find life but where it is created?

Oh, how I laugh with joy when I think of the wondrous ways our Lord works, His miracles to perform! For, if I had never doubted, I would not have questioned and had I not questioned, I would not have found the answer that is so critical to the success of the work I do for myself, for my love, and for His greater glory.

I feel I understand at last the other lady is not a temptation to sin or to despair, but simply a sign that God has put in my path. With her he reminds me that no matter the materials, no matter the physical resemblence, it is the Soul which will illuminate the mere physical details as long as the elixir of life is there to join the one to the other. Without this hour of torment, I would have failed to question and would ultimately have failed in my work. I fall to my knees and humbly give thanks.

Chapter VIII

MOST TRAVELLING PEOPLE couldn't read, but Geordie and Midge Margret, because of their father's insistence that they learn to do so, read tolerably well. Their father had taught them, and though their reading material was admittedly on the strange side, being, like everything else, whatever they could scrounge, they could understand a news sheet. They were going to nick it, Geordie making the pinch while Midge Margret distracted the seller, until they noticed that once people had looked at the papers, they threw them in the gutter. The tinklers found the cleanest copy they could, only soiled a bit around the edges with horse droppings, which had adhered the sheet to the relatively clean middle of the street instead of the disgusting stew swilling through the gutters.

Geordie read it, his breath, like Midge Margret's, coming in puffs. He took a swipe at his nose with his sleeve and said, "'Twere only bones, Midgie. Neither of the lassies would be bones yet."

Midge Margret looked over his shoulder. "No, but then, I wouldnae think if the noddies took oor lassies tae the dochtors, they'd be in the loch onyway. Still, it's a thought. Yer noddies may've put their claes in the loch, maybe, so's the dochtors wouldnae ken who the lassies were or where they coom frae."

Geordie snorted. "The dochtors wouldnae care. No' aboot tinkler lassies onyway."

"Weel, we're gaein' back by the loch anyway, are we no'? We may as weel hae a wee look."

Suddenly, another story caught her attention and she tugged at the paper. "Let me see that!"

"See what?"

"That! Tha's yer young lordship as liked oor sangs. Mr. Walter Scott. He's sheriff here noo."

"And wha' has that tae do wi' onything?"

"Mebbe he'd help us find wha' becoom o' Bella and Leezie. He were a daecent sort. Mebbe he'll mak' the noddies stop killin' folk."

"Ah, Midgie," Geordie said and surprised her by putting an arm around her shoulders and giving her a hard hug. "I was afraid the lout ye married had bate a' the child oot o' ye, but I see it isnae true. Yer Mr. Walter Scott, if it's aye the same man, is older now, and prosperous, and he wouldnae wish his fine friends tae know he'd ever had aught tae do wi' the likes o' us."

Midge Margret knew Geordie was probably right, but part of her stubbornly clung to the memory of how earnest the lad had seemed, how honored he had appeared to have been to be asked into their camp, how much he had enjoyed their songs and sharing their meal. Maybe he had changed and had his head turned, but maybe not. You never could tell about folk.

Geordie said, "I s'pose it wouldnae harum anything tae

tak' a wee peek round the loch. Could be the drainin' will uncover somethin' valuable—or at least useful."

"It's grawin' dark a'ready," Midge Margret observed.

"The street is nae sae lang," he answered. "And the snow has held off. If we hurry, we can see what's tae be seen and mak' it back tae camp by nightfall."

They had begun walking as they spoke and now Midge Margret's eye was caught by some baubles in the window of a jewelry store. She sighed, looking at her own cheap ring of brass and red glass.

Geordie noticed and clapped her on the shoulder. "Seems tae me the hooses look a wee bit poorer than they did when I was last here," he said.

"Prob'ly all the rich folk hae moved intae the bonny new hooses doon below," Midge Margret said. She sniffed. "I think it is worse. There's nae sae mony shops wi' fine things as there were before."

As they travelled farther from the castle, the shops were even fewer and poorer and the sky grew gloomier, the wind fiercer. The houses loomed up on both sides of them, dark and brooding, grimy and stinking.

"And they ca' *us* dirty," Midge Margret growled, then turned as a prosperous-looking woman with a kindly face marched by. "Spare a bit for a puir couple with nae lodgin's tae keep them frae the snow, madam?" she wheedled. But it was no good with Geordie along in plain sight and he had not disappeared quickly enough. A big strong man intimidated the ladies and also lessened their pity—they felt he could work for the money his woman was begging and also that he might take their fat purses by force if they didn't hurry quickly past.

As the tinklers walked through the Lawnmarket, they passed the Mercat Cross, above St. Giles Cathedral. Beyond the cathedral, which had once been Catholic but now belonged to the Church of Scotland, Geordie spotted a man he knew. He quickened his step and Midge Margret followed close on his heels.

"Ryk the Ramrod, what brings ye tae toon?" Geordie asked the man, who was short, stocky and swarthy, with graying black hair and blue eyes that shone with great intelligence and alertness.

"I s'pose I could be askin' ye the same question," Ryk the Ramrod responded. "But I ken the answer as weel as ye do. The winter's driven us in, o' course. Where do ye bide?" He shot a glance at Midge Margret, who used the opportunity to size him up. He was somewhat older than she, but still a young man, and there was good strength in him or she missed her guess. Though it was well into the late afternoon, he seemed sober and his clothing, though worn as anyone's she knew, was mended and cleaner than was the norm among her people, with so little access to water or other means of caring for their meager wardrobes. His hands were rough though, and blackened at the fingertips.

"We're campit oot in the auld forest, wha's left of it," Geordie said. "But there's been trouble oot there. Lassies bein' ta'en frae their beds and carried awa', or snatched while they're oot gaitherin' o' the wood. Folk there before us ken it's the noddies again."

"Lassies ta'en frae their beds?" he asked and glanced again at Midge Margret. "Could it no' be suitors after a bit o' rough wooin'?"

"Rough indeed tae shoot the wee dug tryin' tae protect the family. The dirty bastert pu'd the lass frae her mither's oxters," Midge Margret said.

Ryk the Ramrod grinned and jerked his thumb toward her as he asked Geordie, "So ye were tak'in nae chances wi' yer ain lassie, eh?"

"This is my sister, Margret, ca'd Midge Margret for rea-

sons ye'll ken oncet ye hae been aroond her awhile. She's a
guid lass but can be vexatious as the wee flittin' bug and as
full o' trouble."

Ryk the Ramrod bowed and winked at her and she gave
a little curtsy. "A lass wi'oot spirit is nae use atall. Pleased
tae mak' yer acquaintance, Midge Margret."

"We maun be movin' alang noo, Ryk. My wife, Jeannie,
and our bairns bide at the halt wi' ither families and I don't
like them bein' alane after dark. Midgie and me was gaein'
doon tae the loch tae see where thon lassie's leg were foond
by the Guard. The Bailey family lost their Bella yesterday,
and the Stewarts their Leezie this morning, so we thought
since they found thon skeleton in Nor' Loch, we would look
there as weel."

Ryk the Ramrod, to his credit, asked none of the questions they'd already asked each other. He said only, "Aye,
weel, I'll fetch Red Stevie and we'll cam wi' ye. If there's
murderers aboot, ye'll nae want tae be walkin' hame alane
after dark wi' a bonnie lassie such as yer Midge Margret."

"We'll be glad of your company," Geordie said.

When Ryk had gone, Midge said, "Who is he? Do ye
think we really need him an' his mate? Will they no' slow
us doon?"

Geordie shook his head, his eyes still on the building his
friend had gone into. "Not Ryk and Red Stevie. They're twa
o' the finest tinklers e'er tae live. Ryk the Ramrod understands firearms better than ony man in Scotland and Red
Stevie has made swords worthy o' kings. The pair o' them
are jewellers and welcome in mony's the fine hoose frae In-
verness tae Lunnon. Guid fighters too—though Red Stevie
is peaceable minded and more apt tae talk his way oot of it,
but he's a fine man nanetheless. Naebody's perfect."

Geordie's friend re-emerged, trailed by a tall man with a
red beard and mustache and a red braid swinging across his

back. He looked like a Highlander to Midge Margret, but his face was open and friendly and his eyes, also blue, seemingly guileless, did not fool her. If he was as successful as Geordie said, he would have to be both intelligent and tough. No man of her people could be a fool and mingle with the settled folk regularly and remain in one piece.

"Geordie, guid tae see ye again, mon," Red Stevie said, shaking her brother's hand and nodding and smiling at Midge Margret. His smile assured her that indeed he was no fool and probably received a certain amount of patronage and protection from the ladies in the various houses where the men sold their goods. "And your bonny sister. But say, Ryk mentioned that ye've had some strife where you are at present. Why do ye no' bring your people up here? Wi' a' the buildin' o' fine hooses gaein' on below, mony's the hoose up here is empty and deserted. We hae a complete floor a' tae oorsel's."

"Do ye no get sick smellin' the filth o' it?" Geordie asked, wiping his nose on the sleeve of his coat.

"Ryk burns them sweet smellin' candles he maks frae the floowers he collects in summer. It helps."

"We'll discuss it wi' the others," Geordie said.

"We were talkin' it ower and we think that yer murderers would be unlikely tae put onythin' in Nor' Loch, where the skeleton was found, but St. Margaret's Loch is near as handy, and until the snows began yesterday was yet clear o' ice. It's a wee bit farther oot o' yer way, but there's plenty o' time yet."

Geordie agreed and the four of them half walked, half slid down the steep icy hill past the Tollbooth prison, where Ryk said prisoners were often hanged from a gallows that could jut out from the side of the tall building with the noose suspended over the roof of the shorter building attached. Shops of various kinds occupied the shorter building and

Midge Margret wondered how the shopkeepers would feel having a hanget man dancing above their heads.

"Frae the look o' it, ye'd think hangin' folk was a brisk business here," Midge Margret said. "We've seen twa gallows a'ready in a short walk."

"Ah, and did ye miss the place where the witches were burnt? Geordie, ye're no' showin' yer sister aroond properly," Stevie teased.

They made it out the gate called the Nether Bow Port before it closed for the night. Ryk said that if they decided to return to the city, it might be necessary to bribe or trick the gatekeeper into letting them back in. Midge Margret remembered leaving that gate on the night she fled her husband, but she had not worried then about how to return.

From the Nether Bow Port, Red Stevie said with an airy wave of his hand, it was a straight shot, so to speak, down the Canongate and on to Holyrood House, where Queen Mary once lived. In the old days, there'd been an abbey there and debtors still sought sanctuary on the palace grounds.

"Could the noddies no' be amang the debtors? Maybe they took Bella and Leezie there?" Midge Margret asked.

"I dinnae think so," Ryk said. "Those folk hae mair rules than average, and are close watched tae mak' sure they dinnae leave except for the day a week they're allowed tae tak' care o' business. And there's ainly aboot a hundred o' them. Any funny business would be noticed and reported, you can lay yer life on't. Naebody there wants mair trouble than they a'ready have."

St. Margret's Loch, was, Stevie said, only a wee walk along the Queen's Drive from the palace. The drive was choked with snow but the men plowed along purposefully and Midge Margret followed in their tracks trying to hear what was being said while they pretended she was not there, though she could tell both of the newcomers were well aware of her. She wondered if they had wives.

The Holyrood Park was built around Arthur's Seat, a great mound of earth like a small mountain, still containing ancient battlements and defenses, and flanked in the distance by the Salisbury Crag. Around its edges was a forest surrounded by a drive broader and smoother than some of the roads. Down this road, Ryk told them, the queens and kings would drive their carriages of an evening for a breath of air. Midge Margret well understood why they might like to. The air was much better down here than farther up the street in the city. It was also full of wild game.

"Och, look, there's a fat hare!" she cried. "He'd dae for supper."

"Not unless you're ready tae lose yer head," her brother said. "This is a royal park."

She was about to protest that one rabbit would never be missed, when they saw the glimmer of the loch, rimed with glittering ice around its edge, but its center pewter against the gathering gloom. Swans and geese flocked about, and a few gulls, flapping and swooping, searching for food that was not there.

"Might be bonny in guid weather," Midge Margret said of the loch, clutching her shawl more tightly about her.

"If the weather's dry enough, the loch disappears," Ryk told her. "It overflows from St. Margaret's well during a lang rainy spell. The last few years, it's been here pretty constant, so that the nobility's been discussin' makin' it permanent-like. They enjoy haein' a bit o' a puddle tae gawk at while they're oot takin' the air."

The day had grown so dark, Midge Margret did not think they'd be able to find anything of value, but she reckoned the search was more to comfort Chrissie Stewart and her family than for any real hope of recovering Leezie or Bella.

Red Stevie whistled a bit as he walked with his hands clasped behind his back, sauntering like a gentleman surveying his domain.

The men seemed to take a grim satisfaction in the hunt. Geordie began walking along the shore to the left, while Ryk the Ramrod turned to the right. The footing was chancy. With the ice, where the shore left off and the loch began was difficult to see. Red Stevie had preceded his partner, his long legs bending sharply at the knees like a heron's as he picked his feet up from the snow and put them down again. No other footprints were there this evening.

Ryk cast his eye about the loch, like a hawk looking down from the air for a fat squirrel. This was a good trick for a short man. At last his glance stopped a few feet down the bank and out into the water, just beyond his partner. Stevie stopped and looked hard at the same time and Ryk called, "Steven?"

"I see it," the other man said. "I think I can reach it frae here. It's no' a stick, nor onything ye'd think tae see in a loch in the normal way o' things."

Midge Margret looked to where Ryk was pointing. Geordie made his way back along the bank to join them.

Stevie flopped onto his belly and inched forward on the ice. If he fell in, he'd have a cold walk back into the city in wet clothes, but the ice was firm enough at the edge that it held his upper torso and shoulders as he stretched out a long arm to something that made just the slightest dent in the edge of the ice, and a long dimple in the clear water, such as a half-submerged stick might do.

His fingers grasped the ice-encrusted end easily, but when he gave it a wee tug, it did not come closer to him but stubbornly remained where it was.

"'Tis only the frayed end of a rope but it's snaggit on something," Stevie said.

Ryk, staying carefully on the snow, made his way to where his partner lay and grabbed onto Stevie's heels. Geordie angled himself around to where the ice looked thicker and lay down in the snow, though not extending himself so far out on the ice, which might break from the weight of the two men, and reached out. "If ye kin pu' it a wee bit closer, Steven, I can grasp it as well. The twa o' us should manage."

With Ryk at his heels, Stevie snaked himself forward an inch or two and got both hands on the object, giving it a still careful but more forceful tug. This time it did move and he was able to pull it in where Geordie could help him. The two of them backed up until Stevie was free of the ice, and Ryk joined them in pulling on the rope. It looked as though the men were having a tug o' war with the loch.

As they pulled, Midge Margret crossed herself and held her breath, watching the rope emerge from the water. She was fairly dying to help the men, but there was nowhere for her to stand or grasp. She dreaded that they would find a drowned body, and was more inclined to expect—oh, a discarded jug, an old boot or cast-off carriage wheel, something disappointing. But what came up was the edge of a torn basket that sagged back into the water, as though weighted.

Suddenly it tipped and lightened, as if something gave way, and there was a splashing and small waves on the lake.

The men all fell back as the rest of the basket, having dumped whatever burden that weighted it, bobbed to the surface and sailed across the water, over the ice, and into their hands.

"Ye can ask yer friends if this might hae belonged tae their lassie, I s'pose," Ryk said, examining the basket briefly before handing it to Geordie. "It's no' lang been in the loch, frae the look o' it."

Midge Margret glanced back at the water as he said this, and even in the rapidly gathering gloom saw that the water's surface bore something that had not been there when she last looked. A billow of tartan floated on the surface, with a scrap of lace and some other things. No body, but clothing surely.

So soon Stevie stretched himself out once more and snagged the tartan—a shawl, with splinters among the threads. The others found long branches and snagged the other floating bits and pieces. A shirtwaist, of plain stuff but embellished with soggy fading ribbons, and a skirt of the same quality.

"Puir lassie," Ryk said, when the things were lying in the basket at his feet. "Puir wee lassie."

Midge Margret, her mouth set hard, covered the basket with the shawl and said, "'Twould be Bella's, or I miss my guess. Leezie was ta'en frae her bed. She'd nae basket, and Bella was said to be gaitherin' wood, and there's splinters in the basket and the claes."

She stood, grasped the strap, and said, "Nanetheless, we maun tak' these articles tae the camp. Bella had suitors and friends amang the others. They'll know sartain if these be hers or no'." And she began walking, towing the basket behind her as she had seen other girls do, as she imagined poor Bella must have done.

At the castle, they turned away from the town, through the Water Gate and onto a road Ryk the Ramrod said was the North Bank of Canongate. "If ye're campit oot beyond the new buildin' site, this will be shorter than the way ye've coom," he told them.

They were good company, these two, and they made Midge Margret feel—well, not safe, because the basket she towed was sure proof that safety was even more elusive than usual for one of her kind—but safer, at least, than she'd have

been on her own. Geordie had always seemed well-nigh in-
vincible to her, especially since he'd returned to camp with
sore hands and backed down anyone who tried to say his sister should be returned to her husband. Ryk the Ramrod and
Red Stevie looked to be of the same mettle as her brother
and though they were only three men, she was as content as
she would have been were she a queen accompanied by her
own guard. Surely there were few who would care to take
these lads on.

The moon came out, to her relief, and the stars, and if you
didn't count the smoke from the city, it was a clearish night.
The road might have been filled with snow that morning, but
heavy traffic from the Old Town to the New and back again
had flattened it. This was the Calton Road, Ryk told them,
and it now connected with Princes Street, running through
the heart of the New Town. It was beyond the New Town
that they wanted to go, to the newest town yet being constructed, on the grounds of the Moray Estate.

Geordie and Midge Margret were a bit awed by the fine
buildings now arrayed like formations of stone soldiers in
dress uniform in their straight rows up and down the banks
of the Nor' Loch. The streets were lit with lovely gas lamps
and fine people walked abroad—some had on snowshoes,
some skis. There were carriages with skis on the bottom occupied by people wearing warm, fur-trimmed clothing. Each
block was composed of a long, unbroken face of stately
massive new stone, still unbegrimed by the reek of the city.
That the single façade bore many dwellings could be told by
the doors set beneath fans of etched glass, spaced evenly
apart every twelve feet or so. Each door had a wee porch attached with a graceful awning held aloft by marble columns
fit for the gates of heaven. Most of the doors were white, but
a few were rebelliously painted in hues gay enough for a
gypsy wagon. Lions, eagles, unicorns, angels and demons

were carved into the lintels, besides which each façade bore
a quantity of other elegant ornamentation. Midge Margret
could hardly close her mouth, and all but forgot the sad basket shuffling on its tether behind her.

"It's bonny, no?" Ryk asked her. "In the day, wi' the sun
shinin' on the buildin's, the stane is golden."

He and Stevie talked of the furnishings of this house or
that house they'd visited, which judge, doctor, manufac-
turer, builder, or shipping magnate occupied each one, the
work that they had done for that particular family. "We've a
new sideline, y' see, in fancy door hinges, latches, locks and
knockers, fine fittings—ye cast them much like jewelry and
the quality are ae fond o' oor designs, eh, Stevie?"

"They are," the redhead agreed. "And d'ye ken, Midge
Margret, the studs on yon door? I designed that pattern
mesel'. I wonder did the fine lady who liked them sae much
ken that I had the same design on the door of me ain caravan when I was first on the road. Ye should see the rows of
servant bells in the place! Why, ye couldna hear the kirk bell
for the ringin' of them if a' the servants wis required at the
same time."

Midge Margret thought this well-lit fairy place might go
on for miles and miles, but it stopped with the last gaslight,
beyond which was the ruined landscape of felled trees and
unfinished buildings and roads.

The night fell hard upon them after so much light and
beauty, and the road was less clear than it had been. "They
don't do much work in the winter here," Stevie said. They
had been walking perhaps another hour, and behind them, in
the New Town, the sounds of traffic and human voices had
disappeared from the night air.

Suddenly, almost without warning, muffled horses' hooves
thudded behind them and they looked around just in time to

see a team of black horses conveying a black-covered coach on sledge runners.

Ryk the Ramrod suddenly barrelled into Midge Margret, knocking her backward into the tartan-covered basket. The sledge flew past them like some huge black corbie swooping down upon a bit of carrion. And then it was one with the night and silent.

"Damned fool," Ryk said.

Geordie and Red Stevie were wiping the snow from their clothing and looking into the night where the sledge had been.

The men tried to track it, but the track was confused by others and the darkness itself made the trail impossible to follow.

When they were within sight of the wood, they abandoned the tracking and in a short time were back within the encampment. Geordie and Midge Margret greeted their family and the others.

There was a terrible taking-on when the people in the camp recognized the basket and clothing as Bella's. Chrissie Stewart tore through the things, looking for something that might belong to her Leezie, but found nothing. Murdo and Tam carried on something awful with curses and threats and stampings around. But at last Johnny Faw quieted everyone down and decreed that the things must be burned.

"Should we no' take them tae her family?" Midge Margret asked. "They'll be wantin' tae larn o' this."

Johnny said, "We'll tell 'em when they're foond, but meanwhile these articles are onclean, and maun be cleansed wi' fire."

He grabbed a brand from the cookfire to light the woodpile. It was wet still and would be hard to light, but never would they contaminate the cookfire with such a grisly bundle.

"Haud a bit, Johnny," Chrissie Stewart said, standing between him and the bundles. "We ken these be Bella's things but we dinnae ken if Bella is still in this warld or no."

"She's worse than deid," Tam said, spitting at the ground, "if someone has ta'en her wi'oot her claes."

"Tha's yer opinion," Chrissie said angrily. "I say we keep them a bit, until we ken mair o' the matter."

"I agree," Midge Margret said. "Mebbe she and Leezie can yet be saved. The dugs may be able tae track them or . . ." She didn't want to risk ridicule by suggesting that perhaps the new sheriff could help them, but it was in her mind that lawmen liked bits and pieces from victims to prove a case. If they could raise the dead to give evidence, wouldn't the clothing surely be of some help? But she said not a word, though Geordie gave her a hard look.

At length Johnny Faw threw the brand back into the cookfire and said, "Aye, weel then, Chrissie Stewart, 'tis on yer ain heid. But I ken ye've an interest in the matter, sae we'll leave these claes bide a wee while unburnt."

Red Stevie picked that moment to pull from the satchel over his shoulder a fat hare he had nicked from the Holyrood Park.

This he and his companions spitted and ate. The others had already eaten, though Jeannie had saved a bit for Geordie and Midge Margret.

When all were fed, the men sat around with their pipes and the women their sewing by the firelight.

Ryk the Ramrod told them then of the empty buildings in the Old Town, deserted by the people who had moved into the fine new houses in the New Town and some of the finished houses in the even newer town. "There's plenty of room and the city has nae figured oot who's where tae levy taxes," he said.

The band agreed that would be the best thing to do, if

they could find somewhere to leave their caravans and animals. Red Stevie said he knew a reasonably honest farmer who might keep them over the winter, for a price.

That night Midge Margret heard a girl weeping and moaning and she tried to ask her to come out of the shadows, to come forward and tell what the matter was. But the voice made no answer except to weep all the louder.

PHYSICIAN'S NOTES:

Bloody fool that serves me, I should find a decent brain to put into his skull. He returned my carriage still shrouded and muddy with black slush. The horse was exhausted from being pushed far too hard.

The housekeeper, who first saw him, gave him the wrath of God for abusing the poor animal so, and he looked at her for a moment as if he saw the poor old soul as a potential future component of my love's new body.

I intervened of course and took the knave to my study and to task.

"What is the matter with you, man?" I demanded. "Driving as you must have done to bring the horse to such a lather in this cold, you must have the police or the hounds of hell after you."

"Ah, no, sir, not a bit of it," he said, as cockily as if we were equals. " 'Twas me chasin' them—the bitch of hell and the hounds with her. I saw her again, sir. I woulda had her too, but that bastard of a brother was with her and two other tough-lookin' fellas. She'd do nice for your work, sir. Got good parts, that one. I'll get her for you cheap if you let me watch you do her. Free if I can make the first cut and take her brother as a tip for yer friends over to the butcher shop."

Disgusted by the man's vengeful attitude, I held up my

palm and smacked it down on the desk, firmly. "I've told
you. I choose the next victim. Indeed, I hardly trust you to be
competent to take anyone but this woman. You may point
her out to me, however, and though I don't need many other
subjects before my work is ready for completion, if she is
suitable for what remains to be done, why, of course, I shall
consider her. Though I am somewhat loath to have the new
mortal vessel I am creating contaminated by a woman who
could arouse such animosity. Tell me, what did she do to
you?"

"She married me, the bitch. And left me," he said.

Chapter IX

THOUGH IT WAS only late afternoon by the time the tinklers had made arrangements with the farmer to park their caravans and lodge their horses with him through the winter, the city was all a-gloom once more as they entered by the Leith Wynd, which extended up the hill from the juncture of the Calton Road and the new Princes Street. Once through the gate, they trudged up the long hill leading to the grim fortress of Edinburgh Castle, a castle with no aspirations to grandeur at all, being merely a blocky fortress—a barracks more than a palace.

No longer did any king or queen of Scottish blood sit there, no friend to Midge Margret's people such as James IV had been, issuing edicts protecting the rights of the tinklers. No, now the country was controlled by the old enemy, the neighbor to the south, the Sassenachs, and they were the same who had driven Midge Margret's Highland ancestors onto the road.

A pall of fog mixed in the soup of shadows and smoke

enveloping the city so that Midge Margret could not see her feet before her to avoid the worst of the filth.

Her mother had always said the countryside was best for tinklers, as in the cities the people were so much harder, the charity was scarce and the reek of the chimneys so much worse for a body than the clean smoke of a campfire. It had been the same in her mother's day, during the hard winters when there was no food or fuel, the people must risk their lives and freedom to come mingle uneasily with the settled people. But back then there had been more game. Now there were few forests for the stag and bear and it took many rabbits to feed even a family as small as Midge Margret's.

Mother had liked Edinburgh least of all cities and Midge Margret recalled her saying she never approached it without prayers on her lips.

Of course, for her own reasons, Midge Margret was uneasy here, where she had been betrayed and beaten nearly to death by a man who had promised to love her. What a pitiless place it was where people were beaten for the price of liquor or murdered for the few bob their dead bodies would fetch! The very walls, instead of offering protection from the elements, seemed only to loom ominously, threatening to enclose her in a trap. From the castle at one end to the rocky crag of Arthur's Seat at the other, everything was so tainted by the stinking grayness that the snowflakes themselves blackened as they fell.

Ryk the Ramrod and Red Stevie helped the travelling families find an empty floor three flights up in one of the buildings. The ground floors still held shops, but the upper floors, where the quality had lived away from the stench of the streets, were vacant. In some places the poor had moved up a floor or two, but the exodus from the terrible conditions in the Old Town was so great that there was still plenty of room left. Midge Margret, walking through the narrow close that led from the street to the cul de sac containing the house, felt as if she were being swallowed up—the close was only a narrow walkway between one building and the next—the second floors of all of the buildings in the block were a solid front so that she actually passed underneath the second floor of the two adjoining buildings to reach the house beyond.

When her folk were settled and each family had figured out where it would sleep, it was time to work.

FROM THE WARMTH of the tavern, Scott and his cronies had watched the ragged tinklers struggle up the street, their belongings and smallest children strapped to their persons, while older children with various bundles trailed behind. The snow fell thickly around them and puffs of fog caused the wayfarers to inadvertently play tag with each other, as the gray swirls hid first one person, then another, then two or three more.

"Well, it's official now," Hogg said. "It's a hard winter. The Travelling People have come to the rock to roost."

"That they have," the deacon agreed. "Poor souls."

"Good for the local folk, though," MacRae said philosophically. "Makes your job aisier too, Scott. Every crime committed while they're here, a' ye need do is nab a tinkler for it."

Scott ignored the remark and turned his chair again to look out the long narrow window at the front of the tavern. Under the gas lamp, the wanderers made a ghostly seeming procession—tattered men and women, children hopping from one rag-cloaked foot to the other.

"Ah yes. We should pay them a visit, eh, Shepherd? I wonder if they know Geordie and his little sister."

"Eh?" Erskine asked. "Who's that?"

"A tinkler lad was accused of a murder he didn't do. Our good Shepherd here persuaded the family to stay their hands and saw that the law was sent for, and the—er—witness properly questioned."

"I did ainly what was fair," Hogg said, "and had Plummer been sae wrang-headed as some ither men of the law, it wouldnae done the lad ony good atall." To the rest of their company he added, "After the tinkler laddie was won free, Ivanhoe here had him singin' sangs tae pu' in the *Minstrelsy* books. But I think it was a wee yella-haired lassie he would-hae brought hame if her brother had allowed it."

Scott laughed and admitted, "I've never heard a singer like young Midge Margret before or since. I'd have been a fool not to appreciate her gift."

With the fog and the snow, the features of the people passing by the window were indistinguishable, but Scott thought there was something familiar in the movements of one or two of them. He watched until they were beyond his vantage point. Now that he was sheriff, he supposed it would probably create some sort of conflict to renew his acquaintance, but he sorely wished to if possible.

"I fear that now that winter is upon us, it makes me long for an early departure to my own bed, gentlemen," the deacon said as he stood. "And tomorrow is the Sabbath."

Scott rose as well. "I have a few notes to make this evening on a new idea that's come to mind. I'll walk with you as far as my lodgings if you don't mind, old fellow."

Hogg and Dr. MacRae chose to remain, but the Reverend Erskine joined them, and he and Scott fell into animated conversation as they followed in the wake of the tinklers' procession. Primrose nodded and grunted at all the right moments, but was preoccupied. Scott hoped he was wrong in thinking that the man lingered a bit when they passed the

dwelling where Williamina Stuart and her family currently
resided.

Physician's Notes:

*Once again the Lord answers my prayers using vessels of
the lowliest clay to carry golden inspiration. I obtained a
description from my servant of his wife and her brother and
tonight I saw them. While the woman so detested by her husband, my employee, is on the surface no more or less useful
than any other slattern of her race, there is another who
walks beside her, and she has exactly the element I seek. I
did not know it before I saw her because most women, of
course, do not parade themselves in such a condition. But
these gypsies have no delicacy, and no honor. Though, truth
to tell, the one who is the answer to my prayers has a face
and limbs almost worthy of she who will be the recipient of
this gypsy's unwitting gift.*

*My servant kept watch on them later, I learned, and was
amused to find that they have taken up residence with persons and in a location most convenient for me. I cannot trust
the servant, however, with his own concerns for the one
woman so greatly outweighing my need to acquire the other.
This catch I will make myself.*

ONCE INDOORS, AWAY from the wind and snow, among
her people and with Red Stevie and Ryk joking and making
the *craic*, good fun to add laughter to lighten the work of
moving in, Midge Margret felt considerably better, and
began to smile a bit herself.

She asked Geordie, "Those laddies, are they married?"

He raised an eyebrow and grinned at her. "Here and there
a few times I s'pose. Why, are you interested?"

"I might be. If I ainly knew if I'm married meself or no."

Geordie scowled and turned away from her. He was a very good brother, but on this subject she could not get him to answer. She thought perhaps he wasn't sure himself. They each returned to settling the family in the new quarters, hauling their few precious possessions down the close so narrow that a very fat person could never have made it through. The building was the back one in the cul de sac, which was essentially a bit of space enclosed on all sides by tall buildings. The other houses were fairly decrepit, but this one had some nice rooms on the fourth and fifth floors. Red Stevie said their employer had told them the lower floors were very old, shabby, stinking and infested, where once only poor people had lived, those folk having moved on to the superior floors in another building before the rich inhabitants of this one had moved over to the New Town.

The stairs were narrow and steep but this was no impediment to Midge Margret's folk, who were used to hill-walking, though she wondered a bit that the wealthier people had put up with it for so long. Unlike the warrens on the ground floors of most buildings, these upper stories were laid out like regular houses—the fourth and fifth floors had, in place of the narrow stone stairway, a broad, sweeping staircase of carved wood between them, and great long windows looking out onto the loch in the back. There were lovely fireplaces to lay fires in and the floors made a smoother, softer bed than the ground ever had been.

Johnny Faw insisted that Midge Margret, if she was to keep the things belonging to Bella Bailey, stay apart from the others, in a different room. Her niece Jenny cried, wanting to come with Aunt Midgie, but her mama shushed her and said of course she could not, she was needed to take care of her wee brother, and Auntie Midgie would not be apart from them long. Midge Margret was left to find a place for herself on the fifth floor, in the attic where the rich people's

servants once slept. The other servants' rooms were not
needed by her people, so she had the floor to herself. She
chose a room at one end of the hall, away from the stench of
the street. It had a fine view from its one round window at
the wall, under the dormer. The bad thing was, except for
Geordie and Jeannie, others kept their distance from her
now. She had become unclean, unsanctifit herself, by asso-
ciating with the belongings of a person at least presumed
dead.

She told herself she could put up with that little inconve-
nience for a bit for something so important. Bella Bailey's
people were still being sought in the countryside and when
they were found, they would be invited to return and join the
others. Meanwhile, Midge Margret had it in mind that she
would still take these things to Mr. Scott—Sheriff Scott—
and see if he could make use of them to find the bastard who
had taken Leezie and Bella. If not, then the things could be
returned to Bella's family to be burnt if they wished. Meanwhile, her ostracism was a small matter, and she told herself
she didn't mind, really. She would have preferred to be
below, of course, helping organize things, as she was used
to doing, but for the time being she didn't mind being alone.
She fell into bed exhausted and slept with the bitter taste of
smoke on her tongue.

The next day the fog lifted only slightly. Also, it was the
Sabbath, and according to Ryk and Red Stevie, no hawking
or begging could be done on pain of being dragged off to
jail. The time was spent in organizing their new quarters instead.

Midge Margret arose quite early and put her cleanest
skirt on top of the others and changed into a clean shirtwaist
and apron, then gathered up the basket, clothing and all, and
wrapped it in a blanket of her own, like a bundle of wash.
Then she tripped downstairs past her sleeping companions.

A sharp hiss brought her to a temporary halt. "Here now, Midgie, where do you think you're going?" Geordie asked.

"Well, if I'm no tae be of ony use here, I may as weel mak' myself presentable and see what the local kirks are like. Who knows? I may even want tae join one."

He rolled over onto his stomach and buried his head in his arms, dismissing her.

At the water faucet below, she did a quick wash up. She had to balance the bundle on her head through the narrow wynd, but once out on the High Street, she carried it at her side as if it were little more than a large purse.

One of the Town Guard was striding up the street, approaching her, and before she could turn away had seized her arm, scowling. "Where dae ye think ye're off tae on the Sabbath, ragamuffin?"

"If you would be sae kind as tae release me, Officer, sir," she said in her plummiest tones, quite like the greatest lady she'd ever sold a bit of ribbon to. "I'll gang tae kirk, and say me prayers, that God and the Virgin Mary and the Baby Jaysus forgive the likes o' yerself for impedin' an honest woman . . ."

Still keeping a tight grip on her arm, he doffed his cap and made an elaborate bow. She considered kneeing him in the chin, but thought better of it. He was a large burly-looking fellow with red hair and a full set of red chin whiskers and a big red nose to match.

"Yer elegant pardon, Yer Highness, I was merely gaein' to gie ye a poliss escort sae as not tae let the riffraff annoy yer elegance. Which congregation dae ye belong to, milady?"

"Beg pardon?" she asked. She hadn't considered that. Most places she travelled had only the one kirk. This city had at least five right here on the main street.

"Which kirk do ye attend?" the man asked with a glower that said he was getting tired of their game.

"Weel, normally, o' course, I attends sairvices held in the family castle's chapel, but I thocht, in order tae mak' sure I was at the best ane, I would like tae attend whichever kirk yer new sheriff, that Mr. Walter Scott, was attendin'."

"Och, ye would, would ye?" he asked, still holding on to her arm. He looked a bit surprised to hear that she wanted to be anywhere near a sheriff.

"Aye, I would," she said, staring him in the eye and thinking, *Did I not just say so, ye great lummox?* She didn't say that, however, because though she met his eyes with her own, she was well aware of his big ham hands with their big sausage fingers about to snap her arm in two. "Noo then, Officer, I've answert yer questions and I'm aye aboot tae freeze me arse off. If ye'd be sae kind as tae release me arum and direct me tae the sheriff's kirk, I'll bid ye good day."

He dropped her arm as if it were dirty. No doubt arresting her was too much trouble when he had other things to do, like drinking on the sly or seeing his doxy when he was supposed to be on duty. "If ye tak' my advice, ye little gyppo, ye'll avoid the sheriff and St. Giles Cathedral and git yer frozen arse oot o' toon before them less charitable on the Sabbath than mesel' run ye in."

It didn't even occur to her to be insulted at this abuse, since it was the way police customarily spoke to her kind. "Thanks ever sae much," she said, giving a limp ladylike wave as he stalked up the street. St. Giles Cathedral was dead easy, being just beyond the Luckenbooth stalls. She turned and headed for it. After all, it wasn't work after all she was wanting to see Scott for, but a remembrance of their old friendship, just to let him know she was in town. She'd not say where the others were. And as for giving him

Bella's things, well, that would be an act of charity and she wouldn't be asking him to do something about the snatchings, not on the Sabbath, but rather to pray for the poor girls.

Chapter X

WITH ALL DUE respect to his staunch Presbyterian ancestors and the courage of the Covenanters who had opposed it, Walter Scott was himself very happy to be a faithful member of the Church of Scotland. During his boyhood, church had been an all day family affair with endless hours spent listening to sermons. Now, happily, there was a morning service and an afternoon service and a meal to be had at the end of each.

The Reverend Mr. Erskine drew to the end of his sermon, the choir sang its last hymn, and people were beginning to file out when a ruckus broke out in the rear of the church.

"Tak' yer paws off me, ye great lout!" a female voice cried. "I've as much right tae be in kirk as anybody!"

"Come along, noo, and quietly, there's a good lass, or I'll have to quiet ye doon wi' me baton," came a gruff male voice in response.

Scott rose and turned, holding on to the pew for balance, as he could not use his cane until he was in the aisle.

A great many people were between him and the disturbance, though he craned his neck to see.

"I thought it were a tale of yers, coomin' tae the kirk where yer betters worship, but then I saw ye coom in. Ye'll no be beggin' on the Sabbath and bein' a bother . . ."

"I wisnae gaein' tae bother onybody," she screeched. "I brang somethin' tae gie the sheriff . . ."

"What? Yer dirty auld claes. Naebody would have the poxy things . . ."

"Ow!" she cried, by which Scott took it that the constable had used some minor force in removing her.

"Excuse me, sir, may I pass?" Scott asked the man in front of him, but the woman in front of him had her nanny and two small children in tow and a great heavy lady in many yards of dark blue satin embroidered with green cabbage roses blocked the aisle ahead of them. Behind Scott pushed two other families with screeching babies, and the aisles between him and the door were emptying at a rate of one person every few seconds.

"I beg your pardon," he said to the nanny.

"Won't do a bit of good to beg with these ones," she told him from the side of her mouth. "I try it but there's naethin' much works short o' the hickory switch."

At the mention of the switch, which the children apparently could hear far above the other clamor, they too broke into a bawl.

By the time Scott passed the place where he fancied the fracas had taken place, no one remained in the pew. He was not, indeed, to know anything about it until the following morning.

MIDGE MARGRET HAD hoped by now that Bella's belongings would be with Scott, who would have listened attentively while she explained what had happened to the girl and to Leezie Stewart and then, of course, he would agree to investigate the matter the same as he would for any other kidnapping or murder.

But the brute of a constable had hustled her out of the kirk, where she had sat through that long, boring sermon, before she could find Scott and catch his attention. She wasn't about to leave Bella's things with the constable, who would probably sell them for drink, and so she started back to the family's quarters with a flea in her ear, bruises on her wrist and arm, and Bella's belongings still in tow. She had at least managed to tell that beast of a guard what she thought of Edinburgh justice, but since he had been yelling as loud as she, it was no great consolation.

Her desolation was made worse by the the icy rain that soaked her head and the tartan shawl she had thrown over it. The rain packed the blackened snow into heavy, glassy slipperiness. Although it was only midday, there was less light than in a summer twilight, and the wynd was full of shadows and foul odors as she made her way back to the flat.

She heard the music of Geordie's fiddle before she reached the foot of the stairs, which were very icy indeed. She knew better than to linger on the fourth floor, where the fiddle was playing while people listened to its melancholy strains and a few moved in time to the music, while others slept. Cooking smells came from the fireplace. The band of travellers was taking a holiday from their labors, both to mourn and to settle in, which was wise, since enough of the strict Presbyterian roots of the city remained that except for churchgoers, the streets were deserted, the shops shuttered and all commerce stopped on the Sabbath. As Ryk and Stevie had warned that neither any hawking nor begging was allowed on Sunday, the travellers took a holiday too.

Geordie was intent on his music, and Jeannie and some

of the other women were leading the children in a sedate dance-game, so Midge Margret retreated up the steps, not even cheered by the site of a bowl full of food and a bit of bread waiting outside her door.

She threw Bella's things down in a corner of the room, and looked around at the bare, cheerless place and almost wished she'd provoked the constable into throwing her into jail.

Eating did lift her mood enough for her to begin to wonder what might be in the other rooms on the attic floor, and if something of use or interest might not have been left behind when the owners vacated the floor. Rich people always had lots of bits and bobs they didn't want to trouble over, when they could get new ones so easily.

The other rooms along the hall were smaller than hers, but at the other end of the top floor, though she had to pick a lock to do it, she found exactly what she had hoped for, a storage room, better than any pirate's trove to her at the moment.

She had only a candle and the dilute daylight filtering in from the dormer window when she discovered the place, but found an old oil lamp with a cracked chimney and, of all things, oil still in the base. Lighting it, she could see all the dust and all the cobwebs draped over everything like dingy gauze curtains. She found a rolled-up carpet and returned to her room with it, spreading it on the floor. To her surprise, it was almost new, the nap thick and soft, the pattern bright with reds and golds. Its only flaw seemed to be a large stain in the middle. She tried to imagine being so well off that she could discard a new blanket or rug simply because of a stain. There were old cushions too, these faded and threadbare in places with frayed gold-rope edging, but the insides still plush. Two of these she also took to her room. There were also some rich and lovely clothes, some worn, some not, but she thought she would save those for later, when she chose to make the room known to the others. If they wanted to stick her away up here where all of the interesting stuff was, it was too bad for them if she took first pick. From what little she could see of the color, two of the gowns would be beautiful on Jeannie, with her coloring, and were about her size when she wasn't pregnant. Midge Margret would snag those and surprise Jeannie with them when she'd had the new bairn.

She put the clothes aside and looked around once more and spotted, in one deeply shadowed corner, what at first looked like stacked bricks but turned out to be piles and piles of books. She decided to go through these to find some for herself and Geordie to enjoy and some to teach Jenny and wee Martin to read from when the time came.

The dust made her sneeze but she sat down in it and looked at the books nonetheless.

To her disgust, many of them weren't even written in English, but Latin. She knew a few Latin words, but not enough to make sense of an entire book. The thick, heavy volumes were mostly of that kind and she piled them off to one side to dig deeper into the stacks, building a bit of a wall around her as she eliminated the unreadable or boring ones.

She came to one in Latin that was as boring as the others, as far as text was concerned, but contained a shocking drawing of a naked woman in a stiff, unnatural pose. She closed it quickly and put it with the others. Digging deeper, she found books in both English and Latin, evidently connected with religious matters, as the authors were all Reverend This and Father That. Some of the books were in other languages. She recognized Spanish, French and German from individual words, but one, which she was sure would be in Spanish, as the author was named Miguel de Cervantes Saavedra, she was pleased to see was in English and appeared to be a story. She set this close beside her and found only one other book in this section that looked interesting, one with no title or author, in which the words were handwritten, with dates beside them.

The next section had books which were partially in English but filled with strange symbols and numbers. These too she set aside. She was rewarded at this point by one more of the handwritten books, this one also with symbols, but of a different type, and containing what seemed to be maps and charts, all hand drawn. This she put with the other two.

At last she came upon some books for children, fairy tales and such. These she scooped up. Cramped with hours of sitting cross-legged and bent over the volumes, she rose, set down the books long enough to stretch and pound the dust from her dress and apron, then picked up the armload of books she had selected and returned to her own cozy room.

The oil lamp provided light bright enough to read by, even in the dark. The book by Cervantes was very long and the type set close, so she decided to look into one of the handwritten books instead. She examined the one with the symbols and maps, but could make little sense of it, and thought perhaps some of it might be explained in the other book, so she began to read it. The notes talked of questioning people, most of them women, and getting denials or confessions by employing this or that thing, none of which made much sense to Midge Margret. She finally decided that the writer must have been a lawyer of sorts, because he spoke of trials and verdicts, judges and juries, and punishments.

She skimmed through the book, and stopped when she saw the line: "Burned until her bodie was consumed and cleansed by flames . . ." She threw the volume from her as if the book itself had burned her.

How was she to get to sleep if she read that sort of thing at bedtime? She picked up one of the fairy-tale volumes instead, but it was no better, telling of a woman who married a man with a locked closet. Midge Margret did not know very much about books, but she knew she didn't want to know what was in that closet.

She set that book aside too and blew out her lamp.

She fell asleep feeling lonely, but during the night felt someone beside her, her niece Jenny perhaps, and thought that her family had not abandoned her after all. Except that the smooth and rounded skin of Jenny's little arm was very cold indeed. Midge Margret tried to wake herself to cover her brother's child, and thought she opened her eyes, but then realized she had to be dreaming, because it was not wee Jenny there but some strange woman dressed in a fine gown and lying quite still. Disliking the dream, Midge Margret, still asleep, rolled over and shrank away to the far side of the carpet.

PHYSICIAN'S NOTES:

Only three more nights until the full moon, when all the the grafts and transplants must take place if they are to become part of one whole. My beloved grows impatient, as do I. I told her of meeting the other lady, and of how I knew it to be a sign from God, but that did not seem to comfort her.

I must not dwell on her pain, however, but concentrate on how I shall acquire the final ingredient necessary to our success, the gypsy woman who is to provide the link between body and soul.

Chapter XI

THE INCIDENT OF the skeleton in the loch had given Scott a nudge toward beginning a poem he had in mind based on the Arthurian legend of the Lady of the Lake. He was staring out his office window, pen poised over clean paper, when someone knocked at the door.

The interior whisper that had been speaking the first line or two of the story, just a bit softer than he could hear, broke off entirely, and with studied patience Scott laid down his pen and called for the intruder to come in.

Angus marched in and stood at attention.

"What's got intae ye, man?" Scott demanded a bit more harshly than he would have had he not been interrupted.

Angus looked down at him and apparently saw nothing but the grown-up version of the Borders lad he had known from childhood. He lowered his arm tentatively. "Weel, Mr. Scott, I was just showin' respect, because o' yer new position, ye see. That mak's ye my superior. When I made me report last evenin' tae the captain, he said I maun tell ye of this thing, unimportant though it surely is."

"What thing is it that's so unimportant you have to make a special trip to tell me, Angus?" Scott asked, and then remembered the incident in the kirk the day before. "It wouldnae have to do with a lady in the kirk that wanted to speak to me, would it?"

Angus gaped down at Scott as if the man had pulled the guess out of a crystal ball.

"I was *in* the kirk when it happened, Angus," Scott told him dryly.

"O' course, sir. Ye would be, wouldn't ye?"

"Yes, I gather that's why the lady in question was there," Scott prompted.

"Och, that was why all right, sir, but it 'twas nae lady after ye but a wee divvil of a tinkler lassie wi' a great lump of laundry under her arum. She had the brass tae ask me which kirk ye attended and—weel, sir, I couldnae believe she was serious, sae I tolt her, jokin' like. Then I happened to look down the road and there was the little hoor"—Scott scowled at him. He did not approve of disrespect in reference to the fair sex—"the lassie, sir, enterin' the kirk. 'Course, I could dae naethin' aboot it ontil the end of services, sae I waited and when the last hymn was finished I went in and nabbed—er—apprehended her and the cheeky thing bit me."

He held out his hand to show Scott the angry tooth marks between thumb and first finger.

Scott clicked his tongue and pretended to examine the bite. "Och, tha's a bad wound indeed, Angus. We'll trust she was not rabid. Did you lock her up?"

"Nay, sir. I thocht it best tae speak wi' the captain, and wi' yerself first, sir. Ye see, after I got her oot o' the kirk, she said she was an auld friend of yers, coom tae see ye

aboot a very serious matter. Said she had proof o' what she
was sayin' and she was deid sartain ye would want tae see
her. Said ye owed her and her folk for some help wi' ane o'
yer buiks, Scott, the bold piece. Her that probably wouldnae
ken if she was hauldin' a buik rightside up or no!"

"Did she give you a name, Angus?" Scott asked.

"Aye. Mary or somethin'. I'm sorry, Scott, I didnae think
she wis tellin' the truth."

"I'm sure you did your best, Angus, but if you see her
again, please ask her—politely—to come here to see me.
Escort her yourself, if she'll permit it, so no other well-
meaning officer will intercept her."

A lascivious interpretation of the situation gleamed in
Angus's eye as he relaxed and said, "Aye, Mr. Scott. I'd nae
idea it were that way. But o' course, yerself bein' a bachelor gentleman and all, I s'pose . . ."

"I will forget you said that, Angus, as we're auld friends.
But the fact of the matter is, she is a relative of a former—
client—of mine and they did indeed provide me with some
interesting additions for my *Minstrelsy*. Please do not let me
hear that any other interpretation is being bruited about."

"Nay, Mr. Scott. I'll thrash the gossip that suggests any
such thing, personally, sir."

Angus had left then and the rest of the morning was fairly
uneventful. The words that had begun to form earlier did not
return, as Scott set to wondering what he might say to Miss
Stuart at the reception that was being held by her family that
evening, and what she might say to him.

Chapter XII

ON MONDAY THE tinklers set out to earn their living, most of them by going a-hawking and begging. The Stewarts were muggers—potters—and they had with them some of their pottery. The Gaginos were horners—makers of horn spoons. They and others with things to sell carried their wares from house to house, to sell or trade and to beg for coal as well as bread. Some had to stay behind to protect the children. Ryk and Stevie returned to their own place and their own work in an adjoining building.

The assignments were quickly made by auld Johnny Faw, who had discussed his decisions with the others while Midge Margret was alone in her attic. Once more, the women would be accompanied by men, who would stay out of sight as much as possible so as not to queer the pitch. This day, it was other women who would guard the children.

"Come alang, Midgie," Geordie said when she came downstairs, much earlier than she had intended to rise, thanks to her uneasy dreams. "Ye'll come wi' me an Jeannie.

The bairnies weel bide wi' the Faws. Some folk are ta'en their wee anes wi' them, but I want tae hae the lay o' the land before we tak' them oot."

Begging and hawking in the city was a bit different than in the country. Not so many miles to cover, but up and down the steep hill all the day, and up and down steps as well, to get to the posh places on the upper floors of the buildings.

Jeannie and Geordie stayed below while Midge Margret climbed the long stairs and wheedled food and fuel from the women and servants who lived above the streets. Geordie would come after her, she knew, if she ran into problems, but as the one stairway was the only way to get up or down, no one was likely to carry her off. And Jeannie was too heavy with her unborn bairn to manage the stairs.

Midge Margret climbed and begged, offered laces for sale, thanked those who gave her something, then asked for more, or cursed those who gave her nothing.

One beautiful young woman, obviously preparing for a party, shared some cakes and smoked salmon. Midge Margret normally should have whined and asked for more, but she was so impressed with the amount and quality of the food that instead she said, "You're the kindest person I've met all day, miss. If you'll allow me in tae hae a seat for a wee bit, and haud oot yer hand, I'll gie ye yer fortune fer the sake o' yer kindness." Thinking on it later, Midge Margret couldn't say why she did it, really. Normally, she never would give anything away, especially to someone so obviously well off, but something inside her pushed the words out of her mouth. When she looked at the lady's palm, she thought she understood where the impulse might have come from. She took in her breath sharply.

"What is it?" asked the lady, snatching back her soft white hand as if Midge Margret had burned it. She was so very pretty with her honey-colored hair piled high in great drap-

ing loops, her wide blue eyes and heart-shaped face with its
turned up nose. She was dressed in a gold-embroidered
peacock-colored tea gown, a feather print emulating the
bird's fantastic tail forming the trim of the gown, and the
body the brightest blue-green. Her earbobs were real emer-
alds and turquoises, Midge Margret was sure, set in gold
they were, and giving her blue eyes an exotic greenish cast
to them. The sweeping darkened lashes of those eyes
fanned wide now and the dainty coral mouth formed an O
of alarm.

"No, no, it's nae sae bad, lady. Jist let me hae anither wee
peek, please. There," she said as the lady cautiously extended her hand again. "That's better noo, dearie. Ye see
here, noo, this is wha' caught me eye, and it's this I maun
warn ye aboot. Ye see this line here?" she asked, stroking
the middle horizontal line of the lady's palm.

"Aye. Aye, I do," the lady said, nodding.

"Thas yer heid line. This ane above it here is yer love
line. And this'un here, frae yer thumb doon toward yer
wrist, thas yer lifeline. Noo then, on yer loveline, d'ye ken
these three wee lines branchin' off it like?"

The lady nodded again.

"This 'un, this un is strang at first but fades awa' in a wee
bit until it's verra faint. It significates a gentleman who ye
may think of as a loover noo, but who weel no' be the man
ye loove in the end. He may weel become a guid friend tae
ye, though. This line here, ye see how it gaes up, strang and
straight."

"Och, aye," the woman said, nodding hopefully.

"Noo, thon gentleman would be yer true loove, lady, and
a guid un. But see ye the line here, also verra strang, but rin-
nin' doon across yer heid line till it meets yer lifeline? And
how the lifeline fades here?"

"Aye."

"This man will deceive ye and seek tae cause ye harum. Ye see here where he cooms in, yer lifeline a' but vanishes . . ."

"You—you mean he might actually—kill me?" the pretty lady gasped, and her free hand, the one with the wee golden ring, fluttered to her heart.

"Lady, he may try. Ye understand noo, these lines, they change all the time, they're nae set in stane but in yer ain flesh and bluid. The message in this is that ye maun be as carefu' as aye carefu' can be. If ye hae three suitors, until ye ken which is which, dinnae be alane wi' ony o' them. Always hae yer fither or a brother or e'en ane o' the ither gentlemen within hailin' distance."

"I shall. I shall. But why? Why will this man try to hurt me?" the lady asked. The pink was in her cheeks now and Midge Margret was glad to see it, and recognized it as betokening not just alarm but a very useful anger as well.

She rose, grabbed up her booty, and shrugged. "I dinnae ken that, dearie. Yer palm ainly shows me sae much as I've taud ye. Why does anything happen? Just mind ye that it could and beware, ye ken?"

"Aye," the lady said, and stood up too. "And thank ye, lassie, fer the warning. Here—" She dribbled a handful of hard candies into the pocket of Midge Margret's apron. "Take some extra sweeties for yer bairnies."

"Yer a verra kind lady. I hope the bastert does ye nae harum."

"Forewarned is forearmed. Mind the stairs noo." She held open her own door for Midge Margret and let her out.

By eight o'clock, when the shops closed and some husbands would be on their way home from work, Midge Margret could climb no more. She rejoined Geordie and Jeannie and the three of them sat down to enjoy the young lady's treats. Normally, they would have gone back to eat with the others, but Midge Margret's banishment made eating together impossible there, so they sat in the cold on a doorstep and shared a bit of the salmon and cake. Midge Margret gave the sweeties and the rest of the treats to Jeannie for the bairnies.

By that time it was quite dark and the shopkeepers were hurrying to their homes or to the taverns by the murky muffled glimmer of the gas streetlamps. The fog now rose in earnest from the lochs and from the sea to meet the reek of the city's chimneys as it was pressed toward the streets by the weight of the icy-cold clouds. This fog was much worse than it had been and they could see no more than a few shapes moving about in the dark, and the glow of the lamps on either side of them.

In fact, they could barely see each other, and they knew that after stopping at the few houses between them and the building where their people were, they would need to return for the night.

They had to finish what business they had before ten, when the slops were thrown out, as Midge Margret knew from when she had lived there before.

So the three of them groped their way out from the shelter of the doorway and all but lost each other in the thick, smoky fog.

They hugged the walls to find their way in the unfamiliar place, and crane their necks up to see if there was light in the rooms above the shops.

At one likely looking building, the whole second floor was alight, and with Jeannie taking the farthest door, Geordie lurking in the second doorway, and Midge Margret at the third, they began their tasks.

Jeannie's knocker thumped against its brass plate as Midge Margret lifted the heavy knocker on her own assigned door and let it fall. The fog was so thick she could not see Jeannie, nor could she could see aught of Geordie but his hand and forearm, though he was barely five feet or so away from her.

The door swung open and a man stood there in his night-dress. Very put out he looked too.

"Have you no sense, woman?" he scolded. "A decent body would be in her bed by now."

"And so I shall, good sir, but my little brothers and sisters are starving and I've not a lump of coal to warm them with. Please, sir, if only you would buy or trade for a few of these lovely handmade laces, heirlooms they are frae me ain blessed granny, God rest her soul, I could feed and warm the bairns."

"Awa' wi' ye, ye thieving, lying gypsy or I'll ca' the guard."

"It's you they should be arresting for yer caud black heart . . ." she scolded back. She was launching into the best part, the curses she would bring down upon his head, when she heard the sound of someone choking coming from the space beside her where Geordie was. His hand was no longer visible. "Here, what's that? Who's there?" she said. "Geordie? Jeannie?"

She thought she heard a grunt, but heard no more as her prospect was saying, "Brought your accomplices to rob us then, have you?" Then he slammed the door in her face.

She called out again but no one answered. She grabbed for where Geordie's hand had been but her fingers met only air. Lunging forward, she grabbed again and was rewarded with a small strangled sound.

"Geordie?" she asked, and tripped over something soft, and when she looked down to see it was the still and blood-ied body of her brother, she shrieked and further lost her balance, causing her feet to slide out from under her and her-self to fly headlong into the wall of the house. Her brow slammed against something sharp, and she felt the blood run into her eye before she flopped like a wet rag into the gutter against the building and the blinding pain gave way to blackness and cold.

Chapter XIII

SCOTT TIRED OF Williamina's party early. He had trotted out several of his best stories, read a bit, by popular demand, from the *Minstrelsy,* and generally appeared to be enjoying himself as he usually did in the company of his fellows. The truth was, a number of small occurrences—mere incidents actually, and only one of them truly unexpected—disturbed him.

Willie Forbes was getting quietly, discreetly, genteelly but quite thoroughly drunk as he watched Miss Stuart dancing and flirting with her various admirers.

Dr. Douglas MacRae was also there, quite flamboyantly, if illegally, as the proscription against the national dress remained in effect from before the union with England. He was clad in full-dress MacRae tartan feileadh-mor or large kilt, bonnet, jacket, stockings and gillies. He had a rather unique take on the wearing of the kilt, however, for around his neck was a string of oversized dental work he identified as being the claws of an American catamount, or cougar.

His sporan had a bit of colorful geometric beadwork at the top and his kilt was buckled with a belt of strikingly stamped metal disks. These, he said, were gifts from his friends among the American Indian tribes, whose languages and customs he had sought to document a bit earlier in his career.

Scott saw that MacRae had caught the eye of one of his own favorites among Miss Stuart's younger lady friends, Mrs. Barbara Graham, widow, a voluptuous beauty with flowing chestnut locks, a rather bawdy chuckle, which Scott found particularly likable, and a calm, practical manner not untinged with a flair for poetry. "Were you no' afraid o' bein' scalpet, Dr. MacRae?" she asked, as if knowing that he was, of course, not afraid and thinking highly of him for his sensible attitude.

"Nay, lassie. If I was tae be afraid o' bein' scalpet, 'tis the Frenchies I should hae been fearin', for it was themselves introduced the savage custom by takin' scalps tae collect bounty on the puir folk who had the misfortune tae be livin' on that valuable piece o' real estate ower there when oor Kings and Queens thocht it should belang tae them."

"I've nivver heard it put like that before, Doctor. Ye maun tell me mair."

"Ah, lassie, 'tis very a verra complicatet matter tae gae intae here in such noise and bother. Perhaps ye might care tae accompany me tae my ain rooms. I've mony bonny artifacts that ye may find o' interest there."

He waggled his bushy red eyebrows and Mrs. Graham chuckled her lovely chuckle. She was wearing maroon velveteen this evening with a rather daring neckline and it became her very well. She was not so young as to fail to grasp his meaning and was her own mistress, with her own income, which made her independent if not wealthy. "I'll wager ye do at that, Dr. MacRae," she said.

Mischievously, Scott, who was standing near the pair, turned to Dr. MacRae and said, "Oh, MacRae. I was wondering if you'd had a chance to make your tests on those bones found in the loch the other day?"

"Ainly the preliminary ones," MacRae said, seemingly not at all taken aback in spite of being interrupted in his amatory pursuits. "I had a bit o' water frae the Scryin' Tarn o' Artney an' I used that, but a' I could see, judgin' frae the fashion the images was wearin', was that the lady was alive within the last ten years. Mair definitive tests will need tae wait until I can get oot tae the standin' stanes up on the Dasses next full moon an' place the bones on the lintel stane. That should allow me tae view the subject durin' her final days."

"Will you be able to question her?" Scott asked.

"We're no sae advanced in oor field as a' that, I'm afraid, Mr. Scott. But I should hae an answer frae that vision that will tell me when she was put intae the loch."

Mrs. Graham said, "I feel sae privileged tae be livin' in such enlightened times, don't you, Mr. Scott? 'Tis amazin' what men o' science hae discovered tae tell us mair aboot the past."

Scott agreed that it was indeed amazing, but privately wished that work in Dr. MacRae's field didn't require him to be able to access the actual field in which the stones stood. The Dasses were rocky crags in the least accessible part of Holyrood Park. The stones themselves, no doubt once immense, had weathered until they were little more than his own height and he feared that one day soon in the heat of all of this modernization and building, not to mention Christian enlightenment, they would disappear, broken up or taken to be hearthstones for new mansions and office buildings. Already their energy had diminished until it was only truly accessible at certain times, such as the full moon.

Scott hoped that before that energy disappeared altogether, perhaps some scientist might find a way to make transportable such power as the stones contained. In the meantime, the bones had lain long in the loch. He supposed it wouldn't matter if their origin remained undiscovered a bit longer.

Neither Forbes's inebriation nor MacRae's inability to give him a quick solution to the riddle of the body in the loch disturbed Scott so much as the presence of Corey Primrose. Not that Scott disliked the fellow. In fact, he admired him tremendously, of course, but he had never before seen Primrose at one of the Stuart functions and was a bit surprised that on the slight acquaintance of the oyster house, the man had been invited. But then, he was a prominent citizen of good family and fortune, so why not? Why not indeed. Apparently Primrose shared the opinion that he was as entitled as any to be here and entertain himself as he chose, for he was, as before, making himself charming and attentive to Miss Stuart.

Forbes, like Scott and half the eligible bachelors of Edinburgh, was also besotted with Miss Stuart and this, it took no wizard to discern, was the reason for his decision to become besotted with alcohol as well. Scott looked over at him, and Willie, less drunk than he wished to seem, caught his eye. The two of them exchanged despairing glances.

While Scott was chatting with MacRae and Mrs. Graham, Primrose took the tack of hanging on to Miss Stuart's every word and smiling encouragement for more, looking soulfully into her eyes and finding frequent occasions to kiss her hand. Scott was no mean hand-kisser himself, but it seemed to him he was more likely to make the gesture when he was particularly intrigued by a lady's conversation, as he often was since there were many great intellects and wits among his female acquaintances, particularly those of the older, spinster variety. Primrose seemed to do it whenever the spirit moved him, and it moved him frequently. Furthermore, Miss Stuart blushed prettily every time, and, far from detecting any lack of sincerity in Primrose's behavior, quite encouraged it to the point where she seemed to be keeping her wrist cocked half the evening.

Entranced as she had seemed, however, Miss Stuart surprised Scott. After entertaining Corey Primrose's inquiries and flatteries for what seemed to Scott a tediously long time, the young lady suddenly appeared distracted, extricated her hand from the final kiss, and, forsaking Primrose and ignoring Scott's attempt to attract her attention, sought out three or four of her closest lady friends, with whom she gossiped in an intense way uncommon for the hostess of a party.

Primrose nibbled a few refreshments, and, after frequent glances in Miss Stuart's direction received no notice, departed the affair early.

Scott's friend, Miss Ross, was among Williamina's confidantes, and when that lady extricated herself and prepared to leave, Scott himself helped her on with her cloak and remarked, "Our hostess seems a bit distracted this evening, don't you think?"

Miss Ross smiled indulgently at him. "Och, weel, she met a palm-readin' beggar woman today who tuld her a peculiar fortune. It's put her in a wee dither, I'm afraid."

"Aye? And why is that?"

"Noo, Mr. Scott, I'm sure it's not for me tae say. If ye'd learn mair aboot it, I suggest ye ask Williamina herself."

"Aye, perhaps I will, my dear. Perhaps I will," he said, and handed Miss Ross over to the butler-cum-footman, who led her down the stairs and helped her into a sedan chair.

A queue of chairs and chairmen now lined the street in front of the Stuart home. Scott decided that perhaps the time had come for him to leave too, but he had no need of a chair, despite the fog and darkness. His cane made a quite formidable weapon if he had need of one, and he wished to walk and take what fresh air was available in the smoky haze to clear his head and ponder the events of the evening.

His suit with Miss Stuart was not going well at all, he feared, despite the intervention of various friends recommending him to her and making sure the two of them were invited to the same events, to the same weekends in the country, that sort of thing. He was disappointed, of course. She was a lovely creature but she had so many suitors. And he feared that his own interests—which stirred within him great fires that could be quenched only by further investigation, gathering of information, and ultimately, detailing the matters in novels, poems, stories, and essays—must seem cold and intellectual to such a gay, warm person as Williamina. His dearest friends were actually those he exchanged correspondence with—the time he spent reading and writing, which were the pursuits that most consumed his attention, could be shared with no one, not even his intimates. He cultivated his aptitude for storytelling as a social outlet for those interests, but a wife would grow tired of nothing but the same stories to sustain her. Or some wives would. Scott sadly suspected Miss Stuart would be someone who would prefer a solid fortune, a well-staffed house, and a gainfully employed husband more dependent on a good income than his good name to support her. He had once spoken to her of the dream home he wished to build near Smailholm—he doodled plans for it during the lulls in court sessions. Williamina had seemed most appreciative of the drawings, the details he shared with her for the gas fires and the other modern improvements. But little nuances caused him to feel that perhaps her admiration would be more sincerely drawn by a house whose foundation was other than doodles.

Now, Forbes, a handsome enough man with a family well established in the banking business, for which Willie himself was showing great aptitude, would have made her a good match. However, poor Willie could hardly compare with the dashing appearance, the splendid intellect, the considerable influence and wealth of Corey Primrose. Before Primrose had begun his pursuit, Forbes had been Scott's main rival, but since the two men were good friends, Scott's own attitude had been "may the best man win."

But Primrose was a stranger, and while outwardly congenial, reserved and private to a degree that made friendship elusive. The pubs and oyster houses made quick friends of many old Edinburgh residents, and often quick enemies as well.

Scott dismissed the matter from his mind and began again to consider the idea of the Lady of the Lake, and that led him to ponder the other, more current matter of the lady in the loch. He wished the snow would melt at once so that MacRae might journey to the standing stones and determine more about the original owner of those few poor bones.

The fog on this night was even more opaque than usual, and he clung to the façades of the buildings in order to maintain his sense of direction. The light of the torches bracketed on either side of a few of the doorways was inadequate to give him any sense of where he was, and only the house fronts and numbers provided landmarks.

The beastly weather seemed to have kept most folk in, and aside from the occasional roisterer staggering into or out of a tavern or close, the night was very still.

So when he heard the scream, and very near to him at that, Scott was so startled that he forgot prudence and dashed forward to see what the matter was.

This was very dangerous, the fog being what it was. He could not see what he was getting into or with whom he was

involving himself. Quite possibly the scream was not a cry
for help but a lure for unwary revelers who would be relieved of their purses for their curiosity and might end in losing their lives as well. Equally possible it was a dispute
between persons of a low order who would not appreciate
the intervention of one of their well-dressed social superiors.
But it was a woman's scream, and now that he thought of it,
it had been accompanied by a bit of a scuffle and a muted
thud and crack, as of a body contacting a hard surface. The
scream itself had been more full of outrage and fear than
pain.

All of this went through Scott's mind in the moment that
he stumbled over the bodies and fell across them. Beneath
him, the slighter built and softer of the two bodies let out a
groan. The other one, beneath Scott's head and left arm, was
still warm, and Scott could hear the heart beating, but the
body lay quite still.

Chapter XIV

"HERE YOU, GET offa me," a woman complained with a low, breathy voice, as if the wind had been knocked out of her. "Just 'cause a poor lass is gobsmacked by a building is no reason tae be takin' advantage."

"I beg your pardon, miss," Scott said, trying vainly to get purchase with his cane to raise himself, "I stumbled upon you quite literally, I fear." He was relieved that he could smell no whisky or strong spirits about either of the pair. He was less relieved to see that both of them were bloodied about the face. "Are you hurt very badly?"

"I've felt better," she said. And then, as if remembering for the first time her companion, "Oh, God! Them noddies has killed Geordie! And Jeannie? Where's Jeannie?"

She was feeling about with her hands as if the Jeannie she spoke of might have fallen between the cobbles.

"What happened here?" he asked.

"We was—visitin' these folk—and I was just takin' me leave—me brother and his wife were visitin' the folk at adjoinin' doors. And I heard a wee noise and looked about and I couldnae see Geordie. Geordie?" She was shaking him. "Geordie, 'tis Midgie. Up with ye noo. They've ta'en Jeannie. We have tae get her back before it's too late . . ."

Scott knew very little about medicine but he knew enough to realize Geordie was badly injured. "I'm afraid he'll be no help to you, my dear," he said as kindly as possible. "We'll need to call the Guard to search for Jeannie."

"Guard'll do naethin'," she said automatically.

Before he had time to argue with her, a voice called, "Scott? Scott? Is that you I hear through this soup? Are you in some sort of difficulty? Speak up, man, so I can find you."

"Over here!" Scott called. "A young lady and her brother have been assaulted and another lady kidnapped. I'm afraid the lad is in a bad way."

The girl was patting at his coat with a rag-wrapped hand. "Scott? Oor Mr. Scott? Who likes oor sangs?"

Scott took a closer look at the bloodied, dirty face before him. The pale curls were matted and filthy, but now he could plainly see who she was. "Good heavens. Midge Margret, is that you?"

"Aye, Mr. Scott, wha's left o' me."

"And—oh, my word, this is *that* Geordie. Och, this is terrible."

At that moment Corey Primrose appeared from the fog and knelt beside them. Before he could say anything, Scott said, "You studied medicine. Please, please take a look at Midge Margret here and her brother. We must get help for them. They've been brutally attacked and Geordie's wife has been abducted."

"She's in a family way, Mr. Scott, if yer don't mind me bein' sae undelicate as tae say so," Midge Margret added.

Primrose gave her a sharp look, but turned to Geordie

and with long gloved fingers probed the unconscious man's neck and head. Primrose's white doeskin gloves came away bloodied. "It would be best to take them to the infirmary, where they can be properly tended to. I've nae license, but the man, as you say, is in a bad way."

He turned to Midge Margret and took her face in his hands to turn it so that her injury caught the most light. When he made to pull her hair back from the bloodied scalp, she flinched away from him.

"The woman here will do, it seems," Primrose said, "but it wouldnae hurt to have her looked at as well."

"Very well. Please be a good chap and send for Captain Laing and tell him we need transport for these folk tae the infirmary."

"Perhaps I should stay here with the patients?" Primrose suggested.

"No!" Midge Margret said. "You stay, Scott. We've been tryin' ever sae hard tae find ye. Dinnae leave us noo."

Apologetically, Scott explained to Primrose, "Midge Margret and her brother are old friends of mine. If it will comfort her for me to stay, perhaps I ought, though you are better qualified. Do you mind, auld fellow?"

"It's all the same tae me," Primrose said with a shrug. "I'll return straightaway." He stood, took two steps, and was swallowed by the fog.

MIDGE MARGRET'S TEETH began chattering and she was shivering very hard. Scott removed his own coat and wrapped it around her. The garment was large enough that she was able to cover her brother with the tail as well.

"I t-t-t-tried tae find ye at yer k-k-k-kirk yesterday," she said, "but the p-p-poliss wouldnae let me see ye."

"I heard about it this morning. I'm sorry. Angus was distressed to learn that you and I were, as you told him, old friends and that I was displeased, when you had made such an effort, to find that you were prevented from seeing me. He mentioned something about murders."

"Y-yes. Same b-bloke as did this tae us, or I miss my g-g-guess," she said. "Scott, ye maun send yer men after him before he can k-k-kill Jeannie like he did Bella and Leezie."

"You are for certain that the lassies in question are dead?"

"I ken ainly that Bella Bailey musta had nae mair need o' her claes nor yet her gaitherin' basket, as we foond them in yon loch"—she pointed down the street toward Holyrood Palace to indicate the loch she meant—"the day after she was ta'en."

She bent over Geordie then and tried to cajole him back to consciousness.

Presently there was a sound of tramping feet in the fog and two constables carrying a stretcher between them stopped and set it down, did a military turn toward Scott and stood waiting. They were shortly joined by more guards with another stretcher, and two sedan chairs. From one chair Primrose emerged; from the other, Captain Laing, so hastily dressed that his uniform tunic was buttoned crookedly.

"Wha's that for?" Midge Margret demanded suspiciously, pointing to the caravan of man-carried conveyances.

"To take Geordie and you tae the infirmary so ye can get treatment," Scott said. "Mr. Primrose will see to you. He has connections among the doctors at the university school. Very learned men."

This did not set well with Midge Margret, as Scott quickly learned. She let out a much louder scream than the one that had originally summoned him to her aid and it ended with a moan, "Nooooooo . . ."

Windows opened above them. "Here noo! Wha's a' the racket?"

The constables picked Geordie up, none too gently, and carried him to one of the stretchers.

Midge Margret tore herself loose from Scott's protective grip and flung herself, biting and scratching, at the nearest constable. Primrose plucked her off as if she were a kitten and held her dangling in midair for a moment, still kicking and clawing, while the policemen discharged their duty.

"My dear, you both need treatment," Scott said as soothingly as possible. Her fear and rage distressed him greatly and he could not think how to calm her. "You've nothing to fear, Midge Margret. I will come with you myself and see to it that you get the best of care and that everyone understands that your care is sponsored by me. Now that I am sheriff, no one would dare mistreat you." He couldn't tell whether she could hear him over herself or not, and added to himself, *At least, I hope not.* Nor had he a very clear idea of how he would pay for their care, but pay he would. The *Minstrelsy* was the success that it was partially through the efforts of Midge Margret and her brother and the efforts of others of their kind to preserve the old ballads. He would not let them perish for want of medical attention.

Once the constables had loaded Geordie onto the stretcher and lifted it, Midge Margret quieted and Primrose dropped her—but not before one of her kicks connected with a sensitive bit of his anatomy. She was out of reach before he could retaliate, if indeed, that was what he had in mind, for no gentleman would, of course. She refused the stretcher, however, and walked protectively, if somewhat woozily, beside her brother.

Primrose popped back into the first sedan chair and Laing back into the second. Primrose said through the door, "I'll just go rouse Dr. Knox to come and examine the patients . . ." He cast a wary eye at Midge Margret, who paid him no attention whatsoever.

"Very well, sir," Scott replied.

"Are you sure you'll be safe with her? Some of these tinkler women are very rough."

"I'm safe enough, I think, as long as I don't attempt to force the lassie tae do onything agin her will." He didn't mean it as a rebuke but realized when he'd said it that it might have sounded that way to Primrose, who frowned.

"Aye, well then, I'll be by later," he said, and withdrew.

Midge Margret said, "I thocht ye'd help us, Scott. I nivver thocht ye'd deliver us intae the hands o' the dochtors."

"Deliver you into the hands?" Scott asked. "Forgive me, my dear, but what else would you want me to do when you're injured? Here now," he said, steadying her, realizing he would need to walk beside her, as she still refused to use the stretcher. Her eyes looked huge and hollow in the darkness and her face was a very pale oval, like a ghost's. "I fear you're injured worse than you think, Midge Margret. The infirmary is the best place for you."

"Ah, Mr. Scott, sir, I ken ye mean tae dae the right thing, but it's them as has been ta'en oor folk tae cut up tae see hoo bodies are made."

"That's preposterous!" Scott said. "Where did you get an idea like that?"

Her voice was hard as she said, "On the road, amang me ain folk as has seen the way o' the warld. All o' them taud us hoo the dochtors hires grave robbers tae dig up the deid for the student dochtors tae study, and if they cannae get folk as are a'ready deid, they murders puir folk like us." Her words came in little gasps now as she tried to keep pace with the constables, who were marching double time, bouncing Geordie's stretcher between them none too gently. Scott tried to motion them to slow down but they paid him no mind, descending from the High Street via the southern branch of the street created for the North Bridge.

"How can that be?" Scott asked, also a bit breathless. Finally, as Midge Margret flagged behind her brother, he took her elbow and walked with her behind the soldiers, silently, until she caught her breath, whereupon she took up her complaint again as if she'd never been interrupted.

"Aisy enough," she said. "Yer poliss here would look the other way if it were the fine folk they was paid tae pertekit instead o' traivellin' people sich as me and mine. The deid are guarded by men their families has the siller tae hire, but we tinklers hae nae siller and sae oor livin' bodies is aisier game than the deid 'uns o' the quality. Who d'ye think attackit Geordie and me this nicht and stole away oor Jeannie?"

The chairmen carrying the enclosed sedan chair containing Captain Laing slipped once, and from inside there came a curse and a barked command. The chairmen then slowed so that they carried the chair beside Scott and Midge Margret, who had troubles of their own keeping their footing on the slick cobbles leading down the steep incline.

"Midge Margret, that's incredible. I can't believe—" Scott began to say, but then, looking at the face of Captain Laing, who had evidently overheard much of their exchange, he read more distaste for the tinklers than for whoever had caused their present predicament. "Captain Laing, have you heard of any such problem?"

"Nay, Sheriff Scott. But yer friends there, their kind are nae apt tae be reportin' crimes tae the Guard, since they're responsible for a guid mony of the crimes that tak's place wherever they're tae be foond."

"Ainly becuz ye'd sooner hang onything amiss on the

likes o' us than ain o' yer taxpayin' townfolk!" Midge Margret snapped back.

"I hardly think Midge Margret's own sort would be kidnapping or murdering themselves," Scott said. "So perhaps we should look into this situation, eh, Laing?"

"Aye, I s'pose, Sheriff. But ye dinnae ken these folk as I do. They've wars amang themsel's, ye ken, and murderin' isn't the half o' it. Is that the truth or no, lassie?" he demanded sternly of Midge Margret.

"Aye, it's true enough," she said and Laing gave Scott a triumphant look. "But we're nane o' us at odds wi' onybody nearby at the moment. I taud ye who's daein' this foulness, Scott, and if ye choose tae believe yer hired mon here instead, it's on yer head."

"No need to fash yourself again, lassie," Scott said, again trying to use the calmness of his voice to soothe her as he might a wild beast. "We'll look into it and meantime Geordie and you will be treated well. Here we are, then."

Just past Addams Square, the stretcher, sedan chair, and Scott and Midge Margret turned left onto Infirmary Street. The constables carried their stretcher through the door and into the entranceway of the infirmary. Midge Margret was tottering now as she walked beside Scott, and sagged against him. This unbalanced him and caused his cane to slip, which nearly undid them both. But Laing, seeing the difficulty, swept Midge Margret up and carried her the rest of the way into the hospital. It said something for the state she was in that she allowed him to do it. Scott thanked Laing for his kindness.

"Aye," said the captain, patting all of his pockets when he'd set the girl down on one of the cots, "but ye'd best see that ye still hae all yer valuables on ye."

Dr. Knox and Primrose arrived just as the ward attendants were trying to convince Midge Margret, over her somewhat febrile but still graphically eloquent arguments, that female patients could not possibly stay on the men's ward, nor vice versa.

"Never mind, Lewis," Dr. Knox told the male attendant, ignoring the slatternly looking female one. "They can both go into the examining room. I gather from what you've told me, Primrose, that they were injured in the same incident and I will need to extract the medical history of the unconscious lad from the young lady."

Midge Margret's eyes showed white all around the pupils by now and her nostrils flared at the various smells of illness, excretion, drainage, blood, infection, medicines and a strong smell of whisky, which was used as a painkiller. Moans and groans of misery issued from both wards, for one had to be truly miserable to be lodged in this place for any length of time. The ailments of most folk of means were treated by their family physicians in their own homes.

The two attendants placed Geordie on one examining table and brought in a stretcher on small wooden wheels for Midge Margret to recline upon. The attitude of the attendants toward the new patients was now respectful, even solicitous, with the female attendant addressing Midge Margret as "dearie" and "henny." This with a sidelong glance at Scott, whose name and face were well-known in Edinburgh for a number of reasons. He never could tell if people knew him from his law work, his family connections, his new position as sheriff, or simply because of his literary endeavors. In many places in Europe people were ignorant and illiterate, but the Scottish government had always placed great emphasis on education, and almost every child in the country, and certainly in a sizable city such as Edinburgh, could read, write and cipher.

The woman attendant particularly kept glancing from Midge Margret's face to Scott's and her mouth worked, as if she wished to ask a question. That the two new patients were tinklers was obvious from their dress and, some would claim, the cast of their features. However, since King James IV had within recent memory found it instructive and entertaining to sally forth incognito, dressed as a tinkler, the citizens could not necessarily be entirely sure that a tinkler was always necessarily what he or she appeared to be. No doubt tinklers who were personally escorted and tenderly regarded by literary gentlemen with royal appointments were rather rare.

Midge Margret lay on her side, her wild eyes darting from one person to another. Scott noticed fresh scratches on the backs of Primrose's hands, indicating that Midge Margret had given the poor man more of a battle than Scott had previously realized.

"We shall of course need to keep the young man in care until he regains consciousness or other arrangements can be made," Dr. Knox said, after feeling of Geordie's skull and prodding and poking at him for some time. "And the lassie should bide here a wee bit too, ane or twa nights, perhaps. She has some tenderness that might indicate more problems than are apparent on the surface and we should be alert for signs of brain fever, something not uncommon in cases like this where there's been a sudden violent trauma tae the head. Often such problems will occur in as long as a day or two after the injury."

"Is that all right wi' you, Midge Margret?" Scott asked her. "I shall come tomorrow and see how you're doing and every day, in fact, until you are both released. Would that suit you?"

"What?" she asked. She had been surveying the room and its inhabitants as if trying to memorize them.

"Will you mind very much staying here for the night?"'

Her eyes were calmer now, even calculating as, with a

twitch of her mouth she said, "Aye, I believe it will suit me well enough, Mr. Scott, tae be here where I can watch ower Geordie. In the meanwhile, would you be sae kind," she asked with rather artificially elevated language, "tae inform oor friends and neighbors o' wha' has befallen us and ask that they tend tae wee Jenny and Martin, my brother's children? In particular, if ye'd mention tae a pair o' fellas named Ryk the Ramrod and Red Stevie that they be alert for ony signs o' what may have happened tae Jeannie, I'd be much obliged, sir."

"How will I find these fellows?" Scott asked.

Primrose said, "I can help you out there. They work for me. They acquired lodgings in the building in which I grew up. I'll take you there now if you like."

At this, Midge Margret stared at Primrose with an odd blend of consternation and curiosity that puzzled Scott. Scott patted her shoulder and said, "That would be very kind of you. Tak' care noo, lassie, and please have word sent to me if any change should occur in your brother's, or indeed in your own, condition."

PHYSICIAN'S NOTES:

A very close call this evening. I saw an opportunity to seize the gypsy wench who has within her the agent I require to bind my love's soul to the new body. That agent is a very simple and elemental one—she produces it to nourish the child she is carrying. She looks as though she is close to term and since sacrificing her is not necessary to obtain what I require, I may well allow her to live until I can deliver her child. The mother may be a sinful creature, but the child at least should be baptized and can bear no witness.

My servant's foes, the pregnant woman's husband and sister-in-law, were present at the time, but I prevailed largely because of the cover of fog, and succeeded in disabling, if not killing, the man. If he lives, I will see to it that his child is restored to him, and that perhaps will lessen any grief he may feel on account of his wife, for they seemed fond of each other. The other woman is not needed for my purposes, and since she was taken to hospital, it is unlikely my servant would be able to sell her body to them once he disposes of her, as she is now known to them. Of course, I suppose he could claim she died later of injuries they overlooked and he claimed her body from the grave at that time.

But all is in readiness and it remains only for me to fit together the components I have acquired, animate the resulting creation, and invite my love in to her new fleshly home.

Chapter XV

LAING HAD ALREADY departed with his chair and Primrose had sent the one he had taken away, so on the return to the High Street Scott and Primrose braved the icy slope of Bridge Street on foot.

By now a sharp wind had come up, clearing the fog somewhat, and the smoke overhead so that a few stars were visible and a large full moon that till now had been completely obscured by the murk. Both men wore top hats with mufflers wound around their necks, chins, and mouths. Scott's was in his family tartan and Primrose's was black-and-white checked. The clergy patterns were always done in neutral, of course, just as the hunting version of a tartan was in muted greens and browns, reserving the bolder colors for the dress version of the plaid.

"You surprise me, Scott," Primrose said, looking down from his considerable height, which gave Scott the peculiar vantage point of paying respectful attention to the frost-rimed edges of the man's nostrils. "I had no idea you interested yourself in the plight of the gypsies. That young woman seemed to look upon you with great trust, and I gather that she is not in the habit of extending such regard to many outside of her own kind."

"You give me too much credit, Primrose," Scott said.

"Do call me Corey, as you used to when we were schoolmates," Primrose said with a wide and friendly smile that seemed to warm the night as well as Scott's heart with its good fellowship.

"Certainly, Corey. And I am little different from the boy, Watt, you aince knew."

"Not so. You are very different indeed. If I may call you Walter, that's as much liberty as I am comfortable taking with a person of your present dignity and position."

Scott said, "Whatever pleases you, auld friend. But I fear you give me too much honor. I've never truly taken the charitable interest in the tinklers you ascribe to me. But through some very interesting circumstances, James Hogg and I met Midge Margret and Geordie when I was a student at university."

He regaled Primrose with the story of the lyke-wake and the questioning of the corpse, Geordie's aquittal and the interlude afterward in the tinkler camp. By the time he had finished, they had gained the High Street and Primrose turned down another wynd on the north side of the street.

"It's back this way but why don't you wait here?" Primrose suggested considerately. "I'll just pop up there and deliver the message, and then we might have a bit of something to warm us at the tavern before the 'gardyloo' is cried."

Scott agreed to that readily enough. He managed well enough with his lame leg but the well-lit windows were a good four floors up and he knew that his companion could discharge their obligation to Midge Margret much quicker

than he. Besides, Primrose was already acquainted with the
chaps she particularly wished notified. When he returned to
the High Street, Dr. MacRae was with him and they were
chatting, Primrose relating to MacRae the incidents of the
night.

PHYSICIAN'S NOTES:

*I begin to see the reason behind my servant's dislike of
his estranged wife. She appears to be one of those harridans
typical of her race who throw themselves at their betters and
interfere in things beyond their understanding or intelligence. Her caterwauling made it quite awkward for me to
tidy up loose ends, and she actually had the gall to impose
upon her betters and employ them as errand boys and
nursemaids.*

*With the protector of my "little mother" out of the way,
however, I trust the other girl will provide little more obsta-
cle and can be disposed of if need be at a later date.*

*However, other arrangements must be made for a pair of
gypsy workmen who seem to be sponsoring their fellows in
their occupation of the city.*

*Where they are, the workmen could prove an inconve-
nience to me in implementing plans for others of their kind,
but if they are otherwise occupied, they may not only provide valuable services but also serve as convenient distrac-
tions for investigating authorities should something go
amiss with current plans. Fortunately, their removal to
other accommodations and assignments is easily managed.*

MIDGE MARGRET DID not close an eye, even for a second,
not even for a blink, all of that night. At first, she could not
believe Scott would bring her here, delivering herself and
Geordie into the very arms of the men who paid the body

snatchers to bring them the freshly murdered corpses of
Travellers. But then she realized, seeing how the head doctor and the tall fella treated Scott, that he had become an
even more important man than she'd thought. He was rely-
ing on his importance to protect her and Geordie, and maybe
that was very silly of him. But these medical people seemed
impressed. The woman nurse had not spoken a harsh word
to Midge Margret nor raised a hand to her, but once the doctor had gone, had seated herself at her table and began
downing a bottle of whisky. There were four other women
here now, all of them too sick to rise.

Midge Margret had been around midden heaps that
smelled like roses compared to this place. The bed sheets
were worn and not overly clean, the slops full to running
over, though the jars were covered with filthy wet cloths.

What kept Midge Margret awake as much as anything
was that she needed to relieve herself, but she would no
more touch one of the jars than she would stick her hand into
the filth it contained. To think that the settled people called
the tinklers dirty!

The hospital was horseshoe-shaped and four stories tall.
The central part on the main floor didn't have sick people in
it, but seemed filled with offices. The women's wing was on
one side of the horseshoe and the men's on the other.

The male attendant was asleep over a bottle too, and
Midge Margret crept past him to see to Geordie. He was as
he had been before, out cold. So then she decided to try to
find her way outside to take care of her business and maybe
keep vigil until re-entering the nasty place in the morning.
Cold the weather might be, but it was only the cold of the
body, not the soul-chill she felt here.

She walked back to the women's ward, and paused at the
table where the matron was slumped in her chair snoring. A
ring of keys dangled from the woman's belt and Midge Mar-

gret deftly removed both belt and keys, in case the main
door was locked, and also took the matron's lantern.

Then the only problem was to *find* the main door again.

She had been too agitated to get her bearings straight
when she was first carried into the building. Lighting, then
shielding the lantern, she crept out down the hallway, to
where she thought the door should be. Indeed she found a
door. Four of them there were.

The one directly ahead of her opened without a key. It
contained foul smelling mops and brooms and a number of
other articles for cleaning. She closed the door quickly and
opened the one to the left of it.

She found herself looking into a most peculiar room. It
was a bit like a theatre, or maybe a strange sort of court
room, with chairs on risers so that those in the seats could
gaze down into the center of the room, which contained a
table. That was all. Just a table.

It was no eating table, though; she could see that when
she walked a little into the room and held up the lantern. It
was like the thing they'd laid Geordie on in the examining
room, only there were no linens on it. She shone the light
around behind the table, opposite where the high seats were.
Cabinets lined the walls, she could see that now. Wondering
what might be in them, she pulled on the knob of one but it
wouldn't open at all. There was a wee lock on it. Setting her
lantern down, she took a look at the ring of keys, selected a
small one and held the lantern up again to try the key in the
lock.

That was when she noticed that the smell was different in
here, worse somehow. The stench from the hospital had
filled her nostrils before, but now her nose had cleared of
that enough that she sniffed in this place a horrible chemical
smell mingling with the others of decay and old blood. The

cabinet, she saw close up, was spattered with blood, and the floor had big stains as well. She shuddered.

She hesitated to turn the key. She wanted nothing more than to be away from here, but that was what she'd been trying to do, wasn't it? "Och, well, in fer a penny, in fer a pound," she said softly to herself, and was a bit comforted by the normal sound of her own voice. The key turned neatly and she opened the cabinet. The smell was much, much worse in the little enclosed space. Rows of funny-looking implements lay all neat inside the cabinet. Some were curved, some pronged, some had sharp blades, some were shiny, some rusted; some were crusted with dark stain. Midge Margret's hand trembled as she reached in to pull out one of the sharpish-looking ones. She was afraid the tool would know somehow she had no right to be there and it would cut her with a will of its own. But it just lay there until she picked it up by the handle. She didn't want it at all, but she knew that whoever had taken Jeannie and hurt Geordie and herself was probably still skulking around the city. Maybe he even knew where she and Geordie were, and if he was a noddy, maybe he would be bringing Jeannie by here. She would need herself a good weapon.

After scooting the other implements a bit closer to each other to cover the gap, she closed the cabinet back up and locked it again, pulled her own bloody kerchief from her pocket, where she'd stuck it when she took it off so the doctor could examine her head. She wrapped the kerchief around the blade of the knife, lightly, so the knife could be pulled out of her pocket quickly but the kerchief would keep the blade from cutting through her apron pocket.

And that was when she heard footsteps, out in the hallway, and a lock turning. She scuttled to the far end of the room and held the lantern behind her to shield the light, for once she put it out, she had no way of relighting it.

But the footsteps continued into the room next to the one she was in and she heard another door opening, an outside door.

"It's very late," she heard a man's voice say. The voice sounded high-class and pleasantly pitched, the burr only very slight in his speech, the way Dr. Knox's voice had sounded.

"Ye dinna think I'd be bringin' it early, do ye?" snapped another voice, a chillingly familiar one. She had last heard it low and menacing, as its owner taunted her before crashing his fist into her, a blow she seemed to feel all over again as she listened to that same voice now.

"No, of course not, but you might have let me know earlier in the day you'd be coming."

"I wouldhae done but we ainly jist a bit ago got anither—found anither—"

"Body?" the doctor asked. "Just lying about, was it?"

"No, mon, oh no, o' course not. Anither fresh grave I was aboot tae say, and afore we digs it up, we maun unload this 'un."

"Yes, well, we'll put her on the stretcher there. What's happened here? My God, the poor thing. How did this happen?"

"Coach hit her, I reckon, got opent clean up an' her insides spilt oot."

"Poor child. Very well, ready? Ane, twa, tharee, *lift*."

Midge Margret had heard enough. She might have known. Seamus was the culprit. Geordie hadn't killed him at all, and Seamus had survived to sink even lower than he had been. Now he was killing off their own people—women, like herself, since he had not succeeded in killing *her* on first attempt—and, oh, the very worst of it, selling off their bodies to the school so that the folk he murdered would never rest easy nor go to heaven, but haunt their own folk. He had seen Jeannie and grabbed her, to punish Geordie for beating him. No doubt he thought he'd beaten Geordie to death and would have come back for him except that Mr. Scott and his friend came along first. Midge Margret shuddered violently over and over again as next door, after a brief haggle, the doctor paid Seamus, the door closed and was locked, and the doctor's footsteps retreated toward the hallway while the scraping sound that accompanied Seamus's footsteps faded off the other way.

A door opened and closed, then a few more footsteps before another door opened and closed, telling Midge Margret the doctor had left the infirmary, probably to return to his own home and bed.

Had it not been for the fog, Seamus would have seen Midge Margret this night too when he attacked Jeannie. Then she'd never have called out and Scott would not have found them and she and her brother would have been the next ones to be brought to the door. The lantern light shivered like that of a coach lamp on a rough road as Midge Margret made her way past the table and suddenly realized that this was where they did it. This was where her nice high-class swell of a doctor, the friend of Scott's friend, would cut up bodies brought here by Seamus. And the student doctors would sit in those chairs up there and watch, and ask questions and probably make jokes.

She could not stop shivering until she had closed the door behind her. She knew the door that led to the outside was one of the two she hadn't opened, but she could not possibly leave Geordie alone here now, at night. And there was the body too—Scott should know about the body. Should know what she knew. He said he would visit the next day and the best thing for her to do was wait, and protect Geordie until he woke up and she could tell him what went on and he could protect himself, or until Scott came and she could make him take them both away from here and find Seamus and give a decent burial to the people he had slain.

And then, just as she had decided to return to the relative safety of the ward, where she could comfortably die of the miserable miasma of the place instead of being, say— stabbed, it hit her. The blow to her head must have been worse than she'd thought, either that or it was the shock of hearing Seamus's unwelcome voice after such a long time of hoping he was dead. The body. The body he had brought here, probably in something so low as a wheelbarrow, the body of the woman with her insides spilled out. That might be Jeannie. Poor Jeannie! Poor wee unborn bairnie!

And of course, Midge Margret had to know.

Ah well, the entire place was in darkness save for her lantern, and no sounds except the normal groans of the wretched on the wards. She'd just have a look. If it was Jeannie, Midge Margret knew she must leave the ward tonight, even with Geordie there, and find Scott and get him to call his guards out and deal with Seamus then and there.

And maybe—maybe she had not been thinking this through clearly. Maybe she had to do that anyway, for what if Jeannie was not yet dead, had not yet been murdered? All the more reason for haste, now that she knew who had done it.

How long had she been gone from the wards? What if the matron had roused from her drunken stupor to find her keys and lantern missing? In the state she was in, the woman would likely think she'd mislaid them. But then there would be Midge Margret missing from her bed without even having made a shape to lie there in her stead.

A very hard blow to the head that had been, indeed, she thought, feeling of her lump.

She found a likely looking key and put it in the lock of the door to the adjoining room—and opened the door to hell.

Chapter XVI

THE LAST THING Midge Margret wanted to do was go through that door. Her lantern shone feebly on the room's interior and made out neat rows of cabinets lined with jars of all sizes. Several tables were on one side and the smell of decay and chemicals made her dizzy and sick to her stomach. She could run away as fast as she wanted, but first she must have a wee bit of a look at who was on the table. She must know was it Jeannie or no'.

She could not, absolutely could not, bring herself to close the door behind her, despite the risk of someone coming along and discovering her where she had no right to be. Probably if they did, they would add her to the bodies here. Though from the sound of it, the doctor didn't know the people Seamus brought him were murdered.

She set a foot into the room, and then the other, carefully not looking to the right or left and trying to hold her breath. The lantern caught the edge of a jar, the tip of a pale finger tapping against it from the inside. A deep shudder of revulsion ran through Midge Margret.

She thought that the new body would be in the middle of the room and when she could see the door clearly, and saw that it was not, she knew that the table it was on was lined up, with all those other tables, against the far wall. Each table was covered with a cloth, a cloth with a human-sized hump under it. Thinking the table closest the door the one most likely to contain the newest body, she drew back the sheet.

A half-flayed man lay under the cover. Some of his bones showed, and some of what was under his skin, like the body of an animal dressed for cooking. Swallowing bile, she flung the sheet back over him and moved to the next. This one was also a man, one who had been hanged by the look of his neck, and his chest was open, the skin pulled apart like draperies to expose the ribs and what lay beneath. She covered him and swallowed harder.

The third body was the one, she thought. Under the sheet was the familiar face of young Leezie Stewart, though, as Dr. Knox had said, her belly was open and her insides exposed. She, like the others, wore no clothing. Midge Margret realized she should have known that, inasmuch as Bella's clothes had been in the loch, but the idea of all of those men looking at poor young Leezie as had never known a man, looking not only at her but in her, was truly horrifying. Jeannie, who was so modest and proper about her person, would rather die all over again than endure this last horrible obscenity. Whatever happened, Scott must come here and make the doctors give the body back to the Stewarts to bury. This was indecent, unsanctifit, as her mother would have said.

That was all she had to know really, but just in case, she

checked the other two faces, looking just closely enough to reassure herself that neither was Jeannie.

Then she practically ran, keys jingling and lantern in hand, back to the door. Trying the one door in the hallway she had not tried before, she found what she sought. This one led outside. Once in the cold, she relieved herself at both ends, and felt weak and sick afterward. She thought if she scrubbed herself for days she would never lose the awful smell of that awful room.

But now she must hurry and find Scott and get his help both in retrieving Leezie's body and in taking Geordie away, before anything bad could happen to him. She set off up the wynd toward the high road, wondering how she might find Scott.

SCOTT, PRIMROSE AND MacRae were ensconced in Scott's favorite tavern. Hogg and some of their other friends were already there and well into their cups.

MacRae sat opposite Scott and stared deeply into his tankard, as if to use the dregs of his drink for divination purposes. Primrose was sitting next to Scott, his manner now far more confidential than before. Scott was gratified to think that they might be becoming friends at last. Primrose had been discoursing on philosophy and science.

"It sounds rather as if you miss our student days, old man," Scott said, leaning forward to rest both hands and his chin on the head of his cane. "I know I would if I had been as brilliant as you."

"Do you think I've failed to live up to that brilliance?" Primrose asked with a cock of his eyebrow. "Designing and fabricating the security of an entire city is not precisely art, perhaps, nor science, but it does leave one's footprint for posterity."

"Of course it does," Scott agreed. "And your addition to our city will be lang noted in history. But weren't you more interested in science at one time, philosophy, metaphysical matters?"

"Well, what is science after all than a body of knowledge about that which was once unknown and considered to be magical, more or less metaphysical?" Primrose asked the rhetorical question with a shrug. "I see no reason why science and religion, for instance, should be at odds with each other. The Lord made this world and gave man dominion over it. There is nothing in the Bible that should lead one to think He would wish us to remain ignorant of its makeup and function."

"Oh, quite," Scott agreed. "Unless you count the snake, of course."

"The—oh, yes." Primrose looked mildly annoyed, as if Scott had somehow betrayed him by disagreeing with him, however mildly and facetiously.

MacRae spoke up. "Was it no' an ancestor o' yours, Ivanhoe, who was a great wizard—the way I heard it he was a well-educated man and well travelled also, but cam' hame tae scare the bejesus oot o' the common folk."

Scott smiled. "Ah, yes, the venerable Wizard Michael. Not much of a churchgoer, I fear, but as you say, Lang Davie, well-educated and travelled. He studied at the London court with Dee, the Queen's magician, and travelled tae France and Italy as well, and China too, some say."

"I've heard of him," Primrose said with some of his former enthusiasm. "Philosopher, scientist, architect, political analyst, prophet—even a magician, some say? A pioneer in many fields, master of many disciplines, a Renaissance man." Scott heard in the way Primrose said the term that the man considered Michael Scott and himself to be colleagues in that respect.

Hogg laughed a rather short bark of a laugh. "Funny, folk i' the Borders kenned him as a wily auld wizard it was folly tae cross."

"Pairhaps the man had a sense o' humor," Davie suggested.

"I think you may have the right of it there," Scott agreed. Michael Scott was one of his more colorful ancestors—not his favorite, that was another—but certainly one of the memorable ones. "Folk didnae ken what to make of him since such a learned man was a rarity in the countryside at that time. And I gather he rather enjoyed playing up to the superstition of the locals."

"A dangerous sort of play, wouldn't you say?" Primrose asked.

"For someone, yes," Scott said. "He was also, you see, a very good practical scientist. Known to cast quite uncomfortable spells if his tribute didn't arrive on schedule."

"What manner o' spells did he cast?" Davie asked.

"Oh, some rather potent ones, as tradition has it," Scott said.

"The Wizard Michael Scott was said tae be quite an adept in alchemy, thaumaturgy, and necromancy," Davie insisted.

"It wisnae that he was sae learned," Hogg said, "as that he was canny in the business of usin' what folk thought he knew tae keep himself prosperous."

"Aye," Scott said. "You ken the way of it—the first spot of bad luck a body had, they blamed it on the auld Wizard Scott because they had a guilty conscience ower slighting him his portion for some bit of a thing he'd done for them. And I suppose he was not above a few tricks related to his knowledge of chemistry and physics—that sort of thing."

"I had heard he was an alchemist," Primrose said. "Any tales in the family telling how to turn dross into gold?"

"No. But I believe he had a very fine recipe for cockaleekie soup. And a few other curiosities," Scott said. He was rather amused at Primrose's interest in his wizardly ancestor.

"Oh, so he did leave papers, then?" Primrose asked. "Or were they burnt with him? I assume he *was* burnt?"

"Oh, no," Scott said. "He's buried, quite unscorched, at Melrose Abbey."

Primrose waved his hand in a nonchalant manner. "That settles it, then! He had to have been a real magician to have escaped the stake in those burning times, when he was publicly known to be blackmailing the peasants for tribute while they trembled in fear of him."

"I think perhaps 'trembling in fear' is probably an exaggeration," Scott said.

"Aye," Hogg agreed. "Borderers might be cautious roond a wizard, an' gie him a wee bitty tribute jist tae keep him peacefu'like, and tae gie a favor noo and again, but if they didnae tremble in fear when they was bein' raided nor raidin' themsel's across the Border, nae wizard is aboot tae fright them."

"Perhaps having a wizard in the family explains your tolerance toward fortune-tellers, Scott. Not many would have gone to such pains for the gypsy lassie and her injured brother."

Scott turned to Hogg and MacRae then, and related the events of the earlier part of the evening, and of the injuring of Geordie and Midge Margret, as well as the abduction of Geordie's good lady, Jeannie.

"Thon lassie is no common fortune-teller, Deacon," Hogg said to Primrose. "She's a verra fine singer, and a seventh dochter of a seventh dochter, as was her mither before her."

"*Is* she noo?" MacRae asked. "I'd like a word with her. Could be she could use the Sight tae gie me a clue as tae the identity o' yer lady in yon loch."

"At the very least, it should be easy for her to tell where her sister-in-law has got to," Primrose said archly. "But between us, I fancy she's decided that our celebrated poet friend is an easy mark for a bonny lass in distress. Admit it now, Scott, you are somewhat taken with her, are you not? A man such as yourself, with a colorful imagination full of brave deeds and noble poverty. And there is something about those tinkler girls—a bit wild and untamed."

Scott didn't know whether to be offended or amused. "Really, Deacon! A dutiful wee lassie sich as Midge Margret? She was scarcely bigger than the midge she's named for when I met her—a child. As I told you, her brother had been falsely accused and Hogg here brought the sheriff and myself in to determine the case by a postmortem interrogation of the victim. In gratitude for his release, Geordie shared songs for my buik and persuaded Midge Margret to do the same. That's all. As I told you."

"Perhaps it's the deacon himself has a taste for the travellin' sort o' lassie," Hogg teased. "But dinnae let the roamin' life they lead fool ye, Deacon, the lassies themsel's are nae allowed tae roam far."

"Now, I have heard that said," MacRae mused, "but I admit I've wondered mesel'. Amang some peoples, ye ken, it's common for the lassies tae be as free as the men. Usually this is in cultures where the bairnies a' belang tae the mither, and tak' their lineage frae her."

Both Primrose and Hogg seemed slightly scandalized at this idea and Hogg was quick to correct Dr. MacRae's assumptions. "Well, 'tis no' that way amang the tinklers. The lassies may flirt a wee bit wi' a settled man tae mak a sale or beg a penny, but they're taught to keep their virtue until marriage like ony good girls o' this toon."

"I'm gratified to hear it," Primrose said. "I was simply concerned lest a pretty face and a romantic incident might not have duped our friend here into believing oft-told examples of what is well known to be the tinkler penchant for falsehood."

Scott, who was quite fair in coloring, felt his face growing hot. "The lies I heard that day, sir, came from supposedly respectable men who did not scruple to accuse an innocent man, because he was a stranger and, as they thought, friendless." He smiled at Hogg, who winked back. "Had the respectable men been left to do so, they would have hung the poor wretch and protected the cur who raped and slew his own intended bride."

"No need to defend them to me, old chap. I employ two as my locksmiths and ornamental ironworkers, as I told you," Primrose said. "Fine chaps, as long as they're properly supervised."

Scott was about to rise and go, when there was a disturbance at the front door. "Here, we don't like your kind in here," the publican said.

And Midge Margret's voice said, "I've been hit ower the head wi' a buildin' this nicht and seen cut-up deid bodies and all manner of other ills done tae me and mine, on top o' which I've hunted a' ower Edinburgh tae find where Mr. Sheriff Walter Scott might be keepin' himsel', and noo that I've found the place ye'll no turn me awa'."

Scott was well aware of Corey Primrose's quizzical smirk and MacRae's prurient curiosity as he called to the publican, "No, Mr. Bathgate, it's perfectly all right. The young lady and I are indeed acquainted. Come, Midge Margret. My dear, why on earth are ye no' in hospital where we left ye?"

"I found Leezie, Mr. Scott. Leezie Stewart as was torn from her ain mither's oxters while I listened tae her screamin'. She's layin deid on a table doon at the infirmary, wi' her insides laid open, waitin' for the dochtors tae look at her wi' no claes on and cut her up!"

Scott wondered at the intense satisfaction that lit Midge Margret's face in spite of the distress in her voice.

"And it's no' ainly Leezie I've found the nicht. I ken who kilt her and the ithers as well—who is the noddy and the snatcher o' the livin' tae turn them intae sad corpses for the siller their flesh will bring."

"And?" Scott asked, realizing that he could hardly blame someone with Midge Margret's flair for the dramatic for spinning her tale out a bit, despite the urgency of her manner.

"It's Seamus Connors himsel', him that I was marriet tae until he beat a' the bairnies I coulda had oot o' me, and Geordie paid him back in kind and left him for deid. But he's no' deid. He's sunk even lower than e'er he did before-times and is murderin' oor ain folk. You maun catch him, Scott, and hang the bluidy bastert before he kills oor Jeannie."

"Wait, wait," Scott said. "How do you know all this, my dear?"

"I owerheert him sellin' Leezie tae Dochtor Knox. An I seen her for mesel'. Noo, look lively or he'll be awa'. Bring him back, pu' his hand on Leezie and I'll warrant her wounds will bleed again when e'er his hands touch her."

Scott was already donning his coat and wrapping his scarf around his face, pulling on his gloves, gathering his hat and cane. "They certainly will, my dear, if your surmise is correct. Jaimie, would you please wake Laing and ask him to meet us at the infirmary? We'll need to examine the victim and take Midge Margret's evidence and get a description of the suspect."

"Aye, Watt, that I'll do."

Primrose had muttered something and taken himself off,

no doubt from discretion. MacRae, deeper in his cups than he had appeared to be when seated, tried in vain to linger for the conversation but then seemed obligated to stumble toward the water closet. It was just as well both men were gone. Scott had no wish for MacRae to choose this time to interrogate Midge Margret as to her psychic abilities, nor did he wish for Primrose to repeat some of the slighting remarks he had made about tinklers in Midge Margret's presence, causing *her* to dissect *him*.

Chapter XVII

THE BODY OF Leezie Stewart was a small, diminished, pitiful thing. Scott had not realized she was such a child. Her scalp still bore blood at the roots of her hair, where she'd been dragged by it, and her face was bruised, the dark marks obscenely obvious against the pallor of death. The pity rose in Scott's throat like bile and he felt tears lurking in his eyes. He was a lawyer only, and no hardened policeman to look without the deepest sorrow upon the remains of a girl murdered before she could know much of life. He sighed and cleared his throat. "She was brought here by your husband, Midge Margret? You're certain of that?"

"Aye. I'd ken his voice onyplace."

"And you, Dr. Knox? Do you know the name of the individual who brought you the body of this lassie?"

Knox, rumpled and angry from being awakened twice in one night, this time by the Town Guard, shook his head. Scott found he could barely stand to look at the man. He felt sure Knox would have attempted to block them from entering the morgue had he accompanied them, but he had not. While Captain Laing was rousing him, Midge Margret had used the key from the ring she had purloined from the matron—who hadn't missed it for a moment, but was passed out drunk at her desk, as was her male counterpart. This they learned because Midge Margret, with great anxiety, insisted that they check on Geordie's safety and upon the status of his injury before continuing the investigation. They found that Geordie had roused himself and was parched, muttering for water—a request that went unheeded by the man at the nursing station.

"I know ye mean weel, Mr. Scott," Midge Margret said, "but we'll no' stay here anither day. We'd be safer amang oor ain folk an' I'm sartain one o' the other women can see tae Geordie. Amang them, I cannae do it myself, mind you, as I'm onclean frae a' this bein' amang the deid."

This she said before she showed him the body. When she had done so, he knew very well what she meant. He felt rather soiled himself. And he found he could barely tolerate the presence of Knox, even though his very own grandfather Scott had been a surgeon and an anatomist and undoubtedly relied upon the same resources for his research and teaching materials. But the poor carcass on the table had been a girl of barely fourteen, taken from the cold bed her family had made beneath a wagon, Midge Margret had told him on the way down. Hogg re-covered her.

"We maun hae her back, Mr. Scott," Midge Margret said. "She cannae bide here."

"We need to leave her above groond a wee while yet, lassie. Until we can obtain her evidence that it 'twas your husband who killed her."

"Don't ca' him that," she said. "He's no husband tae me noo." But she was shuddering hard. "She should gae back

tae her mam an' be laid oot proper and waked, and by that
time, why, maybe ye'll hae the bastert in hand."

"Perhaps so." Scott turned to the police constable, who
was still rubbing the sleep from his eyes.

Dr. Knox said, as if seeing the girl on the table for the
first time as a human being who had folk that cared for her,
"Have the constables take my carriage to return her to her
people, Scott. She should not be borne through the streets
like that."

Midge Margret strangled the outrage that rose in her at
the man's hypocrisy. Her eyes blazed. "A handcart was
good enough for her first time, but noo a carriage? Och,
that'll no' mend the harum ye've done her, mon. But a' the
same, bring it roond."

"That's very good of you, Doctor," Scott said, "especially as Miss Caird declines tae leave her brother in your
care and we will need transport for him as well. Constable,
if you and one of your men would bring Dr. Knox's carriage, please? Meanwhile, Dr. Knox, would you be so kind
as to examine the abdominal wound and give me your opinion as to what might have caused it? Once we have obtained
that evidence, I think it would be a great comfort to the family if you would suture the wound closed and perhaps the
matron could be roused to find some sort of gown to cover
the puir lassie."

Midge Margret gave a stiff, commanding nod in the doctor's direction, as if Scott's suggestion was an order from
her.

Captain Laing added, "As she is in this state of undress,
ye maun also examine her to determine if she's been interfered with."

Midge Margret let out a gasp and turned her face to
Scott's chest.

"Certainly I can do that, Sheriff," the doctor said to Scott, and now he seemed not to know whether to be haughty, angry, or contrite. "But all of the bodies procured for us by clandestine means arrive unclothed. You see, while there is no specific law against stealing a dead body, though I'm well aware that it's frowned upon, the procurer *could* be prosecuted for stealing the deceased's clothing."

"Aye, that's true, Doctor, particularly when the clothing belongs to a still-warm body and are removed by the person responsible for the body's demise." Scott was trying very hard to be fair, but the doctor's nonchalance grated on him, although he supposed it was entirely appropriate. He was liking Dr. Knox less and less. But because of Midge Margret's reaction, he said to Laing, "I think we might forgo any further examinations, Captain. It's evident that this lassie has been 'interfered with' in a manner most profound and obvious."

"O' course, Sheriff. As you say," Laing agreed easily enough.

"Midge Margret," Scott said, gently prying the girl away from him to look into her face and make sure she understood him. "I think it best if you and your brother should come tae stay wi' me for a few days, especially since, as you say, you're currently estranged from your people. I have a house-keeper who lives in an adjoining flat and she can be pre-vailed upon to chaperone, I believe."

Midge Margret swiped at her eyes with her fists to clear them and regarded Scott with a narrowed glance as she searched his face for signs of lunacy. At last she said primly, "Tha's verra kind o' ye, Mr. Scott. Fer Geordie's sake, if nane else, I thank you. And this way, I can mebbe gie ye a bit mair help in findin' Jeannie."

Scott nodded. She looked as though she needed nothing so much as warm clothes, a decent meal, and a good night's sleep, that and some relief from fear. But he reflected that had he been similarly attacked, along with his entire family, he probably would not be concerned with all those creature comforts so much as he would care about providing assistance in halting the damage done to himself and his family, and to finding the missing member.

The doctor bent to sew up Leezie's flesh but paused for a moment over the wound. "Odd," he said.

"What?" Scott asked.

Dr. Knox's lips were set in a thin line. "As the tinkler—as Miss Caird can testify, and already has done, I received this body only this evening. I have not touched it except to move it from the procurer's wheelbarrow to this table. And yet, the heart, liver, and spleen are all missing. Not by accident, as I was informed, but surgically removed. See the clean cuts?"

That was too much for Midge Margret, who made it out the door just before she was violently sick.

While she was venting her disgust, the doctor coolly sewed Leezie's poor flesh together over her ghastly wound and the guardsmen removed her pathetic body to the coach, and then, on Scott's orders, returned for Geordie, whom they stretched upon the other seat, his head cradled in his sister's lap. Scott rode atop the coach with the driver, and the men trotted alongside, since the coach travelled at a sedate pace up the West Bow.

Outside the close containing the building where the tinklers were lodged, Midge Margret left Geordie in Scott's care and entered the close, climbing the stairs to the floor where her people were lodged.

Everyone was sleeping, of course, and she was unclean, but nevertheless what needed to be done needed to be done and she shook Chrissie Stewart by the toe sticking out from her heavy woollen sock. Mrs. Stewart came awake with a little scream. "You!" she said.

"Ye maun wake yer menfolk. I found Leezie's body and it's doon below, waitin' tae be brung up and waked."

Mrs. Stewart sat up, rubbing her eyes. Her hair was full of tangled mats, as Midge Margret could see even by the light of the little candle she'd lit at the door, kept there for the purpose of going to the water closet at night and returning without tripping over the bodies lying asleep all over the floor.

"Where's your brother and Jeannie? The wee'uns hae been greetin' a' the evenin'," Mrs. Stewart said and though she could not make it out, Midge Margret knew there would be a hard look on the other woman's face.

"Did the gentleman no' tell ye?" she asked. "Geordie has been sare hurt and Jeannie carried awa' by the noddies. Have ye no' been searchin' for her?"

Chrissie Stewart shook her head as if to clear it of cobwebs. "We searched aye a wee bit when ye nae cam' hame and later there was a gentleman went tae see Ryk and Stevie, but he nivver cam' by here." Then, as if what Midge Margret had said at the first finally sank into her head, Mrs. Stewart said, "Leezie? Ye've foond her? Where?"

"At the infirmary where Mr. Scott took me 'n' Geordie when we was hurt. I wisnae s'posed to go in there but I—" She realized that her status with the Stewarts was not going to be improved if she told them the gory details of the place she had found their daughter. "Nivver mind, woman. She's doon below wi' the poliss. Have yer men fetch her up for layin' oot an' wakin'. Geordie's bairnies, Jenny and Martin, where are they noo?"

"They're wi' auld Johnnie Faw and his missus. They'll do weel enough till their daddy returns."

"We'll find their mither too if ye'll ainly rouse the people tae gae searchin'."

"She'd be deid a'ready, I reckon."

"I dinnae think so," Midge Margret said, and realized she believed it when she said it. Somehow, she thought she'd know if Jeannie were deid.

She left while Chrissie Stewart woke everyone, and heard enough from the stairwell to know that Chrissie had the straight of it. Then she fetched down a few of her own things and the bundle of Bella's clothing and made her way back down the stairs. The people were up now and lighting candles and getting dressed. No one seemed to take notice of her. She wanted to see Jenny and Martin but they still slept. She did not want to be the one to tell the Stewarts their Leezie was missing bits of her insides.

She returned to the carriage and passed the clothing up to Scott, saying, "I'll just gae hae a wee word wi' Ryk the Ramrod and Red Stevie and be back straightawa'."

Scott began to ask something but before he could, the close was filled with tinklers—two of them Stewart men come to claim their own, with Mrs. Stewart close behind. She let out a grunt when she saw Leezie's dead face, that was all.

Midge Margret took the stairs two at a time and pounded on the door to the rooms shared by Ryk and Stevie. When no one answered, she walked in. No one challenged her. She fumbled by the door until she found the candle. Only a small stub lay on the floor, and this she lit with her bit of flint. There was barely enough left of the wax to hang on to.

At that, it was more than remained in the rest of the rooms. All of the tools, the metals, the clothing, bedding, everything was gone. Ryk and Stevie were no longer there.

Why had Chrissie Stewart not said as much? Aye, but did she know? Perhaps not. She'd said that Mr. Scott's tall gentleman friend had spoken to Ryk and Stevie, but she did not mention what was said—if she knew. Perhaps he had sent them off searching, thinking to get Jeannie back in time to care for her own bairnies. But somehow, Midge Margret didn't believe that.

She rejoined Scott at the carriage and, upon arrival at his flat, forgot all as Geordie was settled into one of the comfortable beds Scott's family used when they came visiting from the country. She shivered by the fire, though the flame was bright enough.

PHYSICIAN'S NOTES:

The bloody fool has done it now. His wife, a much brighter individual than he, discovered him delivering the young girl's cadaver to Knox at the infirmary. If Scott and the Guard run him to ground, I doubt I can trust him to remain discreet about his involvement with me.

He'll have to go, but first, I require his help in the final stages of my work. It is a very great waste, really, since I cannot use him for my own work nor even provide his carcass to my former colleagues for their studies, Knox being all too well aware of his health and vigor of recent times.

1 A.M.

All is lost. I allowed myself to be pressured by circumstances into proceeding, though I knew—I knew that the components were inferior, that the spells within my ken were inadequate to augment the surgery enough to make the new body habitable for her.

She knew too. She stood beside me, watching, as I operated for hours without ceasing, taking the parts magically preserved, the graceful arms, the beautiful hands and feet, the legs that danced so beautifully on the stage, the voluptuous torso that would have been so sorely exploited by the wanton upon whom the Lord originally conferred it, the innocent inner organs, and at last, the head of my beloved, still free from death as it was when I stole it from the executioner's basket.

Once the body was assembled and the head in place, I then extracted from the pregnant gypsy a small quantity of the birth fluid which, with the proper enchantments, is the very elixir of life.

All the while she watched me, and I felt her skepticism, felt her shock and distress at seeing her own corporeal head now on the slender shoulders of another's body. Once I administered the fluid, I believed, the spell I had used would be sufficient, the body and head would become a whole entity, and my love could safely enter in and rule it as her own.

But when I had injected the fluid and spoken the words, and looked around for her to enter, she was nowhere to be seen. She whose shade has been my constant companion abandoned me when I would have given her my greatest gift.

The gypsy man made some remark, indicating that he had expected more dramatic results, but I ignored him, to search for my love. I could not feel her in the room, and it was essential that she enter the body within the midnight hour or the moment was lost. I thought she might have drifted to the upper regions, to ponder this momentous occasion, and I ascended the stairs and entered the house to seek her out.

But I found her nowhere. Nowhere. My gift was not adequate. For some reason she could not, would not, enter in. I knew the science was flawless. It was the magic, the magic that was inadequate. All of my life I have known how to perform those feats which have been performed by the best of men in various fields, but the magic is yet, as magic is always, uncharted territory each time it is performed. "Never mind, beloved," I said to the air. "I understand. There is time yet to do this again, to find worthier hostesses for your spirit, to learn whatever I need learn to please you, to exon-

erate myself, to earn your forgiveness and deserve your love again."

I had only just made this resolve when I heard a commotion from the carriage house and rushed to see what was causing it.

The door to the laboratory was open, as was the coach house door. Thinking only that the gypsy had either been overcome by the tinklers' foolish superstitions surrounding the dead or that he had divined my intention of ridding myself of his presence, which has become compromising since his spouse recognized his voice, I shut the doors behind me and descended the laboratory stairs again to disassemble the body, remove the precious head, and make preparations to begin again.

But the table that had borne the composite body was bare, the patchwork creature that had lain there, the creature bearing the face of my beloved, was gone. As was my best scalpel.

Chapter XVIII

SCOTT'S PLAN TO have his housekeeper play chaperone fell afoul of the lady herself, who would have none of keeping a house containing two tinklers. "You mark my words, Mr. Scott, they'll murder ye in yer ain bed for yer charity," she said, and no amount of persuasion on Scott's part could rouse her considerable penchant for charity when it came to Midge Margret and Geordie. The latter was no longer unconscious, but his rest was fitful and disturbed, apparently by wild dreams and fancies.

Midge Margret herself eschewed the settee to sleep on the Turkey rug in front of the fire, covered by an afghan that Scott's aunt Janet had made for him when he first came to stay with her as a boy.

It had been two days since he'd had the two brought to his flat, and he realized that some would consider the situation ruinously improper, but he really did not feel he had alternatives, or rather, he felt that Geordie and Midge Margret had no alternatives that would ensure their safety. He smiled to himself. Perhaps this was house arrest for tinklers. Since most tinklers had no houses of their own, if you wanted to put them under house arrest, you had to provide the house.

Captain Laing took custody of the bundle of clothing Midge Margret had brought from the building where the tinklers now lived.

Scott, who generally slept only four or five hours a night at best, had slept even less since Midge Margret's discovery of the body and her ex-husband's guilt in the matter. Scott had been back and forth to his office and to the Town Guard station, but Laing reported no progress on finding either the man or any other remains.

He had tried to keep his mind and Midge Margret's off the murders and her worry over Geordie, whose improvement was much slower than Scott might have hoped, by regaling her with his little party pieces—anecdotes and stories of his law practice and the people he knew. He told her the stories of his ancestors and of the best fee he had ever received—this from a lockpick, who advised him that to protect himself he should lock his door not with a newfangled locking mechanism but with the oldest, rustiest, most antiquated lock he could find. For extra security, the thief told him, a large dog in the yard could be bribed, but a small yapping dog in the house would frighten a burglar away.

"Aye, sound advice," Midge Margret said, with an expression of professional appreciation. "The new locks are aisy slipped wi' naught but a hairpin, or onythin' the like. The fine locks Ryk and Stevie are makin' for yon bonny hooses below could open as aisy wi'oot keys as wi'." She covered her mouth with both hands and looked horrified, as if realizing suddenly the indiscretion of making such a pronouncement to the sheriff.

He asked her a few questions, but she clearly felt she had said more than she should already. The tinklers tended to be somewhat secretive about their lives and he did not wish to seem intrusive. So he asked her for songs now and then, although his formal research for the *Minstrelsy* was finished.

The night before, Scott's sleep had been troubled by a dream. He seemed to be walking back from the Tollbooth, where the guard station was situated. It was late and in the dream he had been called in to view a pile of bodies that all looked like young Leezie Stewart and were all similarly mutilated. For some reason he was walking past the Nor' Loch when he saw a strange figure crossing the bridge. The figure was obviously female, as he could tell because she had on far too little clothing to protect her from the cold—little more than a bonnet and a single chemise, which would have been grounds for arrest for indecent exposure in the waking world, always assuming she survived death from exposure to be prosecuted, of course.

She was carrying something in her arms and in his dream Scott drew close enough to see that it was a man.

Just before he reached her, she turned sideways, and with strength he would never have believed possible, flung the man's body over the railing and out into the middle of the loch. At that point, he knew he was dreaming and began to wake up. But just before he did, she turned and he saw her more clearly. Her face was beautiful and unscarred, but where it joined her neck, there was a long slash with the sort of sturdy stitches one might use to sew animal skins together. Her hands and arms bore similar scars and her chest bore a large one from the neck down into her bodice. Her hair was matted beneath her bonnet. In the darkness, he could not see the color but he could see on her face an expression of both idiocy and rage.

After that, it was little wonder that he could not sleep.

Midge Margret was curled up so close to the fire, he felt he had to keep an eye on her so that she would not accidentally burn foot or hand while thrashing out, as she some-times did. Her dreams appeared to be deep, but so troubled, he half expected a phantom, perhaps similar to the one in his own dream, to appear in their midst. The horror of the dream had faded somewhat except for a vague wonder about how the woman had come to be both so disfigured and so strong, not to mention who the man was and why on earth she had been allowed out in her chemise on such a cold night.

He sat down with his writing pad on a tray before the fire too and began to write a story about phantoms, both of the kind folk claimed to see but also of the kind that, due to some particularly grievous circumstance, haunted a woman for the rest of her life. He based it on a tale he had heard on his Highland rambles during his summers off from school, when he had accompanied Sheriff Roundtree into the wilds not only to learn more about rural law but also to gather songs and stories for his true vocation.

Midge Margret woke just as he reached the end of his tale. She looked extremely startled to see him, as if he him-self were a phantom, but gradually, as her eyes darted around the room and its furnishings and then back to him in his chair with his tray and pad, she relaxed and fully recog-nized him.

"Good afternoon, Midge Margret," Scott said to her. "Did you sleep well, lassie?"

She broke into a shadow of the brilliant smile she had shown him when they were both much younger. "Aye, Mr. Scott, I did. But I had muckle unco' dreams."

"How was that?" he asked. She stretched as unselfcon-sciously as the cat, who had curled up beside her and now joined Midge Margret in stretching, making a slide of her sleek orange back, with front paws extended in a full salaam on the Turkey carpet, hind legs totally upright, and tail curled above her rump. Before the fire, with the light catching the red glints in Midge Margret's blondie hair and the cat's red coat, they made a pretty picture.

"Shades o' the deid," she said. "And mebbe those who aren't deid as weel. I saw the divvil who was aince my man, but he was in as sad a way as the puir lass he gutted an' brought tae the infirmary. Drooning in a loch and callin' oot as if he expectit *me* tae save him. I nivver would!"

"Sounds like a busy sleep," Scott said.

"Aye, but the ithers was a' welcome if ainly they let me sleep, and I did that and am the better for it."

"I'm happy to hear it. I'm afraid we're on our own as far as tea is concerned, but I've spent time enough in bothies tae ken the way of it. May I offer you some?"

"Oh, that will nivver do!" she said, jumping to her feet. "Ainly let me hae a wee gawk at Geordie and I'll mak' it mesel'. I can cook, though no' sae fairly as Jeannie." Her face fell when she spoke the name of her sister-in-law. Then she brightened and said, "A guid thing aboot them dreams o' mine, Mr. Scott . . ."

"Aye?"

"Jeannie wisnae there, amang the deid ones."

"May all your dreams come true," Scott murmured.

"What are ye daein' th' noo?" she asked, looking at his pad.

"I was writing a story."

"Mair sangs, then?"

"Not this time," he said. "Though I remain interested in the songs, of course. No, this is something of a ghost story. I suppose you've had ower much of ghosts these days, but when something is occurring in my real life, it often gies me ideas for stories."

"Is it a good ane?" she asked, shifting so that she was sitting cross-legged at his feet.

"I don't know," he said honestly. He never knew so soon after finishing.

"I can tell ye. Read it me," she said.

He complied happily, as reading aloud was a sure way to catch his own errors or breaks in the voice he was using. She listened raptly and at the end she was nodding, as if the same thing that happened to the haunted mother in the story had happened to her as well.

"Did you like it, then?" he asked her.

"Like it! That wis the best thing I ever heard! Hae ye ithers?"

"Aye, but nae time for them noo, I fear . . ."

She sighed.

The late afternoon had settled into darkness, and the fog and smoke once more obscured things—it did serve to warm the air a bit, however, as if it were a real cloak and not merely a vaporous one. The fire crackled and the candle burned companionably. Geordie seemed to be settled into a proper sleep. Midge Margret made the tea and Scott offered her some day-old scones he'd acquired from his favorite bakery. As they sipped and ate, he asked Midge Margret of her life to date and she told him.

He was saddened and angered to hear that she had been mistreated by the brutal man for whom they now searched, and though he was not normally a violent man, Scott was gratified to hear that Geordie had taken the knave to task. She prattled on, telling him of how she came to find the clothing in the loch, of Ryk the Ramrod and Red Stevie, and of how she came to be banished from her people because of her contact with the dead girl's clothing.

"It worket oot for the best," she said with a shrug. "They pu' me in me ain wee room toppet the stairs and I found a room wi a' manner o' cast-off articles—lovely books and a new Turkey rug, a'maest like this ane, but it had a stain in the middle. Looked like blood tae me, but that may be 'cause I've seen an awfy lot o' the stuff lately."

"Hmm," Scott said. "Well, perhaps the rug was stained soon after it was purchased and the stain would not come out, rendering it unusable." But they were both ignoring the context, he knew. He made a mental note to look into it. Perhaps Primrose could explain what had happened. He had said the house was once his family home. "What manner of books were there?"

"Every kind. Fu' o' dirty pictures and signs—mair than stories, but 'twas great fun lookin' through them."

"I can imagine. You read, then?"

"Aye. Me an' Geordie both. Fither learnt us tae."

"Very wise," Scott said. He couldn't help noticing the way her eyes took in his possessions and no doubt calculated their resale value, but he felt she did so automatically. After all, folk did give away items they no longer used to the tinklers. He supposed they became quite adept at assessing value. It did not necessarily mean they had theft in mind.

She was once more checking on her brother when there was a knock at Scott's door.

Angus Armstrong stood there, his boots covered in mud and slush, his coat and hat wet with melting snow.

"Good evenin', Angus."

"Evenin', Mr. Scott. There's a thing you must see at Duddingston Loch."

"What might that be?" Scott asked.

"Corpse lights, Mr. Scott. Some folk was testin' the ice tae see if it were ripe for skatin' and they seen lights oot in the loch. It's corpse lights. Mair bodies, or I miss my guess."

"The way matters have been progressing, Angus, I verra much doubt that you miss your guess. I'll fetch my coat and tell the lassie where I'm going."

•   •   •   •   •

DUDDINGSTON LOCH WAS a much larger body of water than the overflow that had become known as St. Margaret's Loch. The larger loch was also located near the road that ran around the royal park containing the volcanic prominence of Arthur's Seat. It was on the opposite side of the park from the little loch where Midge Margret and her friends had located Bella's clothing, however. Between loch and park sat the old village of Duddingston, just outside the park's boundaries and barely within Scott's jurisdiction.

The road from Edinburgh to Duddingston was not cleared completely of snow, so the hired carriage had to be stopped. The investigators strapped on skis and dragged the sleds that had been fastened to the top of the carriage. Upon one of these sleds was strapped a small coracle, a little boat. In it was a long coil of rope. Those who had reported seeing the lights had skied to the loch too, and Scott, Laing, Armstrong, and a constable named Archie Campbell followed in their tracks. Where the tracks stopped, they stopped.

No other persons were near the loch now. Whereas people were very curious about a hanging, and congregated around the gallows as if the occasion were a festival, seeing evidence of the supernatural was not the sort of experience the Scots cultivated. Only too recently had witches been burnt, and indeed, every person who angered another had to fear facing the accusation of witchcraft. Too many people had family ghosts for other manifestations to be a laughing matter. Imagined ghosts might be fun, but the real ones, in Scott's estimation, left folk with such an uneasy sense that they doubted their own eyes, ears and nerve-endings. Most contemporary literature about the supernatural, including Scott's own, tended to rationalize it away, which was all the more evidence that it was not taken lightly nor spoken of easily. "I don't believe in that stuff," people would say, but it was as if they had crossed themselves when they said it. They believed very deeply indeed, but wished fervently that they did not, for one never knew what sort of manifestation one might witness—a reasonable, benign, even slightly humorous one, such as the victim witness who was one of Scott's earliest proofs of the supernatural, or a truly malign one who made the word "haunt" mean that a person would be hounded by its presence, constantly reminded, never feel free of it, never feel quite safe, never know what to expect. This was not the sort of feeling anyone in his right mind relished.

Corpse lights, like the interrogation of the victim witness, were one of the core tools of criminal investigation of the time, another one followed in these days only by duly appointed officers of the court and King. Scott had not previously witnessed them and was actually a bit disappointed when he first saw them.

His first thought, on viewing the quite ordinary-looking candle flame glowing in the dark out across the loch, was that it was a hoax, of course. Someone was standing out on the loch with a candle or a lantern, playing a trick on them. And, as a matter of fact, the mist was rising on the lake so that it would have obscured someone standing under the light. But the light was very high. It would have to have been held by a giant.

Armstrong asked, "You seen corpse lights before, have you, Sheriff?"

"Nay, Angus, I havena," he replied. "There's no' an eerie look tae them, is there?"

"Not at first, no," Angus replied. "You think someone's got a lamp on a tall pole or something like that, but you'll see. What I cannae help wonderin' is how the devil the poor bastard, whoever it is, got way oot there in the middle o' the loch this time o' year. It wouldnae be an auld corpse, for the lights are newly shinin'. Naebody's seen 'em here before."

Scott's dream of the patchwork woman flinging a body as if it were a doll far out into the middle of a loch came back to him. He shrugged and the cold turned it briefly into a shudder.

Laing was removing his skis while Angus, Campbell and Scott did likewise. The constables then linked the sleds with the rope—the little coracle rode on the first sled that was pushed over the ice by the second, toward where the candle flame burned unwaveringly through the mist.

The cold snap had not lasted long, and in a very short time the first sled went through the ice, setting the boat adrift. Campbell, who had been pushing the sled across the ice with his foot, pulled it back up from the water by the rope and set it dripping beside the second sled. They were not far from shore, but it seemed to Scott that the break in the ice happened very close to where the candle flame burned.

Now Scott saw that the coracle was also linked by rope to the sleds, and, pulling it back to where the ice became open water, Campbell very gingerly climbed in. Scott saw a piece of equipment brought forth that he had not seen before. This was a long iron hook, like an overgrown shepherd's crook. Laing handed it to Angus, who handed it to Campbell. The latter rowed a bit toward the flame and when he seemed to be directly under it, he plunged the hook as deep as it would go.

It seemed the water here was not very deep, though the middle of the loch was supposed to be virtually bottomless. The handle of the hook still protruded from the water a good six feet while the hook probed as low as it could go. The candle flame seemed to retreat a bit, leading the boat forward.

In another yard or so, the iron hook went into the water again, and this time it caught on something. "I think I hae haud o' him, sir," Campbell called back.

"Then haul him oot, there's a good fellow," Laing called. Campbell hauled. He was a large, stout man but he was hampered by a heavy overcoat and gloves. Still he pulled on the hook, and when it came up, something limp and cumbrous and wormy-white came up with it, dangling from its middle like an oversized clump of seaweed.

Campbell did a masterful job of hauling the corpse into the boat with him, and rowing back. The moment the corpse came out of the water, Scott noticed, the corpse light vanished from the air.

"Good Lord," he said.

"Looks a bit more supernacheral noo, does it not, Scott?" Angus asked, as the two of them helped haul the coracle in.

It took some time for them to haul boat, Campbell, corpse and hook out of the water, pull them back to a point where Campbell could safely disembark and the others help him move the corpse from the boat onto two of the yoked sleds, then pull the lot back onto the path.

"Och, wha' a mess this one is," Angus said.

"Do any of you know him?" Scott asked the policemen.

"Aye, I think I do," Campbell said. "Brawled a bit, this one. Looks like he got on the wrang end o' a broken bottle this time."

"Aye, or something like it," Angus agreed. Scott just nodded. The corpse was the blue and white of the frozen and drowned, though not much eaten by fish, which confirmed the evidence of the corpse lights that it had not been long in the loch. His ginger hair was a stark contrast to the flesh, which gaped in new raw mouths in dozens of visible places—cheeks, eyes, neck, along his nose, crosshatched.

His clothing was cut to ribbons too, and no doubt the flesh beneath it.

"One battle too many for oor Seamus," Campbell said.

"I beg your pardon?" Scott asked. "What did you call him?"

"Seamus. Seamus Connors. Bad for the women, didnae ken how tae say 'please, missus, may I?' and walloped on 'em if they complained."

"His reputation precedes him," Scott said dryly. "He's our body snatcher, according to his wife's evidence."

"Aw, weel then, that'll save the city the expense o' burial," Angus said.

"Right, then." Laing pointed toward the carriage. "It's gettin' nae earlier. Let's load 'im an' be off."

They tried dragging the sleds with the body behind them, but too many bits of the late body snatcher kept flopping out and catching in the snow, so in the end, Angus and Campbell shouldered the first sled, Laing and Scott the second, that is when Scott could, for his lame leg still made skiing a bit awkward, let alone skiing and carrying something heavy on the shoulder above his good leg. At length they reached the carriage, attempted to turn it around on the drive, got stuck, had to push it from behind while the horses pulled from the front but became mired in drifts and freshly thawed mud. In the end, they had to unhitch the horses and gently lead them out of the bog and onto the road again, then all of the men turned the carriage, rehitched the horses, loaded sleds, coracle, corpse and all into and onto the coach.

As they were driving up the Canongate to the guard station, Scott spied Primrose emerging from St. Giles Cathedral. Primrose tipped his hat in Scott's direction, but Scott beckoned to him.

Angus and Campbell had dismounted and were beginning to unload the body. "My dear Corey, come see. We've caught Midge Margret's wayward husband, our body snatcher. Looks as if he caught a live one this time and became the corpse himself."

Primrose peered down at the body. A wisp of some emotion, possibly only revulsion, passed briefly across his countenance before he said slowly, "Aye, it does indeed."

"I'd appreciate it if you could spare a moment to examine him and tell us what manner of weapon might have made these wounds and which of the wounds could have been the fatal one."

The constables carried Connors into the station and laid him on a rough wooden table—the same one they sometimes used for meals or to interview witnesses, and once, Angus had told Scott, to deliver the baby of a female miscreant.

"Scott, you ken I didnae finish my medical training," Primrose said.

"Only because you could have taught the professors a thing or two while still in college, from what I've heard," Scott said. "After the other night, I don't trust Knox or the others without corroboration. Please, have a look. You see here, the throat wound. Can you gauge how deep it is without instruments?"

"Aye," Primrose said, pulling off his white winter gloves and tucking them in his coat pocket before examining the wound Scott indicated and several others with a professional interest that seemed to grow livelier as he investigated. "You were wise to exclude the doctors, Scott. I would say a scalpel is responsible for these wounds. And yet, they in no way indicate a skilled hand but rather a fierce rage."

"Well, we know from both Midge Margret and our ain good constables that the late and apparently unlamented deceased enjoyed mistreating women. Perhaps he mistreated or attempted to mistreat the wrong one."

"The force and depth of these wounds is rather remarkable for one of the fair sex against a powerful man such as he appears to be," Primrose said.

"Aye, well, I thank you. Looks as if all of the blood was drained oot of him with his wounds, does it not?" Scott asked. "They're not pinkening even in the warmth."

"No, I shouldn't expect them to," Primrose said. "If that's all then, perhaps I'll see you later."

"Certainly. Thank you so much for indulging me."

"My pleasure," Primrose said, and touched the brim of his hat in a perfunctory way, turned on his heel, and left the station, which had begun to reek of death now that the corpse was warming. Scott looked after him for a bit, and back to the wounds.

"We should hae a' the dochtors poke roond on him, Sheriff," Laing told him. "You know how it is wi' this kind o' murder. If the murderer should touch the victim, the wounds will bleed again as if fresh."

"Yes, yes, I had considered that possibility when I asked Deacon Primrose to examine him," Scott said, worrying his chin with his fingers. "In order, of course, that we would have a thorough examination by an uninvolved party before we ask possible suspects."

"Och, aye," Laing agreed.

Although the body had been identified by Angus, Scott decided to fetch Midge Margret himself to view the remains of her husband. He wished to avoid further alarm to her, to check for himself on Geordie's condition, and to draw her out further on her husband's character, habits and acquaintances.

He hated to leave the warmth of the stove in the police station, for the chill of the loch with its corpse candle was deep in his bones in a way that the cold had not bothered him previously. But he dutifully resumed his hat, coat, muffler and gloves, and found, once away from the stove, that he was glad enough to escape the rising stench of the corpse.

Chapter XIX

MIDGE MARGRET HAD never before been left alone in
someone's house. Not that she was exactly alone. There was
Geordie, of course. She didn't think he'd ever been left
alone in anyone's house either. Such a lot of things settled
people had! Even someone like Scott, a bachelor man on his
own, not too well off for all the respect it seemed to her he
was shown. She had been inside enough houses when the
owners were there to know that his things, some of which
were old, a few of which might be valuable, were not new
or costly or lavish by the standards of the day.

Most of his things were books. There were chairs and a
table in the main room, a bed in the alcove, some fairly nice
china and silver in the wee small kitchen, no doubt sent up
from home by his mother, but there were few ornaments. A
letter opener shaped like a dagger, somebody's skull, and a
pair of real swords hanging over the fire. That was about it
for ornaments. Otherwise it was all books and papers.

For passing the time, the furnishings could hardly have

suited better. She looked through the stacks on the floors, on the sills, on the table and desktop, piled beside the chairs, lying open on the mantel.

Many of these were about law, but some were on other subjects. There was enough reading material available that she need not choose a single book at all, but could while away hours just reading the titles of all the books. Some were religious, some had words that were much bigger than she could read. She wondered if perhaps there was a dictionary. The dominie in one little town, less frowning and severe than the usual sort for those teachers, especially when it came to the tinklers, had told Midge Margret about dictionaries, that they contained all of the words that there ever were. Most words were not a great deal larger than the ones in the Bible, but some of Scott's books had very long titles indeed. The dictionary the dominie had showed her was a very large book. She thought it would be close to hand perhaps in one of the piles nearest the desk, but the shelves were the easiest place to check first since the stacks were in such a muddle she didn't think she could ever replace the books all in the same order, so he wouldn't know she'd been looking. All of the largest books, she saw, were on the top shelf.

She dragged over a hard-bottomed chair and stood on it to reach the top shelf, but she was still too short. So she found a little stool in the kitchen and set that atop the chair seat. She could reach now. Almost at once she was sure she was in the wrong area because most of these books had a thick layer of dust on them, as indeed they would have had they been hers and stuck up so high.

They were also wedged tightly together, and she broke several already bitten fingernails past the quick trying to dislodge one book from the other. Then she noticed that the one on the end was put in the wrong way, and it had a metal

buckle and a strap to hold the pages shut. She grasped the
buckle and pulled—and five books pulled loose at once.
She started to shove them back in, and then saw that behind
the pages and the buckle, there was no book. The "books"
were a front for a little secret door. When she pulled it
open, there were some other books and papers back there:
three large bound books and several smaller, thinner ones,
plus loose papers. She pulled them out and carried them
down, one large book at a time, then the smaller books, and
finally the stack of papers, being careful in case there was
jewelry or money hidden among the pages. Not that she
would take such things. It was only that she thought there
must be something there besides just books and papers.
Otherwise, why hide them like that?

   She put them on Scott's dining table, along with the
stacks of books already there, and opened the first of the
large books. The pages were made of funny stuff that felt
more like leather than paper. The handwriting was spidery
and the words were spelled strangely, with *f*'s where, if the
word had been the familiar one she thought it was at first,
there should have been *s*'s. Part of it was in Latin, she was
sure, like what the priests used when one of them chose to
come from his church and do a Mass for the tinklers. Not
many Catholic churches remained in Scotland at that time,
but a few had come back and these were anxious to embrace
any believers that could be found. The tinklers didn't believe exactly the same way the priests believed, but so long
as they didn't tell the priests, and they didn't, they had allies
on their journeys, shrines to shelter in as well as to pray at,
and someone to church the dead.

   The book also contained some of the same symbols she
had seen in the strange volume at the house where her people were lodged. Stars with six points, crescent moons, as-
trological signs she was familiar with from the tarot cards,

and other symbols she took to be arcane. She dearly wished she had already found that dictionary.

The three great books were all in the same cobweb hand-writing, brown with age on the leathery pages. The other, thinner books seemed newer, and were all in English. Possibly they were translations of the larger volumes, and the loose papers appeared to be puzzles of some sort, that started with symbols or odd groups of letters and numbers and then solved them, with notations at the bottom.

She felt a little disappointed. It was surely an important discovery, but she had no idea what any of it meant and did not know of anyone she could ask except Scott himself. How could she ask him? It occurred to her that she could just explain what she had been looking for and what she had found and that her curiosity prompted her to look further. Of all the settled people she had ever met, Scott was the most unusual in his kindness and lack of suspicion of her and her kind. He seemed bent on treating them as if they were anyone else in the town. He did not, in fact, seem to notice that they were any different. She must have a talk with him about that when all of this was over. He would get badly taken advantage of by some if he didn't learn to be more discriminating. She would have to teach him how to tell who he could trust, and who not. She took the large books back to the shelves, and set the stool back on the chair seat, then climbed up and down three times replacing them, closed the trick door to the hiding place, dismounted, returned the stool to the kitchen and the chair to the dining table. She would try to read the translations next, but in the meantime, if Scott returned, she could pick her own time to discuss the books instead of risking him getting angry at her.

It took a moment to find out which of the smaller books was the first one, but it was numbered and said, "The mas-

ter works of Dr. Michael Scott, known as the Wizard, translated from his own writings."

Who was this wizard? Some relative of Scott's? An ancestor, maybe, judging from the age of the bigger books.
Geordie groaned and gave a loud grunt and she hastily
shoved the books and papers to the bottom of one of the
other stacks, again to hide the evidence of her investigations, and went to check on her brother.

He did not look as good to her as he had earlier. The pur-
ple shadows beneath his eyes were not from the candle glow
alone, and he was sweating a lot, though his lips seemed
cracked and dry. She stuck her finger in the glass of water
she had left beside his bed earlier and dropped some of the
water onto his lips and into his mouth, then dipped a
washrag into the glass and bathed his face with more of the
water. The bedclothes were disarranged from his restless-
ness and these she straightened beneath him and over him.
She hoped Scott returned soon. They needed to send for a
healer, if all of the doctors in this town were butchers.

Wiping her hands on her apron, she returned to the main
room, her eyes downcast and full of worry about her
brother. Which was why she didn't notice at first she was
not alone.

A tall figure stood in the doorway, his hat in his hand.
"Good afternoon, Miss—Midge Margret."

"Good afternoon, indeed!" she said, staying well away
from the man. She recognized him right enough as a friend
of Scott's, but he was no friend of hers for all that and she
didn't recall his name, though his superior air was ae familiar. "How did you get in here?"

"The door was unlocked. I knocked but heard no answer
and presumed Scott was writing. Where is he?"

"Out for a bit. He'll be back any time now. What do you
want?"

"Why, I came to see how you were doing, how the investigation is going, and to ask to borrow a book actually. I don't suppose you'll have seen it. It belonged to an ancestor of Scott's in whom I've taken an interest."

"Why did you take an interest if it's Mr. Scott's ancestor, not yours?" she demanded. Something was not right about this man and she knew it. He was smiling at her, and had she never been with Seamus, she might have thought it a lovely smile, but she saw around the teeth the same cruel twist to the thinnish mouth she had come to recognize in her husband, and that the eyes were crinkled not with good humor, but with amusement at the malice he intended.

"That, lassie, is a matter between Mr. Scott and myself and not for discussion with rabble Scott has seen fit to take in off the street," he said, his voice growing nasty now that he had been standing there long enough to be sure Scott wasn't within earshot.

"Mr. Scott's left me in charge o' his hoose while he's awa'," she said, trying to look more like a housekeeper and less like a housebreaker. "I think ye'd best wait until he's hame again tae borra a book."

He grunted and went to the bookshelves without another word to her and began pulling volumes from the shelves and throwing them on the floor.

"Here, what are ye daein'?" she demanded, and reached for his arm to make him back away, but he simply gave her a shove that sent her across the room. "I'll tell the poliss, I will," she threatened, but he only laughed.

"Aye, and whatever I've a mind tae do, I'll tell them you did it. I'll say while Scott was gone you vandalized and burglarized the place. Who do you think they'll believe, you daft hoor? An honest upstanding citizen like me or a gyppo beggar like you?"

And one after another he threw the books on the floor,

never minding that the pages got torn and rumpled, all of Scott's beautiful books.

"Wait, you'll ruin everything and you'll nivver find it," she said. "If I gie it tae ye, will ye gae awa' and leave us be, and later, bring it back in good shape?"

"Of course," he said. "It's you who are angering me and causing me to do all of this damage. If you knew where it was, you could have spared your benefactor all of this mess. It's your fault for getting above yourself, you know, just because someone believed your wild stories and took you in."

She was about to get the chair and stool again, but seeing as how he was very tall and could reach the shelf without standing on anything, she said, "Up there. Them books as are the last five in thon row there, they're fawse. Ye open them by the buckle o' the end book and inside are the auld books."

"I find it odd that you know what I'm looking for right away. Are you a witch that you seek out the knowledge of the old wizard?"

"No. I was lookin' for a dictionary and foond the hidden door by mistake. I'm nae witch."

"I'm happy to hear that," he said in a ringing voice that reminded her of a preacher's, "for the sake of your immortal soul, if you have one. And I'm not sure I believe you. What if it's a trick or a trap. No, you get them down yourself."

"But—" she began, and he started pulling books from the shelf and continued to do so until she set up the chair and the stool and handed down the first book.

She had the third in hand when she felt the stool jerked out from under her. She fell flailing, and as she did, the man reached out with what seemed to be a tablecloth and threw it over her head. It smelled funny, in a way that made her sick, and though she tried to fight it off, she found she hadn't the strength.

By this time she knew that the attack on her and on Scott's library was not personal or even because the "guest" hated tinklers. Why he needed Scott's books she didn't know, but she was sure it had to do with the murders. As certain as she had been the night before that Seamus had committed the crimes, she was equally as certain that this man had something to do with them as well.

But the chloroform-soaked cloth over her head made her mind woozy as well as her body and, though she was dimly aware of the sounds of more books being mangled, Scott's mum's nice dishes being broken, and then, to her horror, Geordie's feverish grunts and groans as the man was no doubt attacking her helpless brother, she could not lift a finger to prevent any of it. She did not even know how long it took before she was hoisted upon the man's shoulder and carried some distance before being deposited painfully into a conveyance that could have been either a sedan chair or a carriage. The smell from the cloth over her head intensified and she stopped thinking anything at all.

PHYSICIAN'S NOTES:

God deliver me from a poet who thinks of himself as a crafty enforcer of the King's laws! Did Scott really think that if I had dispatched Connors to his appointment with the devil, I would have touched the corpse in front of witnesses? The incident provided me with the information that the body I created for my beloved still lives, after a fashion, and perhaps even without the soul of my dear one is able to entertain some rudimentary emotions. Hatred being the one that springs immediately to mind.

The animated body spared me the trouble of dispatching

Connors myself, but now I have the task of reclaiming it and dismantling it, as I fear the exposure it has undergone without being properly inhabited and guarded by my magicks have rendered it subject to swift deterioration. All but my love's head of course. This must be joined with a new assembly of parts.

I can feel that my love wishes to know why, if Miss S.'s countenance so resembles her own is available, I do not simply meld my beloved's spirit with the body of Miss S. I try to explain that I mistrust the seeming ease of this procedure because one can never be sure in these matters how complete the transfer of personality, or spirit, is, and how much survives of the original individual. Besides, while my love's own dear face is available, if somewhat the worse for the harsh treatment the body has subjected it to, I would not like the new version of my love to wholly resemble any other lady. This is both because I wish her new form to be as completely my own as she once was and also because I should not like the relatives or acquaintances of the other lady to recognize her in her new identity as my wife. That would be extremely awkward and questions would arise. I could, of course, take Miss S. herself to wife and then make the transfer. But I cannot bring myself to wed another woman, even for my beloved's sake, or to lie before God of my intentions toward Miss S. when He knows my heart remains with another. And if we made the transfer totally to Miss S., my love would be an unwelcome guest in that body, not the possessor of the new vessel I have vowed to make for her solely for her use with her own lovely eyes gazing out of her own dear face with gratitude for what I have been able to accomplish for her.

So: to the task of assembling yet another body. Fortunately, the pregnant woman possesses some fine features that can be harvested without causing death before the birth of the child.

Neither she nor the little baggage who is the wife of my former assistant, however, is a virgin and for the sake of the magic, virginity is necessary. For that, I believe the genteel Miss S., whose breeding and decorum, so similar to my loved one's, will serve nicely.

Of course, it is always possible that there are stronger spells and more sophisticated methods in the books of Michael Scott, and if so, perhaps I can prevent any recurrance of the last unfortunate incident, when seemingly the inhabitants of the body parts took over before my love could gain control of the body. It is possible that I may keep alive some of the donors after harvesting what I need and do further study and perhaps use one in a ritual sacrifice to enhance the magic. My choice for that would be Scott's wee tart.

She may have Scott fooled with her wiles, but he is a foolish man where women are concerned. She has shown herself to anyone with an ounce of discernment to be cunning, sly, and stealthy, besides which she is willful, rude, disobedient, and no doubt a thief. How else can she have known where the books were hidden? Had she not challenged me, I would have searched in a calmer way, or waited for Scott to return, but her fishwife manners and anger have sealed her fate. While she is certainly not fit to be an integral part of my love's body, she is comely enough in a purely physical sense that I am confident she will do nicely for spare parts. Scott says she has a lovely singing voice. Perhaps I'll be able to use her vocal cords.

Chapter XX

THE VANDALISM COMPLETELY surprised Scott, but more surprising was finding Geordie Caird dressed and collapsed in the doorway. Angus, who had come with Scott, surveyed the scene with a cynical glance. On the way from the guard station, the two of them had met James Hogg, Dr. MacRae and young Murray, who, Scott understood, were coming home after an evening in the Star and Garter. MacRae and Murray instantly bent over the unconscious tinkler, and Hogg, with Scott, bent to begin picking up the jumbled and broken books.

"What did ye say tae the wee witch tae mak' her dae this, Scott?" Angus asked.

"Not a thing," he replied, scratching his head and trying to think if he had missed some nuance of mood, some hint of instability in Midge Margret's demeanor. But there had been none. "We parted on the friendliest of terms. I had read her a story and invited her to make free of the library. While worried about her brother and the murders, Midge Margret seemed most gratified by the arrangements provided for her and her kinsman. I dinnae think she did this."

"He musta helped her, then fainted awa' again before he could escape too," Angus observed.

"Certainly not," Scott said. "He has been unconscious or the next thing to it since his injury last evening."

"This man couldnae hae moved himsel'," MacRae said.

"He's faking," Angus insisted. "These gyppos, they're a sneaky lot. He's actin', like."

"He's barely breathing and there's a fresh wound on his head," Murray said.

Scott looked where the young medical student indicated. "That is no' a fresh wound. That is the auld one, freshly bleeding."

Hogg picked up an overturned chair, and a broken stool that belonged in the kitchen. "I can't think why either of them would want to break the kitchen stool."

"Unless they wanted to"—Scott's eyes rose to the top shelf of his ravaged bookcase—"reach something. Midge Margret is a wee bitty woman."

He took the nearest chair and climbed up on it himself. Usually he would have used the kitchen stool. She would have needed both. He saw, as soon as he neared the secret hiding place that what he had taken for a slight space between the edge of the door and the case was indeed a gap. He pulled open the door by the buckle on the nearest book and it revealed an empty interior.

"She found auld Michael's books," he said.

"Yer auld wizard ancestor?" Hogg asked. "What would a lassie like Midge Margret want wi' such things."

Scott shrugged, trying to think of an answer himself. "She was a curious lass, and clever. I've nae doot she would hae found it a great game tae discover them, perhaps while looking for something else. But she'd nivver ken what was inside just at a glance. That was all in the notebooks of translations. My great-great-aunt did them long ago."

"If it was spells and such were in them, mebbe the lassie was thinkin' they'd help her at her fortune-telling," Angus ventured. "A' them tinkler girls are witches onyways."

"Don't be daft, Armstrong," Hogg said. "If the tinkler lassies were a' witches, there'd be mair rich tinklers, would there no'? Thon lass were nae witch, but she was, as Watt says, curious and bright."

"Bright enough tae run aff wi' them. Unless they're still here in this mess. Are they, Sheriff?"

Scott abandoned the mess on the floor and made his way to his desk, hoping that Midge Margret or whoever had made a wreck of his home had not destroyed the draft of the new story or any of his other work. To his relief he saw that his work was shoved to one side and a place large enough to set the great tomes of the wizard's had been cleared.

He kept searching, in case the books were still there.

"Well?" Angus asked.

"Aha!" Scott said, beginning to pull and restack books from a previous stack. "There is an irregularity here after all!"

"Wha' might it be, Watt?" Hogg asked.

"Great-Aunt Sophia's translations, shoved in amang these books. Noo, I wonder, why would they be there? If Midge Margret did take the big books, these would be of far more use tae her in discovering the meaning of the text. They were hidden up on the shelf with the originals the last time I saw them."

"Stupid lass probably didn't know the difference," Angus said.

"Now that is where you would be wrong, Angus," Scott said. "She's nae stupid."

"Aye, weel, and I'll lay ye odds this laddie didnae cam tae be at this door under his ain power," MacRae said.

"Gentlemen"—Scott turned, still holding the notebooks, and sat on the edge of his table—"I do not know why the books were taken, except perhaps as a ruse. I do not think, for one thing, that Midge Margret could have taken a' three volumes without making more than one trip. They were muckle hefty books and she is strang, but nae sae strang as a' that. My guess is that the murderer was watching us a' the day for anither chance tae strike at Midge Margret and Geordie. He may have ta'en the books as a ruse tae lead us astray. But still, even sae likely a theory leaves us wi' one big question."

"Aye, and what is it, then?" Angus asked.

"Why, we were assuming the murderer was the churlish wretch we fetched frae Duddingston Loch less than two hours ago. But the corpse lights were shining ower his drowned body before I was fetched tae find him. How could he then have returned here to wreak his revenge on his poor spouse and Geordie when he was drowned and dead?"

"Not anither ghost!" Hogg said. "This business is unco' enough."

"No, not anither ghost, my friend. Anither murderer. Dr. Knox found that some organs were already missing from the Stewart lassie when oor loch corpse delivered the body tae the infirmary. Someone had already taken what was wanted frae her and passed her along." He smiled ruefully. "We are, gentlemen, looking for a *thrifty* slaughterer o' young women."

"Waste not, want not," Angus muttered.

"That's as it may be, Angus. But unless I am entirely misreading this incident"—he swept his hand to indicate the vandalized room—"he has taken a young woman I value to slaughter as well. Murray, if you would be so good as to remain here with our patient, it would greatly ease my mind. Normally one of the doctors frae the university would be called, but they are implicated in these crimes at present. Dr. MacRae, while I realize your specialty is not strictly medical doctoring, I wonder if you might not find an examination of the body of the body snatcher of great interest."

" 'T'would be good tae recognize the man sae that when I am finally able tae make my final analysis o' the lady in the loch, I'll be able tae say for certain whither or no yer man had aught tae do wi' her death."

"My thoughts exactly," Scott said. "Meanwhile, I wish to make another visit to the tinklers and question them about the abductions. Hogg, will you come along and advise me?"

"I will," Hogg said.

"And finally, Angus, I wish you to convey tae Captain Laing that a search must be made for this killer all through the city, and every nook and cranny be poked for Midge Margret, or"—he swallowed, remembering the bright elfin face with its intelligent, though rather sad blue eyes staring up at him as he read that afternoon, a face so mobile that each emotion of the girl's soul showed upon it like clouds blowing across the summer sky on a windy afternoon—"her body."

"Fair enough, Sheriff," Angus said, and marched off.

Dr. MacRae also made his departure, closely followed by Scott and Hogg, bound for the dwelling now occupied by the tinklers.

THE BUILDING WHERE the tinklers had been staying showed no light in any window, though the hour was not yet late. Hogg had a candle stub in his pocket and it provided light to negotiate the flights of stairs.

Three doors on the way were closed and bolted, but the

fourth stood wide open, and gave back a wordless echo. No lamp remained to light, but even by the little candle and the murky moon and starlight that filtered through the smoke, the fog, and the filth on the windows, Scott could see plainly that no tinklers remained.

Hogg crossed to the fireplace and put his hand to the hearth. "Still warm," he said. He held his candle stub higher so that he could see more of what lay within the fireplace. "Scraps of cloth, broken bits of things."

"Hiding evidence?" Scott asked.

"Nay. My guess is they burnt the deid girl's things sae she'd no' come back for them. There'll nae doot be a fresh grave in some unused corner o' a kirkyard tomorra, wi' no marker. That'll be yer deid lassie. The ane ye foond at hospital."

"I suppose Midge Margret could have gone with them," Scott said. "Do you suppose they've quit the city or simply found anither building?"

Hogg shrugged. "The weather is warmin'. From what you say, they've had a bad time o' it here. Still, it's early yet and bound tae freeze. I dinnae ken what I'd di mesel' in their place."

To Scott's surprise, he found they were whispering— here in the darkness, surrounded by trash and the burned remnants of a dead girl's belongings. The room seemed massive and colder than the out-of-doors. A brisk wind had come up and rattled the windows and chimneys.

Hogg swung around, lighting a circle around them to illuminate as much as possible the remainder of the room. Scott saw the staircase leading upward, and at the same time the wind rushed almost visibly through the upper floor so that it seemed there was someone there.

"Very well," Scott said more stoutly than he felt. He was bone-tired from the lack of sleep the previous night, the dredging of the corpse from the loch, and finally, the shock of viewing his vandalized quarters and worrying over the activities and fate of his guests. But none of this began to find the murderer nor to locate Mrs. Geordie Caird before she met the fate of her predecessors. "Midge Margret mentioned to me that there was a bloodstained carpet upstairs and some curious books. I'd like to have a look at them as long as we're here."

As they began to mount the steps, a door slammed somewhere above them, and footsteps seemed to scurry like large rats across the upper floor. Hogg and Scott exchanged glances over the candle stub.

"Naught but the wind?" Hogg said, but it came out a question.

"Aye, that's right," Scott answered. "A very strong wind tonight. It will blow away the fog but likely cause another freeze, wouldn't you say?"

"Och, aye," Hogg said, but, on achieving the top of the staircase, looked around himself most carefully before setting foot farther into the hallway. "'Tis—verra—windy—indeed." The foot went down as softly as dust falling.

Scott, with his cane and lame leg, had not the option of being so silent, but he followed his friend nevertheless. At one point his cane sunk into a rotted place on the stair and he fell forward, muffling a groan instead of allowing himself to exclaim as he might ordinarily. From somewhere on the floor, a shriek answered him.

"A ghostie?" Hogg wondered. But he asked it with less caution than that with which he had observed the wind.

"A right lusty one, if so," Scott said, for the voice had a human timbre to it.

The staircase split the top floor into two sections. The only light came from two dormer windows set far apart on each side on the wall opposite the staircase. Rags of pale curtains inhaled and exhaled with the wind as it gusted and sighed through the cracks between pane and frame, frame and sill. Between these windows protruded the knobs of rows of doors set so closely together that the rooms beyond them had to be very small indeed—servants' quarters, for the house's glory days when the entirety of it belonged to a single family. With a nod to each other, Scott and Hogg turned to the left and, Hogg on the right side of the hall, Scott on the left proceeded to open the doors, and inspect the monastically bare rooms, smelling sourly of human sweat and other bodily odors, the seeped in stink of old cooking smells and the ghosts of slop jars whose emptying had been neglected through the day while servants attended to their duties for their employers.

The rooms were windowless, airless, and unpopulated by living or dead souls, as near as the men could make out. At the far end of the hall, another door and another knob waited. Each man closed the last door on his side and then faced the northernmost end door together. The candle stub was growing so short by now that Hogg had to set it on the back of his pocket watch so it would not burn his fingers. Armed with this, he nodded to Scott, who turned the knob and opened the door.

More wind-troubled light writhed across the room from the small circular window in the back wall. It played across a homely hodgepodge of cast-off articles: trunks, clothing, books, and, fortunately, another half-burnt candle, this one in a holder. Hogg took it up and entrusted the light of his trusty stub to it before extinguishing the stub and returning his somewhat waxy watch to its proper pocket.

"Ah," Scott said, still from the hallway. Hogg had been blocking the doorway but the two men could see, if dimly, the entirety of the room, which was much crowded but not large. "This is the box room Midge Margret referred to. Her

own quarters are at the opposite end from this room, as I recall she said."

None of the small rooms on the other end of the hall revealed anything remarkable and they quickly moved to the
southernmost door. The door seemed stuck when first they
tried it and then, from muted squeaks and grunts on the opposite side, it seemed to Scott that they were being opposed
by a tug o' war team of particularly large rats. At last the
doorknob gave way and came apart entirely and Scott stumbled back and would have fallen but for Hogg, while on the
other side of the door shrieks and explications indicated a
similar fate had befallen those inside the room. These
shrieks were not rodent in nature, but were uttered in a very
low order of Scots.

Scott regained his composure and pulled the door his
way. Two small forms tried to barrel past him but he
grabbed hold of one and though he fell once more, retained
his grip, while Hogg grabbed on to the other.

Even by the inadequate light the dextrous Hogg had managed to preserve while in combat with his small captive,
Scott saw that these children were remnants of the departed
tinkler band. He guessed, from their frightened and abandoned expressions, that they must be the niece and nephew
Midge Margret had mentioned. The others had possibly
abandoned them, or, more likely, Scott thought, the children
might have hidden themselves to wait until their missing
mother, father, or aunt returned for them rather than travelling on with the rest of the band.

Retaining his own captive with one hand, he let go his
cane, which would no doubt be an object of fear to such
youngsters, and fished in his pocket for a penny instead,
which he held up so the light gleamed on it. "Haud a moment, child, and I'll give you this coin."

The child was immediately all business and stopped dead

still and foresquare, holding out her hand demandingly while glaring up at Scott through narrowed and suspicious eyes. She appeared to be no more than six years old. Scott bent down to hand her the coin. "I'm a friend of your aunt Midge Margret, you know. She and your father are staying at my house. Has she been to see you lately?"

The girl shook her head, but eagerness and relief had joined the suspicion and wariness in her tiny heart-shaped face at the mention of Midge Margret's name, and Scott knew he was correct about the identity of the pair. The little boy, barely able to walk, had his thumb in his mouth and seemed dangerously close to tears.

Hogg hunkered down and asked the girl, in a kindly way, "So, you two takin' up residence here, are ye? Is it no' a bit cauld and lonely? Are ye no' a bit hungry?"

"We're verra cauld and hongry, sir, and we're ainly wee bairnies," the lassie began. Scott guessed it was her practiced whine when out begging.

"Why did the others go off and leave you here?" Scott asked.

"They were afeert o' the patchwork lassie, sir," the lassie replied.

"Patchwork lassie?" Scott asked, his recent dream coming back to him in a rush.

"Aye, she cam' whilst we was wakin' Leezie Stewart," the wee girl said again.

"Did she hurt anyone?"

"Nay, sir. She ainly stood there. But she were deid, sir. Awfy deid an' aw. Onybody could see it. The ithers ran away but we couldna go wi' Mommy and Dad and Auntie Midgie still here so we hid. The patchwork lassie didnae do naethin' wrang. She just picked up Leezie and carriet her aff somewheres. But everybody else left too. The ithers weel no be back and oor mommy and dad and auntie havena coom hame an' it's aye dark and cauld here."

"There there, child," Scott said, fetching out his own clean handkerchief to wipe the little face, its layer of dirt now running with fresh tears and snot. "Dinnae greet. As I said, your daddy is safe at my house. Would you like tae come wi' us?"

The lassie took the hanky from him and gave her face a businesslike and impatient swipe and demanded to know, "And who might you be when yer at hame, sir?"

"My name is Walter Scott."

"Yer the sheriff what writes buiks?" she asked.

"That's me."

"Aunt Midgie says ye'll help. Weel then, Marty, cam alang. We're gaein' hame wi' Mr. Walter Scott. He will tak' us to oor dad and mak' us a great feast of sweeties and pu' us in a bed saft as saft can be." Her words were spoken half as inducement for her brother but also were half a statement of their terms to Scott. "Int I right, Mr. Scott?"

"Och aye. Sweeties and a soft bed it will be. And perhaps the cat Grimalkin will allow you to pet her and Mr. Hogg can be prevailed upon to tell you a story."

That agreed, wee Martin suffered himself to be carried by Hogg while Jenny led the way out of the building, pausing kindly for Scott and Hogg to catch up with her at doors and cautioning Scott where to beware of rough places that could trip him up.

Dr. Murray was sleeping with his face on a book laying open on the side of the bed where Geordie Caird slept.

He woke when the tea kettle whistled and had tea and cakes Scott had bought the day before at the bakery, shortly after Midge Margret and Geordie came to stay. These particular cakes hadn't been to Midge Margret's liking. The ones that had been had long since vanished. The remaining cakes suited the children well enough, however, and they gobbled them down to the last crumb.

"Ye look awfy tired, Watt," Hogg said when the children were fed and tucked in next to their father. "Why do ye no gae to the tavern and hae a pint? I'll look tae the bairnies for a bit."

"No need for ye to miss your pint, Mr. Hogg," young Murray said as he licked the last of the cream cake from his fingers. "I've studyin' tae do and it's quiet here. I can stay wi' the patient and the bairns while you and Mr. Scott gae oot investigatin'."

"That's verra good o' ye, laddie," Hogg said.

"Aye," Scott said, clapping Hogg on the back. "It's very good of you, indeed, Murray. We shouldn't be long."

PHYSICIAN'S NOTES:

I had intended to acquire Miss S. this evening, and would have accomplished this goal but for the necessity of taking Scott's gypsy slag in hand.

She so sorely tried my patience that I could have cheerfully killed her but the brood mare, whom I cannot keep sedated without endangering that lifeforce she will supply for us, ceased her hysteria on seeing the newcomer. So I left them locked together in the cell in the laboratory and returned to town, only to find that Miss S. was not in this evening. I left my card and a note that I would be stopping at the Pen and Sword, in case she cared to join me there later. At the tavern, I hoped to glean the news and see what has been discovered, what is thought, and what course the investigations take into the most recent developments concerning my work.

It would be a bonus if the lady met me at the tavern. Although I have lately sensed a resistance within her quite foreign, it seems to me, to as pliable a character as hers, I have no doubt that she is smitten and longs to be with me. Her eyes and body say so, and her unspoken words yearn for my company even as she pleads other engagements. It is perhaps a ploy to make herself more desirable, but futile, of course, even pitiable. My beloved had no need to stoop to such behavior to gain and hold my ardor.

Chapter XXI

MIDGE MARGRET ACHED all over and her head felt full of
fur and razors. Her eyelids and mouth were gritty and she
could taste her own blood. She was in jail, she thought at
first, seeing bars around her. But then she saw that the bars
stood alone in an otherwise open room. A cage, then. She
was in a cage. In one corner of the cage Jeannie lay on a pile
of clean rags. Fast asleep she was, all in, but sound and
healthy as far as Midge Margret could make out. She herself
had been lying in the middle of the floor of the cage.

The room around them was very large, with a high ceiling raftered in iron, stone walls and an iron staircase spi-
ralling up toward the ceiling. The moon spied on them from
an overhead window—a skylight. No other windows in the
room, only cabinets and bookshelves. It smelled and felt
much like the rooms in the infirmary—the big one with the
theatre seats and the other, horrible one with the bodies.
There were no bodies here now, but there were tables, with
straps on them, and she knew without a doubt that bodies

had recently lain on these tables, and furthermore had the distinct and uncomfortable feeling that the straps had been needed to stop whoever was on the table from writhing in pain.

Other tables and cabinets held bottles and jars of various liquids and substances she did not wish to examine too closely, of strange-looking curled wires and glass tanks likewise suspect. The smells coming from them were not those of decay but various caustic substances that burned her nostrils.

The room was entirely uncarpeted, and unheated as well, which made her suddenly aware of how very cold she felt. Jeannie, she could see now, still wore the coat she'd had on when they went hawking—could it only have been the night before? She herself had lain beneath a blanket and now she pulled it up over her shoulders and wrapped it tightly around her. She heard nothing but the sound of Jeannie breathing and a bit of a whistle and rattle from the wind playing round the skylight.

Otherwise it was altogether silent.

Then an unseen clock gonged once, and again, and the moonlit air around her shimmered and drew itself together, gathering into the rough outlines of two women. She strained her eyes looking for details and they appeared, focusing gradually until she saw that one of the figures was a small pale lady with long, softly curling hair that seemed made entirely of the moonlight. She was wearing a flowing, vaguely Oriental gown of the kind the ladies called a "combing robe." The other was a tinkler woman, buxom, shapely, and with a look about her that clearly said she thought she was something where the men were concerned. Men ghosts, maybe. The tinkler woman glared at the back of the small lady with an expression that said clearly if daggers still worked for either of them, her ladyship would be done for.

Midge Margret looked at the ghosts and they looked back at her. The lady's mouth moved, and the wind rushing across the skylight, the shifting of Midge Margret's own garments, the still-gonging clock, seemed to be forming low, whispered words.

"You'll have to speak up, madam," Midge Margret said.

That was a mistake, for suddenly a voice bellowed inside her head like a clapper in a bell, "I think Herself here wants tae ken if ye can hear her. And I bloody weel hope ye can. There's been nane but me tae hear her greetin' and moonin' aboot the place when thon daft handsome booger she married is awa'. When he's here she's hooverin' beside him and when he's above"—the tinkler shade jerked its head toward the ceiling—"ye'll no' find her ladyship here. And she's been carryin' on somethin' turrible ever since the murderin' bastert cut aff me ain head an' put me figger and her heid taegether, which did neither of us ony good."

"Ye'd be Bella Bailey or I miss my guess," Midge Margret said aloud.

"Aye, yer a bleedin' genius, you are. I sure as hell ain't thon puir bleedin' wee Leezie lassie he dragget the guts oot o' to stuff intae me figger. Didnae think me heart was pure enuff or some such rot, daft bugger."

"Wha' does he think he's doin'?" Midge Margret asked. "Why's he ta'en folk awa' and killin' 'em sae the likes o' Seamus Connors can tae 'em tae the infirmary for the dochtors tae butcher?"

"What're ye askin' me for? D'ye think he esplained his reasons tae me, then asked me nice, 'Miss Bailey, dearie,' if I'd mind dyin' sae he could use me bits an' pieces for his project like?"

The lady gave Bella Bailey an impatient look and stared

hard at Midge Margret again. Midge Margret figured she could see and hear the ghosts because she had the so-called gift, which was more of a curse most of the time. And then she'd had Bella's clothes with her, which sure enough let Bella haunt her. But Bella was a familiar sort, being one of her own people. The lady was strange and sad and edgy-like. More like what Midge Margret thought a ghost ought to be, if it was going to be properly scary. So sad and quiet and unpredictable, you'd no idea if it was going to beg you for a coin or murder you.

The lady drew closer to Midge Margret, and then all of a sudden was right in her face. Vaporous white fingers with their ghostly rings touched Midge Margret's arm, and a patrician nose touched Midge Margret's own nose, as pale, still breast met Midge Margret's, which was bobbing up and down like a bird looking for a worm, so hard did her breath come and so strong and fast was her heart beating, Midge Margret felt a terrible chill come upon her, colder than ever the cold, cold room had been before.

As bad a place as she was in already, Midge Marget had never felt so sad and so angry and betrayed at the same time, so desolate, so haunted herself by the ghost of a new and hopeful love and the terrible, final certainty that all was lost.

THE PEN AND SWORD was the closest pub, less than a block from Scott's flat. He was glad it was no farther. The cold bothered him more as he grew wearier from the unaccustomed exertions of the day. Just outside the pub, he felt a particular chill up his spine, as if he were being watched. He saw no curtains fall back as he looked around him, nor did there seem to be anyone else on the street besides himself and Hogg. Stamping the filthy snow and mud from their feet, the two men entered the pub.

"Good evening, Hyslop," Scott greeted the proprietor. "Mr. Hogg and I have come for a spot of sociability."

"You're in luck the nicht then," Hyslop said. "They're a' here, a' yer auld cronies, ladies too, in the inner room."

"Speaking o' ladies," Hogg said, and made a sweeping bow as two of the fair sex entered the room, along with a howling burst of wind that shook the furs trimming their bonnets, cuffs, hems and necklines. "Miss Wullie, what a pleasure."

Scott had been about to decline the company of his fellows in order to return to his quarters, take much needed sleep and see to the welfare of Geordie Caird. But he could not resist lingering to speak to Williamina Stuart and her companion, none other than Miss Ross.

The drinking club was in session. The Reverend Erskine was in great spirits, as were several others. Captain Laing was there as well, and from his exhausted expression it was clear he was there mainly for a restorative tonic before resuming his duties. The deacon appeared a bit morose, and it seemed to Scott he had been having perhaps a tad more whisky than was decorous, but decorum was never the aim of the drinking clubs. The other indecorous thing about the man was Miss Nancy Clelland, who was self-designated in the club as La Passionata. She had her head turned so that it came in under the hand Primrose was leaning his chin against while his elbow rested on the table, as if the weight on his mind was too great for him to bear unsupported. Miss Clelland was babbling half-sympathetically, half-brightly at the man, who seemed to be ignoring her while he listened to the others.

They were all in the process of another of those tedious rounds of toasts to "save the ladies."

"To Miss Ross!" said the Reverend Erskine, with a nod

to the older lady, forgetting that he was to use her club name. "The soul of wit and intellect."

"Is that all?" Laing asked.

"The Deacon's no' toasted onyone," Nancy Clelland teased, rubbing against the man like a cat.

Primrose looked up and straight at Miss Stuart and raised his glass. "To the la Passionata," he said, turning to Nancy Clelland with a smile. "The most beautiful and affectionate lady in the room."

Scott almost felt the heat rise from Williamina's cheeks as she turned on her heel and walked back the way she came, Miss Ross with her.

Scott wished to go after her, but she could well consider such witness to her humiliation an impertinence. He glared down at Primrose, who smiled in a supercilious fashion. Nancy Clelland cuddled closer to him and he shoved her away so hard she fell against the wall. Primrose did not spare her a glance but called for another glass.

"Sir, do you take pleasure in being unkind to ladies?" Scott asked, walking round the table to attempt to be of assistance to Miss Clelland, who was swiping at her face and groping for her coat.

The Deacon looked surprisingly, if momentarily, wounded, and then resumed his rather supercilious smile. "Why, sir, it was no unkindness to let one lady know that there are far too many others to make her haughtiness of any interest to me, while making another aware that she is behaving like a fool in her attentions to me. For indeed I yet mourn the death of my beloved wife and have not scrupled to say so to either that stuck-up piece or to any other who would lack the natural feminine reticence and throw herself at my head regardless of my reluctance."

Nancy Clelland did not even bother to put her coat on before stumbling for the door.

"Clearly if that is your attitude, the lady was ill-advised to do so," Scott replied when Miss Clelland was gone. His hand itched for a duelling pistol, although duels were long out of fashion and he himself thought them to be foolish and barbaric. Still, he could not bear to see two ladies so soundly humiliated at the whim of the arrogant lout Primrose was showing himself to be, at least while drunk.

"Come, come, sir," Primrose practically drawled. "Just because a person wears a skirt is no reason to believe her more worthy of having her faults overlooked than if that person wore trousers. Boldness in women is most unbecoming and perhaps unnatural."

"Surely, my boy, you might have—" the Reverend Erskine began. He sounded shocked, though certainly he had seen enough of humanity in its cups that little should surprise him.

"Oh, really, Father," the Deacon said with a sardonic lift to his brow. "You of all people should understand that there are those of the fair sex as perverse as any man. Was it not your own mother, sir, who was of such a foul temperament that her own husband had her kidnapped by Highland brigands and spirited away to live out the rest of her life on some secluded island? She was the daughter of a murderer, if I remember correctly, and his evil temper inhabited her soul no less because it was housed in a female body."

Erskine said nothing, but Scott could tell the remark had wounded him. The view of Erskine's parentage put forth by the Deacon was the one commonly held. Scott had never heard his clerical friend express himself on the matter.

"Aye, weel, I have heard it said," Laing said, leaning across the table to meet the Deacon's languid surveillance of his fellows, "chust in passin', mind ye, that yer ain mither was nearly murdered on several occasions by yer fither and that had it no' been for the intervention of a fortune-teller, she would ne'er hae known that the man attempted tae marry anither woman while he was awa' in a foreign land, and, when confronted by her brother, who chanced to be there, murdered the puir mannie."

Scott couldn't help but intervene, lest the quarrel turn his party into something far more serious and tragic. "Gentlemen, I think we have seen from this conversation the point of how our ancestry shapes our attitudes and what a profound influence the ladies may play on our lives. Why, I'm minded of my ain ancestor, also Walter Scott but known as Auld Beardie, when he had grown too fond of his own hearth, would be reminded of his duties by his lady, my grandmother, formerly known as the Flower of Yarrow, who would set before him his dish, upon which she had placed his spurs, as a sign that the larder had grown empty during his languor and it was time once again for him to go raiding."

Scott had trotted out the anecdote before and it had provoked laughter but the atmosphere in the tavern was strained and tense now, and the story drew not so much as a chuckle.

The Deacon gave Scott a gracious smile, making Scott wonder momentarily if the man had realized the folly of his behavior and was after all more sorry for it than he would allow himself to seem. Pleasant and charitable as it would have been to believe so, Scott's past experience told him such repentence was unlikely.

"Mr.—er—the Deacon's—most illustrious ancestor, known as 'Pricker' Primrose, would have appreciated your grandmother's domestic statements," the Reverend Erskine said to Scott.

The Deacon smiled amiably as far as his upper lip. His eyes were lidded and seemed to be studying his claret with great concentration.

"One with the ladies too, was he, this 'Pricker' ancestor of yours, Deacon?" asked Lang Davie.

Primrose's face was stony.

Erskine seemed to be remembering something he had read or heard now, and his attitude toward Primrose was that of someone who had received unpleasant enlightenment regarding his fellow man.

"Nothing so merry as that," he told the jokester as well as the other drinking companions. "Pricker Primrose was a very famous interrogator of witches."

"Aye," Laing said. "Why, I ken where I've heard the name noo. It was this Primrose whose gentle persuasion caused puir Lady Glamis tae compromise her innocence enough tae alloo her tae be burnt."

"He was an exemplary public servant," the Deacon said. "And a servant of God, of course."

"Yes," Scott said, "And Lady Glamis was an innocent woman, by all accounts." He was divided as to his opinion of witches and their persecution. He knew that many had been the victims of political and economic plots to deprive them or their families of land, goods, and power, or, in the case of Lady Glamis, the widowed Lady of Glamis Castle, born Janet Douglas, simply because she had the wrong ancestors. The King had been raised by a Douglas kinsman of hers and hated the man and vowed vengeance on all Douglases. The innocent and well-liked Lady Glamis had been the victim of this hatred. For a while it had seemed that she might escape the stake, as no one could be found to testify against her, but the King kept her in prison until she was old and blind and lame and at last allowed herself to be worn down by Primrose's ancestor.

"That may or may not be," Primrose said. "But it was his job and he did it well for Kirk, King and country. I would loathe such a task myself."

Scott wondered. Williamina Stuart had been warm to himself and even more so to Primrose until the night of her party, when Miss Ross intimated it was the result of a fortune-teller's prediction that had unsettled Williamina so that she distanced herself from her suitors. Had this information been obtained by Primrose as well? Did the antipathy to witches and sorcerers run in the family so that Primrose would bear a grudge to a fortune-teller—or even to a sorcerer so much as to wish to stamp out any trace of his work? The connection between the incidents was far too slight for Scott to make an accusation, but suddenly he needed to be out of the pub, needed to speak to Williamina as soon as possible and learn the description of the fortune-teller mentioned by Miss Ross. That might explain why Midge Margret had disappeared, and if Scott knew that, then he could perhaps find her before harm, or more harm, befell her.

"Excuse me, gentlemen, I fear that duty calls. I must prepare for a wee excursion tae the country tomorrow. Good night."

"I'll be by in the mornin'," Hogg called, remaining in the tavern to glare over his glass at Primrose.

Chapter XXII

THE LADY'S WRAITH clung to Midge Margret as obstinately as the tinkler children clung to a mark until they had drained his pockets and good will of every last farthing, and had the pocket watch, wedding ring, and other jewelry besides. The part of Midge Margret that still thought like herself was in profound sympathy with the mark as she never had been before. The wraith clung to her, and the ghost's cold took the warmth from Midge Margret's body, her will, her clever ideas, her very self, and replaced all but horror with numbness and ice.

Instinctively, Midge Margret backed away, tripping over Jeannie and pressing against the back bars to free herself of the phantom. "Here now, ye lave me be. Gi' awa' frae me," she cried, and with great searing pain yanked her arm loose from the ghost's fingers and began slapping at it.

The lady's ghost, rather to her astonishment, receded until it was once more hovering outside the cell. A triumphant smile seemed to play across the specter's face before it retreated into the ether. Bella's ghost remained where it was.

"Don't think that Herself will be bidin' lang in her wreck of a carcass," Bella's ghost's voice said. "She kens noo that ye hae the sight and that means she can use ye. And she'll use ye a' up if she has tae, when the time cooms."

"*What* time?" Midge Margret asked, but Bella too began to fade.

"Midgie!" Jeannie called. "Oh, Midgie. It wisnae jist a nightmare was it? Ye've been ta'en too and noo we're bathe o' us doomet."

"Don't act daft," Midge Margret said, relieved beyond belief to be speaking with the living rather than the dead. "We're nae doomet till we're deid and that we're not. Are ye arright, Jeannie? Has he hurt ye? And yer wee bairnie, how is it?"

"We're fine, henny, fine. I can feel the bairnie kickin' yet. But, och, Midgie, wha' are we tae *do*?"

"I havenae had time tae think on it yet, Jeannie, but we maun be quit o' this place and soon."

"But how?"

"Wha' are we, then, wee settled toon lassies wi' nae thocht in oor heids but parties an' shops that we cannac pick a lock? Gie me ain o yer hairpuns."

Her family were not thieves, but knowing how to pick a lock was only good sense, as such a skill was likely to come in handy fairly often. Red Stevie and Ryk the Ramrod, she suspected, had learned to make locks from learning to pick them. This lock looked new enough. No doubt Stevie and Ryk themselves had made it before the cage was installed. She hoped they had not done too good a job, but recalled hearing Ryk say that their locks were made more for looks than locking and it was true enough. The casing of the lock, as she could feel when she touched it, was scrolled with intertwined knots. Those knots might have held the door closed better than the lock, which clicked open after she'd fiddled it with the pin for a bit.

"Be quick, Jeannie," she said, and bundled her sister-in-law out of the cell and onto the cold stone floor of the room. After running across what seemed like miles of floor to the iron staircase, she began to hope that they might make it. "Up you go noo, dearie," she whispered to Jeannie, not sure whether to guard her from behind or in front but hoping that if escape was to be made, Jeannie might make it first as she was less well able than Midge Margret to look out for herself.

The iron stairs clanked with their footfalls and the railing was nearly as cold as the lady's ghost. Jeannie paused halfway up, panting, holding her stomach and unable to continue for a precious second. Midge Margret thought now she heard something other than the wind beyond their room and prayed it wasn't so.

The door at the top was locked as well, but this one she opened even more quickly than the one on the cell. Midge Margret had given no thought as to where the door might lead—whether into open country or perhaps the inside of a house, where Primrose might be even now plotting how he was going to murder them.

But this place was neither field nor house but some sort of shed—a carriage house, she thought. At first it was the smell of horse and leather that made her think so, but as they lingered a moment longer her stomach roiled again with the smell of the vapor that had been in the carriage, had stopped her struggling and made her sleep until she woke up caged. The same must have happened to Jeannie.

Midge Margret looked carefully around her. Her eyes were well-adjusted to darkness by now and as she turned, she saw that the door through which they had come was no longer visible against the wall of the carriage house, but blended in with the wainscotting and plaster and some shelving cleverly placed across it to make the wall seem continuous. Another, a proper door, was set in the wall farther on, and when she cautiously turned the knob and peeked inside, she saw a papered hallway with polished floors and rugs, pictures on the walls, a hall tree now bare of coats and hats. She closed the door as softly as she had opened it. The large double carriage doors were not locked, and gave when she tested them. She swung one wide enough for Jeannie to escape through and gestured to her to go.

"But—" Jeannie turned.

"I'm right behind ye," Midge Margret reassured her. "Aff wi' ye."

Jeannie slipped through the door and broke into a waddling run as she passed the great house, with its columns and porticoes and other doodads casting eerie shadows onto what was not yet a lawn but a rubble of slush and building materials, mud and tree stumps. It was one of a very few finished houses in this new bit of town. No neighbors about to question odd comings and goings or screams in the night, Midge Margret thought. Though probably the screams couldn't be heard aboveground. Else how would the man entertain fine guests while poor tinkler lasses lay suffering below?

She was considering whether she might be able to burn down enough of the place to call attention to it so he couldn't use it to harm anyone else, when she saw something separate itself from the shadows ahead of Jeannie. It moved a bit like her, at a stiff waddle, and seemed to be coming to meet her.

Midge Margret started to shout. She started to run. But

hands as cold as only the ghost lady's had ever been clamped over her mouth and around her throat.

"If it ain't me dear wee wifie," growled the unmistakable voice of Seamus Connors. "Now, now, darlin', you maunnae be leavin' sae soon. Himself will hae plans for ye, I'm sure, if he's gone tae a' the trouble tae bring ye here in his fine carriage."

SCOTT TOLD HIMSELF all the way home that he needed to calm down, make lists, think things through, but the idea that somehow the blood of Pricker Primrose in Corey's veins and Midge Margret's disappearance were related would not leave him.

Geordie and the children were sleeping, and it seemed to Scott that the father's rest was a more natural, peaceful one with his bairns tucked in close to him. Young Murray had stretched out on the floor beside the bed. Scott took Midge Margret's place near the banked fire and tried to compose himself for sleep, thinking that he would send word requesting an interview with Williamina the next morning before he left for the country with MacRae.

He found that despite his lack of sleep, he could not settle comfortably, and so he lit a candle, trimmed a quill, and began writing the note.

After several drafts he realized he could not make it sensible, nor could he impart the urgency he felt to Miss Stuart, that she should overcome the antipathy she had demonstrated to his company and was likely to continue to demonstrate after he had witnessed her humiliation this night. And the longer he thought about it, the more urgent the situation seemed. Primrose no longer seemed a familiar if somewhat estranged school chum. The man's actions to both women that evening had been calculated, callous, and deliberately hurtful, taking into account no other pain that the ladies might have that would be influencing their own behavior toward him. True, Nancy Clelland had behaved overfondly, but Nancy had lost her father and brothers in England's war with the Americas when she was a slip of a lass and ever since had been seeking someone to love and protect her as they had done. She had a considerable fortune of her own now and lived with an elderly aunt off Princes Street in the New Town. Most of the eligible men in Scott's circle knew her history, and even those who did not care for her were kind to her and quick to protect her against some who would take advantage. Scott was the only one of his company who knew the circumstances of the usually delightful Miss Stuart's recent withdrawal, but she was well-liked enough that most would have realized her reticence to be unusual for one of her nature.

Remembering her as the dear friend she had been to him until recently and recalling the gentleness and care for others that had so marked her character as to make her the object of his dreams for marital bliss, Scott knew he had erred. He urgently needed to speak to her, and learn what had been said to her by the fortune-teller and if the woman matched Midge Margret's description. Perhaps Willie would find his unexpected visit odd or lacking in propriety, but he was on the business of the law and not courtship in this instance and she would have to realize the distinction.

Wearily he resumed his clothing, allowing himself a change of shirt, and left his sleeping guests.

The wind had acted as a broom throughout Edinburgh, sweeping away the trash and muck on the ground, and overhead, whisking the customary pall of smoke away to the south along with the clouds, fog and gloom that had characterized the skies for days. Now a huge white nearly complete orb of moon frowned ferociously down upon the city, as if to expose its secrets and cast long night shadows upon even the most innocent of structures and persons. Willie Stuart's house stood almost opposite Scott's across the Canongate, and the trudge from his door to hers was nearly a level one, but it was hard going with the wind trying to bowl him down the street with each step. He reflected that a spike on the end of his cane might be a wise precaution in such weather, to dig into the ice and assist him in staying upright. Somewhere in the night he smelled smoke of a sort other than that which normally hung over the city, but he thought it might be some wretch trying to keep warm.

He reached Miss Stuart's door and knocked, but there was no answer, though lights still shone from the windows of the upper floors. He knocked again, harder, and still received no response, and the door was locked. This house was occupied only by Miss Stuart now, in the absence of her parents, who were abroad. The servants did not live in, but there was a kitchen and a door into it for the cook so that she would not have to awaken the family when she came early to prepare breakfast.

Scott made his way round to the back, which faced out onto one of the many closes whose other houses were now abandoned. The smell of smoke was much stronger here and again he looked around but saw nothing.

By the brightness of the moon, he saw scuffed human tracks in the snow, a man's, rather deep, and those of two other men, widely spaced, as if carrying a chair. The kitchen door swung open easily, for it had caught within it a swatch of fur of the sort he had seen on Williamina's ensemble earlier in the evening. A bit of torn cloth was attached to the fur. The lady had left in haste, and, unless the graceful Williamina had recently become clumsy and careless, under duress.

At once the puzzle was complete for him, and his poor friend had answered wordlessly the questions he had been going to put to her.

The wind had shifted so that it was at his back, the smoky smell much stronger as he hurried back to his own quarters and entered quietly so as not to wake his guests. He did not pause. He took only long enough to load a pistol, conceal a dirk in his boot, and, as a last thought, gather up the notebooks with the translations of Michael Scott's books. Then he hurried back outdoors, just as the night erupted with screams of "Fire!" and he saw the fire truck being carried on its poles by the firemen, one of their fellows running along before them, swinging his wooden rattle and echoing the cry of "Fire!" to those who had not heard it the first time.

Miss Stuart's residence was ablaze. Scott cursed to himself. Not only was it a fine residence, but with the houses of the town cheek by jowl, no fire could be allowed to burn unchecked or the whole of the city would be destroyed. People were pouring out of their houses to form a bucket brigade down to what remained of the Nor' Loch. All at once the smell of smoke and fire became foul, and by this Scott knew that the muckrakers, the folk who gathered manure from the streets, had joined in the fire fight. Manure put out a fire as quickly as water, but it smelled to high heaven, of course. Scott pitied Willie's servants trying to salvage what would be left from such a mess.

At the North Bridge Scott stopped briefly. The snow here was almost untrammelled, despite the furor on the Canongate and the High Street. The marks that he saw were those of horses, and carriage wheels, and alongside them, the prints of two men, standing apart from each other the length of a sedan chair.

So, Williamina had been taken—yes, he feared, taken—

on foot only a certain distance before being put into a waiting carriage. Dismayed, and knowing the Guard would be
busy with the fire, Scott hurried across the bridge, though he
feared that without the aid of a carriage he would arrive too
late.

Chapter XXIII

MIDGE MARGRET TURNED in the grip of the cold hands that held her and raised her knee sharply to where Seamus's groin should have been. She connected only with more desperate coldness, and now that she was turned around she could see why. Seamus, the man she feared the most of any in her life, who had haunted her nightmares since the first time his fist hit her jaw, was now fit for nothing *but* haunting. The once dashing Irishman was now nothing much to look at. Indeed, though she could feel still his desperately cold hands on her neck, he was otherwise even less of a presence than the two spooks below, and was little more than a disturbance in the air.

"Seamus Connors, why are ye no' in hell wi' the other divils where ye belong?" she asked, unintimidated by fists made of vapor, however cold.

"I was waitin' for ye, darlin', to see the master do for you as he's done for others and watch while he cuts ye up for spare parts, ye blackhearted bitch."

"Like the pair of ye did for Bella and poor wee Leezie? I knew you for a drunk and a brute, Seamus, but never did I think ye'd stoop tae murderin' oor ain folk for the pleasure o' some twisted *gorgio*."

Jeannie screamed a long, thin scream and Midge Margret twisted in the phantom's grip. Jeannie had fallen to the ground, clutching her belly, and over her stood a tall, misshapen figure wearing something thin and white and holding an object that glittered in the moonlight.

The cold fingers pulled away from Midge Margret's neck and she broke and ran from the carriage house to try to reach Jeannie before it was too late.

SCOTT WAS PERSPIRING, despite the cold, by the time he reached the New Town. The notebooks in his pockets, the pistol, his heavy clothing, all weighed him down and the need for speed caused him to slip and slide as he walked. He could not really run and the faster he tried to go, the worse his good leg pained him and the harder he limped.

He had been to visit Nancy Clelland's home only once, and that was at a party. The houses in the New Town were, block by block, solid façades of imposing stone with similar ornamentation. A few distinguished themselves with a bit of stained glass or a door of an unconventional color. Now that he thought of it, was not Nancy Clelland's door red? He seemed to recall some light jest about red doors being considered lucky because of some fairy belief, and that Nancy had added with a giggle that it was also the color of passion. The remark had been aimed half at himself and half at Forsyth, who had brought Miss Stuart to that particular party.

He paced off the blocks, trying to remember which one contained her house—he thought she lived on a corner—

when he saw the black carriage parked opposite the next corner. A tall man in a tall black hat with a muffler wound round it to keep it on his head stooped by the gate, over what could have been a bundle of rags.

Scott knew by the man's bearing, by the movements he was making, that this was Primrose. No amenities now. He pulled out his pistol and pointed it as he advanced upon the scene. "Stop where you are, Deacon, and stand away from that girl. You'll do her nae more harm."

"Nor will anyone else. Scott, my God, man, has the responsibility of your position completely gone to your head?"

Scott was within a few feet of him now. The apparent rags were the expensive cashmere coat and shawl worn by Nancy Clelland earlier in the evening and it was Nancy's ginger hair that spilled out of the fashionable bonnet. The clothes were slashed and covered with blood and Nancy's face did not bear looking at.

"Poor wee lass," Scott said. "Was it no' enough tae wound her honor before the whole pub? Did ye have tae murder her too, when she'd gone away and let you be?"

"Scott, I swear to you, I found her like this only a few moments ago. After you and the other gentlemen castigated me, I felt I needed to apologize to both her and to Miss Stuart for my ungallant behavior . . ."

"Aye, and what have you done with Miss Stuart? Her hoose is burning doon and I found a wee bit of fur in her back door."

"Oh, dear, in her haste to come with me to comfort Miss Clelland, I fear she may have tipped over the candle she carried to the door. That must be it surely. Please, keep your voice down. I don't wish to alarm her further. She insisted on accompanying me to see Miss Clelland, whom she knows to be an excitable creature, but she was weary herself, poor girl, and fell asleep in the carriage. Regrettably my driver is off for the night and I had to drive myself."

"Why did ye no' mount a horse like any other gentleman?" Scott asked.

"Because my original intention was to ask Miss—dear Miss Clelland—to be my bride." His voice broke as he looked down at the bloody bundle.

"Ye've an aye strange way of declarin' your love, man," Scott said. He didn't believe Primrose for one moment and kept the pistol trained on him.

"Scott, I swear to you I would never again have said the slightest thing to wound my poor Nancy. Miss Stuart was coming with me in case Nancy would not see me after this evening. Please, Scott, I may be able to revive her yet by sharing my own blood with her if only we can get her to my home on time."

"What do you mean, sharing your own blood?"

"It can be done, I tell you. I've learned extremely advanced techniques while studying abroad in France and Germany."

"I thought you'd given up on medicine."

"I've given up on nothing, including Nancy. But if you do not permit me to carry her to the carriage and help me with the procedure when I have her safely home, I will not be responsible for the consequences."

"Carry her, then," Scott said tersely. He wanted very badly to put away his pistol, believe the entreaties of his old friend, and assist him in tenderly lifting Nancy into the carriage, but there were too many questions as yet unanswered before he could believe that Primrose was indeed wholly innocent of these crimes.

As the man lifted Nancy, however, Scott did notice that she bled no more, and with great reluctance he pocketed the pistol and opened the carriage door for Primrose.

Williamina Stuart was slumped in sleep against the far door.

"For Christ's sake, man," Primrose said, "get in and help me with her. God only knows we'll have two dead women on our hands if Miss Stuart wakens to see she has a new travelling companion in such a condition."

Scott could not but agree and followed Nancy's bloodied slippers into the carriage. It was only when the door was firmly shut and the vehicle rumbled into motion that he noticed the peculiar odor inside the coach.

As the carriage jerked forward, Williamina fell away from the door and slumped at an awkward angle against the seat. Scott tried to reach forward to help her into a better position but found he no longer had the strength or attention to dislodge himself from Nancy's feet, which were resting on his lap.

He tried to take the pistol from his pocket, but his fingers fumbled and his hand fell away to dangle lifelessly before him.

His head was swimming, his senses filled with the cloying scent that filled the carriage, when the vehicle jerked once more to a sudden halt. The coach lifted slightly as a weight was removed from the front, there was the sound of feet thudding onto the ground, and the carriage door beside Scott's right arm was pulled open.

Primrose snarled as he shoved Scott to one side and thrust his hand into Scott's pocket where the pistol was. "I'll just relieve you of this, old man."

The door stood open. Primrose knew very well about the fumes, of course, and fully expected Scott to be incapacitated. Had he the sense to do so, Scott would have cursed himself for a fool.

As it was, he closed his eyes in dread when a shot rang out and he heard Primrose bark, "Get away from her. You,

woman, herd the brood mare back to the house. No, stay
away. No!" Another shot rang out. Midge Margret? No.
Primrose's voice was disgusted when he spoke to her, but
he'd sounded almost afraid when he gave the command to
stay away.

"Damn. All right then, you two help me with her. Carefully now."

He was suddenly beside Scott, pointing a brace of smok-
ing pistols at him. Scott's own gun lay abandoned on the
ground. "You, you're the least dead weight. Up top with
you. If you attempt escape, I'll shoot your little protégé first
and then ruin your good leg for you."

Shoving one pistol into his coat, Primrose grabbed a
handful of Scott's collar and jerked him from the carriage so
that the sheriff fell hard onto the frozen ground. Midge Margret and the pregnant lass, her sister-in-law, were struggling
with a large, half-naked body. Primrose shoved the pregnant
woman aside and finished hoisting the body inside, piling it
on top of Williamina. Scott wondered if it was his stupor
that made him think the body very much resembled the one
he had seen in his dream, throwing Seamus Connors into the
loch.

Midge Margret tried to turn back to Scott, but Primrose
hit her over the head with the pistol butt and shoved her in
after the corpse, then indicated to the pregnant woman,
Jeannie, that was it, Jeannie—Scott's head was clearing now
that the fresh air filled his nostrils—should follow her in the
tangle of arms, legs, skirts and heads that filled the carriage
as if it were a charnel wagon making the rounds during some
bizarre plague.

Scott feigned more difficulty than he actually experienced as he climbed atop the coach. It occurred to him to
grab the reins and drive everyone to safety, but the vapor
he'd inhaled still slowed him, and before he could act, Prim-

rose was beside him, reins in one hand, pistol in the other, urging the horses forward. The wind whipped their manes and tails as it did Scott's hair, now that he had lost his hat. Primrose's hat had blown off or been knocked off as well, despite the muffler.

They drove only a short distance, past the entrance to an imposing stone mansion. The building had an attached carriage house.

"Get down and open the doors," Primrose commanded Scott, who did so with some difficulty, lacking his cane.

While Scott was complying, Primrose turned the horses around so that he was able to back the carriage into the building once the doors were fully open.

Primrose forced the two tinkler women, both groggy from the fumes inside the coach, to drag Williamina Stuart between them down the steps. He then reached in for the half-naked creature and slung her over his shoulder.

"I fear I cannot carry Nancy," Scott apologized, to his own detached amusement, as if for some error in etiquette. For the first time since boyhood he felt absurdly embarrassed and ashamed of his slight infirmity.

"Never mind. Leave her. I'll come back for if she's needed. Down the stairs before I shoot you and leave you here. I would too, but I've lost my former assistant and you will have to suffice."

"Then your remarks about trying to revive her were a ruse?" Scott asked innocently. He recalled belatedly that there was no doubt another function he might serve for Primrose to keep himself alive. Primrose would have been the one who stole the wizard's books, as well as abducting Midge Margret.

Primrose did not answer him but gave him a scathing look and gestured with the pistol for Scott to precede him down the stairs.

The room was larger than a ballroom and featured a modern, fully equipped operating theatre with two tables and a laboratory. The jarring note was an animal cage placed beyond the operating tables.

Once inside Primrose locked Midge Margret and Jeannie inside the cage and laid Williamina on one table and the patchwork woman on the other. He ordered Scott to strap Williamina down, as he proceeded to do to the patchwork woman. Scott was both glad the man had left him free, and slightly shamed but mostly annoyed that Primrose did not deem his crippled schoolmate enough of a threat, once disarmed, to restrain him.

The floor was stone except, Scott noticed, for a pattern of small mosaic tiles inlaid around each operating table and linking the two. These were in the forms of two interlocking pentagrams further interlocked with a larger, all encompassing one.

"You will pull that toggle over there, Scott, and it will lower the lamps. I will light them myself," Primrose said and then, to another person Scott did not see. "It will not be long now, my love. Patience."

FOR SCOTT, PERHAPS because of the vapors he had inhaled, perhaps because it was simply his reaction to such a shocking situation, time slowed dramatically. Part of him seemed to detach itself and stand away, watching himself, a large disheveled, pale-haired lame man, leaning on the table where a lovely young woman lay strapped, watching a madman at another table preparing tools with which to cut up a parody of a woman strapped to that table.

"I don't suppose, just for old time's sake, you'd mind telling me what it is you're doing and why it is you've been doing it?" Scott asked.

"Certainly," Primrose said. He seemed oddly cheerful now that everything was arranged more or less to his satisfaction. "You're a romantic, Scott, judging from your literary reputation. I doubt you will ever write or read a story more romantic or tragic than ours, eh, my love?" he asked the unseen presence.

Scott doubted it too. Primrose's past and present crimes were already rather too sensational and lurid for Scott's readers, or so he hoped. Nevertheless, Scott realized that he was treating this situation with the same detachment as if he were reading the scene rather than living it. The large underground laboratory with the skylight. Why a skylight? Natural light for a cellar room with no windows of course. But how to prevent anyone from looking down into the room and getting quite a shock in the bargain? He wanted to ask and then he thought—possibly it was concealed inside a conservatory, surrounded by plants but open to the glass roof above. Everyone who was anyone had a conservatory if they had a house, so Primrose was certain to have one as well.

"You were aware, of course, that I studied abroad?" Primrose asked. "I'll need you over here, old man, to clamp off things and hold forceps and such. Yes, fine that will do." He began snipping stitches. Every time his hand touched the miserable misshapen body, it gouted blood. No doubt about his murdering this one. "Clamp that off there, will you— yes, that one. There's a good fellow. Anyway, as you surmised, though the medical school here in Edinburgh is one of the top in the world, I was nevertheless bored with my studies. A mind such as mine requires variety, diversity, and then too, I have always been one who sees the disciplines, separately though they are taught, as each being merely an element that blends into the divine whole, a whole which I sought to know as much of as possible. Oops. Rather a gusher, that one. Got it!"

The man might have been heading roses rather than a woman for all that it bothered him, Scott thought.

"At any rate, I became involved in French politics early on. It really was quite dreadful how the poor were dispossessed, their labor exploited while the King and the aristos spent money like water. Not a thrifty bone in the lot of them. I went to many political parties but also, in conjunction with my studies, met the cream of Parisian society as well. I had all but despaired at that time of finding a woman I wished to make my wife. The suitable girls I met at the society parties were shallow, silly, vain, or stupid, rather like your Miss Nancy Clelland. Whereas the ones I met at political meetings were altogether too clever, too plain, too fat, too domineering, too superior. They had opinions, pasts, seemed to hold me responsible for things other men had done to them, no doubt through their own lack of discretion. We're to the jugular now. Careful, there, there, quickly now, clamp! That's it. Got it. Very *good*. My dear Scott, I do believe you missed your calling."

Scott was not sure whether or not it was prudent to thank him for the compliment, if it was such, and let a nod suffice.

"Then one day I was walking along the Seine, thinking actually about your ancestor, if you want to know the truth, and old Dee and Nostradamus and how much we all had in common, how quick the world was to condemn us. I had broached the subject, you see, at a political meeting, of how the stars presently dictated conditions, and how a conjunction was coming that would alter circumstances so that they were more in the favor of the common folk. I was laughed out! Literally. At any rate, I was pondering these things when I saw her."

"Your wife?" Scott asked.

"My wife, my life, my love, my Veronique, sitting on the grass beside the river, her long, fair hair waving gently in the breeze." Primrose paused in his snipping and slicing to stroke a lank strand of the dirty matted hair on the head he was severing, to lightly stroke its cheek with his finger. "She was wearing a spring frock, white with green sprigs, and she looked so—so serene, so at peace. I loved her at once. I sat beside her and took her hand and looked into her eyes and knew I could tell her my hopes and dreams. I could, and she was always so wise, heard me out so completely, answered so quietly and intelligently, immediately comprehending all that I said and seeing the grand plan. We were wed within a few days, so eager was she to be mine. We had so little time to be together. I was called back to London for some examinations and although she begged to go with me, I would have had little time to attend her there, and so, loath as I was to be parted from her, I left my wife with her family.

"It wasn't as if they were aristos or anything. She was, like myself, bourgeoisie, middle class, merchant class, though of a well-to-do family. My own family never got to meet her, but they would have approved my choice. She was so afraid to be parted from me, however, that her serenity drained away, her cheeks grew paler, her attitude more agitated. I realized that the revolution, building as it was then, terrified her. So I showed her a bit of my more arcane studies, and from an ancient book I'd found among some Parisian antiquities, I cast a preservation spell upon her, just to keep her safe."

"I take it the spell worked?" Scott asked, and immediately worried that he had been too forward with the madman.

"In a sense. I heard that her family had been arrested and were to meet the travelling version of Madame Guillotine in their country home. A huge bonfire had been built in the town square. Her mother's body was being cast on it as I arrived and Veronique herself was being led to the guillotine. She saw me but did not cry out, would not endanger me. Before I could reach the cart, she was kneeling, the blade flashed, and her lovely hair, cut short for the execution, was being used by the executioner for a handle to hold up her lovely face and show all that she lived no longer. Except—she did. Her eyes opened as her face was turned toward me and she smiled gently. It was the spell, you see. It saved her, after a fashion. But it did her little good, as, again, I was too late to save her poor body, which was cast upon the fire and burned with the rest. Perhaps it still lived too, but I rather hope not."

"Oh, I do see your point," Scott said. "Ghastly business."

"Quite. Not the revolution of course. Necessary to cleanse the arteries of la belle France. But at the same time, it had taken from me my own belle. While attention was turned away from the pile of heads awaiting pikes or some other public display, I suppose, I rode by, snatched it up, and rode as hard as I could to the port. There I purchased preservation agents and also an Oriental rug in which to wrap Veronique so that she would not be discovered. A severed head would have been an awkward thing to have found in my possession, to say the least."

"Oh yes," Scott agreed. The head was halfway off the unfortunate and ill-matched neck and shoulders by now. "People simply wouldn't have understood."

Primrose looked at him sharply and he feared he had gone too far. He had to remember that the man was only mad, not stupid. But Primrose said, "You've more perception than I've given you credit for, Scott. Of course they wouldn't have understood. Though to all appearances, the head was as dead as any other severed head. Never again did it smile at me or acknowledge my presence in any way. But neither did it decay or decompose in any way. I brought it here, to the home I had asked my father to prepare for us. No sooner had I carried her head over the threshold than I began to perceive that her shade lived with me here. I consulted her on every detail of decor, on every furnishing, but it was not the house of stone and mortar she longed for but a mortal housing of flesh and blood for her soul and I always knew that. So I studied and worked, read and researched, until I felt that I knew how best to prepare a new body for her head to grace."

"To this end?" Scott asked, nodding to the pathetic and now nearly headless creature over which they worked.

"This is not the end, merely an experiment which did not work as well as I hoped. The science, you see, was correct, but I am a relative novice at magic."

"How did you become interested in magic?" Scott asked, and when he dared to glance up, saw that, within the cage, neither woman was listening to what was being said. Midge Margret stood muttering to herself while Jeannie looked on anxiously.

"Because of that ancestor of mine, Pricker Primrose. Many of the witches he prosecuted were liars, and confessed falsely, but there were a few genuine sorcerers among them, and sorcerers are known to keep books—grimoires, they're called, full of their spells. My ancestor impounded these but did not, for some reason, destroy them. Ah, now for the other jugular. Careful, careful. There. Got it! You see how it is with his spell? While there's little blood in the body, what there was seems to have been held above the original cut in order to oxygenate the brain. I can't say scientifically at this point exactly what the physiological effects are, but perhaps I can use the spell on another, less precious patient, Miss Stuart, maybe, or your little friend, or the pregnant girl, and have more leisure to experiment and find out." Primrose looked up and smiled brightly at his assistant. "Of course, I'm thinking of the women because they will already be somewhat damaged. It would be fascinating to put you back together after a long time, old man, and see if you still had it in you to write. With women it's always difficult to tell if their brains ever worked properly or not, isn't it? Och, come on, Scott, think of the opportunity you'd have, man. What a medical pioneer you'd be. And the auld Wizard Michael would be proud of you. Now, do pick up that forceps you just dropped and clamp here, would you? There's a good fellow."

Scott found his detachment had deserted him and he was once more very much in the midst of the nightmare. His mouth was dry and he felt the cold of the room profoundly. He could not form another question, but fortunately Primrose, so taciturn and controlled in society, was relaxed and voluble in his own setting, performing the grisly work with which he was so familiar.

"Those early grimoires were my childhood reading, much as your folktales and romantic stories were yours. I began searching for them in secondhand stores, the attics of acquaintances and friends, though I of all people realized my little hobby needed to be kept quiet. We haven't burned any witches here for the last fifty years, but one never knows when such barbarities might return to fashion. The sad thing is, these grimoires, for all of the mumbo jumbo about the devil, basically contain formulas for chemical combinations coupled with the sort of alienist principles that have recently begun to be explored by eminent men in Vienna and Austria. The power of the human mind, suggestion, that sort of thing. The more mysterious spells, like the one I just used, are rare indeed, and will work even more rarely. It takes a mind such as my own to perform the rite correctly and then to have the courage and skill to manipulate its components and experiment with it to uncover the scientific and mental basis for it."

Scott could not decide whether the man's maudlin attachment to what remained of his wife was his true motive, as Primrose claimed and seemed to have convinced himself, or if the whole thing had actually become an intellectual exercise turned obsession.

"There. Now, then. You're on your own again, my dear," Primrose said to the head, which he set tenderly aside with another brush of his finger against the cheek. "Just for a bit. Mr. Scott and I have a bit of research to do so that we can construct a better body for you this time. I think overall our raw materials are better and I'm hoping the great wizard will have something to say about turning the sow's ear into a silk purse without the purse retaining the shape of the ear. We don't want the seams to show this time, and of course, instant healing will be our priority. That should be easy enough since the more powerful wizards have always claimed to be able to do miraculous healing."

"Do you count our Lord among them?" Scott asked, shocked.

From the cage, Scott heard Midge Margret's voice, oddly distant and distracted, saying, "Och, here comes anither ane. Oh, it's you, wee Leezie. Poor bairn. Was it you then kilt off Seamus while you were in yon monster? Of course it were. The thing had your heart, didn't it? Your spirit went with it. There, there. This is me brother's wife, Jeannie. Leezie says she'd never hae kilt you, Jeannie. She kent you were the one give her life again and she were ainly tryin' tae help you oot there before auld bloody bones cam alang in his great carriage . . . Ye ken Seamus weel enough, but he'll nae be hurtin' the likes o' you noo, nor us nither. He couldnae haud me when I ran frae him. Wi'oot his great bluidy muscles, he can ainly frighten folk noo."

Primrose, with the focusing and concentration powers of the very brilliant, seemed not to hear Midge Margret's apparent monologue at all. He continued as if she were not speaking, and Scott forced himself to stop listening to her as well and pay close attention to the madman who had once been his schoolmate.

"Of course! He was the greatest of them all. And for that reason, it is a travesty that people of such powers, who studied and prayed to be allowed to use them, should have been persecuted even more harshly than the Lord Himself, and their inspiration deemed and assumed to be diabolical."

"And yet," Scott said, and would not have continued if he could have prevented himself from doing so, as he knew it was a foolish thing to do, but the words came pouring out of him without his will or permission, "look here at what you have. The remnants of at least three murdered girls, another young lady who admired you, and your servant, deid, and three more young lasses you propose to butcher all to gain this—what else can it be but diabolical?"

"My dear Scott," Primrose said almost affectionately as he undid the straps holding the now lifeless patchwork body. "You do have such a flair for the melodramatic. No one of any consequence died to make up this body—gypsy girls who were little more than animals, parasites living off the hard and honest work of others, breeding beasts ready to bear bairns for any man who could lay hands on them. No loss to society whatsoever, and gaining by my work the chance to become a part of someone superior, someone lovely beyond their imaginations and valuable and valued beyond price. As for the randy Miss Clelland and my former servant, I am innocent of their lives. My creation, I'm afraid, took exception to the role Seamus played in gathering her parts for assembly, and chased him from the laboratory with one of my best scalpels once my back was turned. Miss

Clelland's attentions may have excited the jealous wrath of
the part of my creature who was my own Veronique."

"But how could she—the creature, I mean, have managed the strength to throw a grown man far out into Duddingston Loch?" Scott asked, marvelling at that, in spite of
the other marvels he had seen.

"Oh, that was an aberration in the magic spell. It's basically a variation on the Kabbalistic ritual for creating a
golem, you know, and they're very strong, golems. It's one
of the features I wished to modify in the new spell.

"Now then, if you'll just dump the cadaver onto the floor
for now, Scott. I do regret having to damage this creature, as
I might have benefitted from being able to study her physi-
ology, but with her strength and willfulness, I could not
allow her to live as she was. She didn't matter otherwise.
Veronique rejected the creature as her earthly vessel from
the moment I had her completely assembled. Now then, I
found that your ancestor used a rather unusual notation sys-
tem. His symbology is far more sophisticated than any I
have thus far encountered. Of course, I've only had a chance
to glance at the books . . ."

Scott glanced over at Williamina and was horrified to see
she was now fully awake, though pale with shock and shivering with cold. How much of Primrose's ranting she had
heard, he had no idea. "Actually," he said to Primrose, "I an-
ticipated the books would cause a problem. An aunt of mine
made some notes on how the texts could be translated,
which she deciphered from clues the wizard left behind for
the family. Once I figured out that it was you had taken the
books and probably Midge Margret as well, I brought them
along thinking to trade them to you for her life—"

"How gallant! You do have the soul of one of those
knights you're so fond of!"

"Thank you. I hope that you will at least reward my

thoughtfulness in bringing the journals by allowing me to unstrap Miss Stuart and lend her my coat—she would no doubt be more comfortable awaiting her demise with the other ladies in the appalling quarters you've provided."

"You are a true gentleman, Scott. I think I have never before appreciated what a fine fellow you truly are and I shall be very sorry to have to dispense with you when the time comes. Your request is most considerate and reasonable. I daresay we could even repair with the books to the warmth of the house for a while before continuing. A glass of whisky would not go amiss, eh? We can bring a bit to share with the ladies, if you like, though surgeries go better if there's no food or drink on the stomach beforehand."

Scott unstrapped Williamina and assisted her to her feet, which seemed to have fallen asleep. Though awake, she was all but in a swoon. Primrose, impatient with their progress, swooped her up to carry her and unlocked the cage door.

And then, abruptly, Primrose's arms dropped to his sides, dumping Williamina to the floor, where she might have been injured had she not clung to Scott on the way down.

Primrose was staring wide-eyed at Midge Margret.

Scott followed his glance to see what it was about the tinkler girl that so arrested Primrose's attention.

Midge Margret was not herself. Not at all. Her features seemed to have changed entirely. Her mouth softened, the lips were larger and fuller, her eyes also larger, more widely spaced, their color more brilliant, her lashes darker and longer and more curling, her complexion paler, more lustrous and creamy, her brows arched more delicately. Gone was her wary expression as well as her oddly acquisitive innocence. Even her hair fell more softly to her shoulders, in waves, its color more that of dark honey than the flaxen shade of the bouncing curls that normally peeked from beneath her scarf.

When she spoke it was not in her normal, full, somewhat roughened voice in its accustomed broad Scots, but rather with a velvety soft alto whose words were either in French or accented with the Parisian version of that language.

She reached through the bars with a hand that was no longer dirty and callused with nails bitten and broken below the quick, but slender, pale, elegant, and smooth as porcelain, with nails a perfect crescent above each delicate finger. *"Mon amour,"* she breathed, and stroked Primrose's cheek, as he had caressed the cheek of the ugly, empty head that had once been hers.

"Veronique! My darling! You've come back to me. Just a moment. You mustn't stay in there, in the cold." Primrose's hands were trembling and a line of spittle traced its way down his chin unnoticed in his excitement. "But how did you manage this, my love? And why now and not before?"

The transformed Midge Margret stepped out of the cage as if alighting from a carriage, her wrist arched, her fingers resting gracefully on Primrose's sleeve. Once free of the door she melted into his arms and they embraced in a manner so passionate that if Scott had not turned away to gesture Jeannie and Williamina toward the stairs and freedom, it would have been embarrassing to behold.

Their kiss was long and ardent and stilled his questions. How nice if undeserved for Primrose, Scott thought, to have a living, breathing, warm and God-created woman in his arms instead of the hideous travesty he had planned. But was Midge Margret a consummate actress to have achieved the appearance of his late wife, basing her performance on what she had just heard? Even so, even to save her own life and those of all about her, how could she so lovingly and hungrily embrace the man who had been the death of so many and who promised for her only torment and murder?

Scott spotted his pistol lying on a table where Primrose had placed it along with his own guns once he began his macabre surgery. Unfortunately, since Scott was not a man prone to violence, it had not occurred to him to bring materials to reload the thing once the first shot was fired, as it had been into the body of the unfortunate creature.

He knew he should regain it, however, or take one of Primrose's, or take himself to the stairs with the others, but he could not leave Midge Margret, despite her apparent willingness, in the grip of the deranged Primrose.

She laughed a musical, ever-so-delicately bawdy laugh, the sort of laugh that was perfectly acceptable for ladylike amusement in the drawing room, but would hint to a man of other delights in different, more private surroundings. "*Mon pauvre petit.* I wish I might have spoken to you before now, but I had no voice, not that it would have mattered to you, eh? All of the time you are thinking it is a most particular body I need to return to you, a body you must create to be uniquely my own, and yet, I need—you see?—only one body, whose conformation did not matter. The mind and spirit were what mattered. I needed one who was receptive. *Vous comprends, mon coeur,* it was not I who rejected your creature. Your creature had not what was required to receive me.

"But this one, *la petite romanichelle,* her mind, her body, suit me admirably." She manuevered Primrose's bloodied hands in a lascivious way that caused Scott to look away again.

"And we can be together always, my love?" he asked in a half-growl of passion.

"*Toujours,*" she replied in one zephyrlike breath and they locked once more in an embrace.

Scott thought that if he was to rescue Midge Margret now, he must escape with the others and return with spiritual help, preferably a Catholic priest if such could still be found in Edinburgh.

"Your skin is so cold, my darling," Primrose said, looking only into her eyes. "Come, we'll go upstairs and make use of our home as a proper living married couple should."

Scott, ahead of them on the stairs, wondered that they could negotiate the spiral staircase so closely entwined and without looking where they were going. He would have to remember that such ardor was possible if he had need to summon it forth for some future scene in a story.

It was not until the couple was almost at the top of the stairs where Jeannie and Williamina huddled in a cold and frightened embrace with only Scott between them and their would-be murderer that Primrose seemed to notice them.

"I fear your appearance has caught me entertaining far too many involuntary guests, my love," Primrose said. "I'll just bid them farewell . . ."

From beyond the door came the scraping of footsteps on stone and men's voices in puzzled conversation. "Mr. Primrose, it's me, Ryk, and Stevie. Primrose, your horses are perishin', man. I'll pu' them up for ye if ye like. Mr. Primrose? Sod the man!"

"Ryk!" Jeannie cried out, and turned to pound on the door. "In here!"

At that moment Primrose lunged for Scott, but the woman with whom he was so closely entangled changed, crying out, "Ryk the Ramrod? Stevie? Thanks be to Jesus!" She shoved at Primrose. "No ye don't, ye murderin' bastert!"

He stepped back of his own volition. "Veronique?"

Pounding at the door, then another voice, "Here, Stevie, you did this lock. Undo, it, man. There's folk in trouble doon there."

Scott could not take his eyes off Primrose and the woman still half in his embrace.

Midge Margret disappeared once more as quickly as she had surfaced, and Veronique said, a bit sharply, "You are once again undone by your excess of zeal, *mon amour.* Before I went to my death, my tormentors when forcing me to watch the beheading of my father and mother told me the travelling guillotine was your suggestion, long ago, in one of your political meetings, to stamp out resistance to the revolution throughout the land."

It was still quite amazing to Scott, after all these years, how passion, once aroused, could transform itself from a loving aspect to an angry one.

"The little spell you did, a mere sweet pretense, so I thought, to keep me safe, has instead only kept me from paradise to witness your misery, your madness, and the decline of morals until you sacrificed innocent women and children, as you said, for my sake. But did I approve? Did you ask? *Non!*"

"Oh, Veronique," he said, clasping her again. "Please, please, don't be angry, love, I beg you. You said that we could be together always . . ."

The door broke through, pushing Jeannie and Williamina down a stair. Williamina automatically reached out and grabbed the hand of the pregnant Jeannie, who grabbed Scott's shoulder to keep from falling. Scott clutched the rail to retain his balance, and used his free hand to clasp hold of the woman in Primrose's arms.

Perhaps it was the touch of Scott on the flesh of the girl he had befriended. Perhaps some of Veronique was Midge Margret acting a part, or perhaps it was what Veronique's spirit had planned all along, but Midge Margret's body pulled loose from Primrose's caress to fall hard against the stairs above her and against Scott, while her hands flailed both to find further support and to fend off Primrose.

And then Primrose was falling, tumbling down the spiral

stairs another twist and then off them and onto the stone floor.

"Toujours," the woman resting against Scott's lame leg . said softly. *"Vraiment, toujours."*

Scott was not clear on what happened next, for there was much noise and commotion as two tinkler men bundled the frightened ladies out the door and descended to see what the problem was and to help Scott as well.

But the woman against his leg seemed to empty out somehow; her erect yet languid posture changed, the temperature of that part of her body he could feel through her clothing and his own seemed to warm, and when she spoke, as she did next, a vapor like that of cold, except of a more defined shape, seemed to leave her mouth and plunge toward the man lying on the flagstones. "She didnae say she was going tae bide here, ye bleedin' booger," Midge Margret said savagely. "But yer ae free tae join her and she's ower welcome tae ye."

Chapter XXIV

PRIMROSE WAS NOT quite so lucky as Midge Margret's words had indicated. The fall had not killed him, but had broken his spine so that he was completely paralyzed and could no longer speak nor see. The doctors thought he could hear, but the man had no way of responding and for the rest of his life needed everything done for him. As a madman, he would ordinarily have been kept in an asylum to receive such care as the keepers could spare him, but as a murderer he spent the rest of his life in prison. His money and home were seized by the city and the Crown, though Scott used his influence with the court to allow enough to pay a special jailer to care for the man's physical needs. Nevertheless, justice was perhaps purposely not swift for a man who had betrayed those with whom he had been raised, been responsible for the death of a wellborn and well-liked lady as well as for the deaths of several other people, and the abduction and terrorizing of another gentlewoman. There was indeed no case to try, with the Sheriff of Edinburgh as chief witness, and the judge, a friend of Miss Stuart's father and a former friend of Miss Clelland's family, on hearing Scott's evidence, declared that it would be unseemly to hang a man who could not walk to the gallows nor stand long enough to have the rope placed round his neck. And so Primrose's once diversely brilliant mind, his long, skillful fingers, his active and athletic body, remained in the prison of his own ruined flesh, and that flesh was itself imprisoned in the grim dungeons of Edinburgh.

Geordie, who recovered from his injury with only a slight headache to show for it, Midge Margret, and the children moved out of Scott's home and back into their former lodgings. Jeannie had her baby soon afterward.

Ryk the Ramrod and Red Stevie returned to their old quarters as well, where they could keep an eye on the Cairds. The two men said that Primrose had ordered them, quite suddenly, to move their tools and other belongings away from their fellow gypsies and down into a cold makeshift workroom in the kitchen of one of the new homes being constructed. As it was a good job, they had complied, and had been passing by his home on their way back up to the Old Town and the company of their friends when they noticed the open carriage house and the condition of the horses. They had, of course, had no idea what the man was up to and thought that perhaps he had been angry with them for having brought the other tinklers to live in the old building.

It took Midge Margret some time to return to herself again, even though she was no longer Veronique and claimed to have no memory of the time the ghost had occupied her body. She cried often, Geordie said, and was fearful. Ryk had become most protective of her and she, who was once so independent, could no longer bear to be alone.

Scott was surprised one day when Ryk and Stevie

brought her with them to his office. "The lass has sommat tae ask ye, Mr. Scott," Ryk said.

"Yes, my dear Midge Margret," Scott said warmly, and rose to take her hand. Instead she threw her arms around his neck and embraced him tightly, as if he were her lifeline. "Och, ye poor wee lassie," Scott soothed her in his Borders Scots, as he had been soothed by his grandmother and his aunt Janet. "Shush noo, henny, what fashes ye, girl? How can I help ye?"

"It's like this, sir. She's lost a part o' her life, has Midgie. She kens the ghost o' Mrs. Primrose had it, but she doesnae ken what she did then. Jeannie willna say onything. And she doesnae want Midgie travellin' wi' 'em nae mair. Says she's unsanctifit, says she behaved somethin' hoorish and e'en though it helped tae save her life and that o' her child, she cannae forget it and she doesnae want Midgie roond the bairnies."

"Oh, dear," Scott said, and, holding Midge Margret, for a moment had a shameful and confused memory of his reaction watching her being held in a similar fashion while possessed by Veronique. He gently put her away from him. "Oh, dear. What a shame. And it was not her fault. Not at all." He explained to her as best he could, using the gentlest and kindest language at his command, the conduct of the ghost while occupying her body and why Jeannie might be wary of her. She appeared by turns ashamed and angry, revolted—at one point he thought she might vomit right there in his office—and then, thankfully, interested in how it might all have happened. She was an intelligent girl after all, and though she had been a married woman, she blushed when he described some of the ghost's behavior and once snuck a look at Ryk, who was trying to find something to do with his hands.

Stevie stood by the door with a broad grin through the

whole thing and finally said, "Nae matter, henny. We'll explain it tae Geordie as best we can and if he and Jeannie
need tae gae wi'oot ye this time, ye can bide wi' us for a
bit."

"I couldna!" she said. "I'm ruint already."

But Ryk took her hands in both of his and kissed them
tenderly. "Not really," he said. "There's ways aroond it, ye
ken. I've always liked ye right weel but ye were sae proper
and I've been aroond aye lang and havena ony use for a
lassie wi'oot a bit o' heat to her."

"Ye might as weel gang wi' him, Midgie," Stevie said.
"He's a stubborn man."

Midge Margret changed again before Scott's eyes. She
gave Ryk an uncertain smile that grew when he nodded and
grinned back at her. Suddenly, the old Midge Margret was
back, laughing and full of joy as she tucked herself neatly up
under Ryk's arm. To Scott's amusement, her laugh now
contained a bit of the bawdiness he had heard from her while
she was possessed by Veronique.

THE FULL MOON rose slowly over the crags, casting long
shadows from the standing stones and from the select group
of people who stood nearly as straight and still as the stones
themselves.

The snow lay in clumps on the jagged rocks and the remains of icy drifts reflected the white moonlight from the
hollows. Most of the snow had melted now, driven off by
the warm rains of the past month, but here the coldest winds
blew. It was a steep climb and the rains had made the boggy
ground treacherous, while the mist rising from the moist
ground made it sometimes difficult to see one's footing.

However, Scott wished finally to identify the remains of
the lady found in the loch, to learn her story and lay her soul

to rest. Since Primrose had offered at the time of their discovery to pay for the burial of the bones, Scott could only
presume that the pitiful skeletal remnants belonged to one of
the wretched man's victims and that a sense of, if not guilt,
at least proprietorship, had caused Primrose to make what
had seemed a generous gift of Christian charity.

So what would normally be little more than a forensic
test by Dr. MacRae had become something of a wake. Scott,
Laing, and Armstrong were there as official witnesses. The
Reverend Erskine, now giving a preliminary prayer for the
soul of the departed, was there to provide spiritual guidance
for the departed as well as a modicum of protection for Scott
and the others from any misplaced ghostly wrath that might
be called up along with the memory of the woman's last moments.

Barbara Graham was there because, as she explained to
MacRae, she thought the soul of the girl might be comforted
by the presence of a sympathetic woman. A cold wind
flapped her hair and skirts around her, lending her shadow
an eerie undulation, as if some dark death goddess from the
Old Religion was there just behind them, waiting to claim
her own.

Reverend Erskine's voice mumbled to a halt and he nodded to MacRae to begin.

Solemnly MacRae opened the cloth bag, and from within
it there came a slight clatter as he extracted the bones and
laid them, one by one, upon the recumbent lintel stone between the two taller ones that flanked it. Then he stepped
back and waited.

Scott had read of the procedure but had never seen it performed. He thought there might at least be words, as there
had been at the lyke-wake so long ago. He glanced inquisi-
tively at MacRae and started to ask him if there was no invocation of spirit, no chant or charm that might hasten the

wished-for manifestation. The wind was cutting through his trousers and burned his face and, though he didn't mind so much for himself, Barbara Graham was shivering, and the Reverend Erskine, though not as frail as he looked from the way he had scampered up the crags, was no young man.

As Scott turned away from the stone, however, the wind whistled low. The ground mist, like a living thing, rushed at the stone, leaving the land all around as clear as it might be on a sunny summer's day.

Above the bones on the lintel stone was now what seemed to be, not a whirlwind so much as a whirlpool, formed solely from the moisture of the mist. It revolved rapidly above the stone with its vortex over the bones, sucking them up into itself.

Suddenly mist, whirlpool, and bones all vanished and a girl knelt there, her hands raised in supplication. Her face was plain, long-jawed and pitted about the cheeks, but her hair was clean and sandy brown and seemed to have been pulled loose from a bun at the nape of her neck to straggle onto the tartan shawl around her shoulders. Her skirt was of patched brown homespun and pale rings at the hem showed it had been let out many times.

The wind gave her a voice. "I didn't mean tae snoop, Master Cornelius! If ye say the heid belangs tae yer wife, why then, whose business is that but yours? Please don't hurt me, Master. There's naught I wouldnae do for ye." And then the kneeling figure fell over and seemed to come apart, the wind still screaming between the teeth of the skull that once more lay upon the stone.

Barbara Graham gasped. "Poor wee Susan!"

The men all turned to stare at her.

"Susan Carstairs," Mrs. Graham told them. "She and my youngest lassie were at school taegither until Susan's parents died. They left little for her care and I heard later she had gone into service but that her new employers died as well and she disappeared."

"Aye," the Reverend Erskine said. He swallowed, and looked rather guilty. "She was a maid for the Primroses. I remember seeing her at the funeral. Now that I recall, she was standing just behind young Corey and kept looking up at him, and I remember thinking it was a good thing the young man seemed to have such a strong moral fiber, for there was a lass who could easily be led to ruin by her new master. When she stopped attending church, I wondered, of course, if perhaps after all she had not placed ower much temptation in his way and had been sent to the country to conceal a delicate condition. Naturally, I didnae ask questions for fear of embarrassing the boy." He shook his head. "I fear naebody else did either."

Barbara Graham said rather bitterly, "They wouldnae, would they? Thank God my Michael left me a business and a home for me and the bairnies or it might have been me and mine lyin' in the loch all those years."

"I suppose if the lass grew up in the city and wi' a decent family, Primrose couldnae give her tae the medical school for fear she'd be recognized by a student who would question how she died and how he came tae have the body," Laing said.

"She must have been at least one of his first, if not his very first, victim," Scott said, and gave a deep sigh. "Poor little lassie. At least we know who she is and where her parents are buried and may use her murderer's money to bury her next to them."

MacRae slowly and reverently picked up the bones and replaced them in their carrier. They were now what was left of a real person, and not merely oddities left in the noisome mud of a stinking cesspool when the sewage had been drained away.

As the witnesses trudged back down the hill to the carriage, which would return them to the city, Scott reflected that had the bones not been found at the same time that Midge Margret brought the other disappearances to his attention, no one would ever have known what had become of the little serving maid, Susan Carstairs, and the identity of the lady in the loch would have remained forever a mystery.

AUTHOR'S NOTE

STUDENTS OF ENGLISH literature and history beware! I've taken a leaf from Sir Walter's book and messed about with lives, places, and events as suited my story, and while there are many facts in this book about Sir Walter Scott and Edinburgh, it is most definitely a work of fiction and of fantasy.

While Sir Walter did, of course, write the *Minstrelsy of the Scottish Borders,* grew up both in Edinburgh and in the Borders, did indeed go gathering folklore in the company of rural sheriffs, and was himself appointed Sheriff of Selkirk, he was never Sheriff of Edinburgh.

By the time my story takes place in my fictional Edinburgh, the Nor' Loch had already been drained and St. Margaret's Loch, a creation of Prince Albert, was not yet created.

Body snatchers and "resurrectionists" did practice their grisly trade in Edinburgh and Aberdeen, thanks to the proximity of Scottish medical schools. Travelling people were prime targets for these "noddies," as the body snatchers are

called by the Travellers, and their stories are believed to pre-
date the arrest of the infamous Edinburgh murderers Burke
and Hare.

According to the research I've been able to do, there have
never been any standing stones in Holyrod Park, but it's the
sort of place they *might* occur.

Sir Walter Scott, in addition to writing his famous books,
had a very full and interesting life. It is thanks to his efforts
as Edinburgh's chief public relations representative to the
King of England during the royal visit to Scotland that Scots
reclaimed their right to wear the tartan and play the pipes.
Scott also found the long lost crown jewels of Scotland, the
famous cannon Mons Meg, and convinced the government
to spiff up Edinburgh Castle so it looks as regal as it does
today.

In his novels, Scott was never one to let chronology or re-
ality stand in the way of a good yarn, so I like to think he
wouldn't mind if I am similarly careless with the truth when
fictionalizing Sir Walter himself in this book.